Christie—

Enjoy!

ECHOES
OF
DARKNESS

ROB SMALES

Books & Boos Press ◆ Hebron, CT

Books & Boos Press
PO Box 772
Hebron, CT 06248

Cover design © 2016 Mikio Murakami

"A Night at the Show" first appeared in *Wicked Seasons*,
© 2013 NEHW Press
"Maxwell's Silver Hammer" first appeared in *Zombies Need Love, Too*,
© 2013 Dark Moon Books
"Photo Finish" first appeared in *The Ghost IS the Machine*,
© 2012 Post Mortem Press
"Mutes" first appeared in *Dangers Untold*, © 2012 Alliteration Ink
"Playmate Wanted" first appeared in *Dark Moon Digest #5*,
© 2011 Dark Moon Books
"One Sock, Two Socks" and "Those Little Bastards" first appeared on
www.robsmales.com, © 2012, 2013 Rob Smales

1. Smales, Rob—Author. 2. Fiction—Horror. 3. Horror stories.

Manufactured in the United States of America

First edition

ISBN-13: 978-0-69-260957-6
ISBN-10: 06-9260-957-1

Have you ever had a bad dream or a dark thought?
Then this one's for you.

CONTENTS

From Merriam-Webster:

echo *noun* \ ˈe-(ˌ)kō\
- the repetition of a sound caused by reflection of sound waves
  b : the sound due to such reflection
- a repetition or imitation of another
- one who closely imitates or repeats another's words, ideas, or acts

darkness *noun* \ ˈdärk-nəs\
- evil; wickedness

INTRODUCTION

I'd like to say a word about the title of this book.

We all have darkness within us. Most of us try to keep it hidden, but it's there, tucked up in the out-of-the-way corners of our minds, and secreted down in the shadowy recesses of our hearts. I don't mean the darkest of darkness, the blackness you'd find within the heart of a monster: the serial killers, pedophiles, and politicians.

No.

I mean the everyday darkness, the kind we all feel and maybe even recognize.

Ever shouted at another driver sharing your road, whether they could hear you or not?

Darkness.

Ever been out somewhere and had the urge to tell a mother that maybe if she spanked that child once in a while, they'd know how to behave—and considered offering your services, if she was feeling a little squeamish?

Darkness.

Ever been in line at the store, and the customer currently at the register is taking *way too long*? Maybe they're rummaging through every coupon ever printed to find the one that'll give them another ten cents off an *already* discounted sale item.

Maybe they're just being loud and pushy, trying to get a little something extra, to which they clearly have no right. And maybe—just *maybe*—you find yourself wishing, for a moment, that something would happen to them. Nothing terminal— you're not a terrible person, after all—but maybe something *embarrassing*. Sudden onset laryngeal paralysis, perhaps? Or a gushing nosebleed? How about a case of explosive diarrhea?

Darkness.

You see? Our darkness is harmless! Sometimes—imagining the customer ahead of you suddenly browning their trousers, for example—it can even be *funny*! It doesn't have *anything* to do with what you would find in the heart of the Dahmers, Gacys, and Mansons of the world, right? Right.

Or does it?

Just like darkness out here in the real world, the shadows we see—or, more accurately, *don't* see—every day, our darkness within is a matter of *degree*. Out here in the real world there are shadows, and gloom, and dusk, and night, and holes in the ground where the sun never reaches, and our pupils dilate enormously in a futile effort to penetrate the utter, complete blackness. Out here in the real world we beat back that darkness: once with fire, then with gas lamps, and now with electricity. Out here in the real world we try very hard to stay in the light.

And within?

Within we do the same. Within, unlike the Dahmers, Gacys, and Mansons of the world, who stand firmly amidst their shadows of the mind, we *normal* people act very much as we do without: we walk around our darkness. We avoid it, maybe skirting the edges on occasion on our way to a lighter place, coming to rest comfortably in one of the brighter spots in our hearts and minds. Those darker places exist within us, but most people ignore them, uncomfortable with the thought of examining the blackest places of their souls. I mean, who knows what they'd find?

I do.

Every writer spends a certain amount of time looking within themselves—that's where the stories come from, after all. The writer spends time poking about in the recesses of their own soul, looking for ways to connect with the recesses of yours. The romance writer tries to connect with the romantic part of you; the adventure writer looks for ways to touch the part of your soul where passion, excitement, and pride have set up house; and the horror writer . . . the horror writer probes their darkest places, searching for ways to stretch out a psychic finger and point your dark places out to you. Maybe even give them a poke.

Our dark places speak to your dark places.

They don't speak directly: there isn't any fantastical mental communication, or sci-fi telepathy at work here—there is no *real* psychic finger. We take the things we find within our stygian spaces and we shape them. We give them feature and form, pour them into voice and verse, couch them in pleasing phrases and mold them into compelling stories, then set them loose upon the world within the pages of a book.

Like *this* book.

As you read this book—taking in the dialogue, learning about the characters, discovering the plots—those hidden spaces you try to ignore, the places in your psyche you so carefully step around, will hear those echoes of my own darkness woven into the pages. And no matter the subject—be it peckish zombies, a crashing plane, a mother trying to protect her daughter, or even just a simple case of missing socks—those echoes imprinted on the page will, like a sound of the proper pitch when it arrives at the waiting tuning fork, *resonate.*

All great stories resonate with the reader. The reader connects with the story, experiences it along with the characters, sometimes even feeling a sense of loss when it's all over. A story that has really *worked* for the reader will have them putting the book down when it is done and saying *Holy crap, that was good.*

That's what I'm shooting for. That is my goal. In the thirteen stories that follow, I've tried to capture at least some of the darkness that resides within me, some of the darkness we all share, and polish it up. I've tried to gift-wrap some echoes of that darkness and aim them toward your secret, hidden tuning forks, hoping for that resonance: *holy crap, that was good.*

Have I aimed my echoes properly? Have I gotten the pitch *just* right?

Turn the page and find out.

Rob Smales
December 27, 2015

DEATH OF THE BOY

Bits and pieces. Images. Sounds.

His father, panicked, screaming at the horse to "Go! Go!" The bright, sunny world racing by as the wagon bounces and jounces over rough terrain.

His mother, eyes round with fear, looking about for escape. Finding none.

Her hand on his head, pushing him down—"Stay in here! You'll be safe!"—before the thud-thud of her fist tamping down the lid. Her "I love you" forcing its way past the pounding. His father shouting. Mother crying out too, as, inside the barrel, the boy feels the wagon shudder. Slow. Tipping, the barrel sliding this way and that, battering the boy, though it remains upright. Mother's shotgun booms. Father's revolver fires twice, then a third time, and then there is only screaming.

He huddles in the barrel, listening as the screaming goes on forever.

Until it stops.

Silence.

Silence and the smell, the terrible, rotten stink oozing between the shrunken barrel-slats, clinging to the inside of his nose, the back of his throat, making him gag.

Not silence. **Almost** silence. He makes out feet shuffling. Cloth ripping. Wet sounds . . .

Chewing.

1

*He knows **what** they are chewing. And though he's been told time and again they can hear quite well, he simply can't help himself. He begins to cry.*

Feet shuffle. Many. Moving closer as he tries to muffle his sobs. He clutches at his own traitorous mouth, trying to force the noise back in, but it's like pushing a handful of water upstream in a river; the sounds rising from his hitching chest simply flow between his fingers, around his hands, until the top of the barrel is torn away, and strong, cold flesh twines into his hair in the exact spot Mother's warm palm had rested upon to push him down.

A sudden, scalp-loosening yank, and he gibbers, begging them to leave him alone, please, leave him alone, but hands grip his shoulders, grab at his clothing, and pull him out, into the bright sunlight.

His sobs become a scream.

Gunshots.

"Wake up."

The words accompanied a sharp blow to his thigh. The boy opened his eyes to find the old man standing over him, dusty boot drawn back for another kick. Noting the boy's open eyes, the old man returned the boot the ground and squatted, bringing his harsh, leathery face so close the boy choked on his breath: coffee, and at least one tooth going slowly bad.

"Them things can't smell nothing over their own stink, and they can see pretty good, but they can hear better'n you and me, so far as I can tell. You gonna be making noise, you want to be awake for it, so's you can choose to run or fight if one of 'em comes along. Y'unnerstand?"

The boy nodded. The old man stood in one fluid motion.

"Then quit'cher sleep-squallin'. Time to be up and moving, anyway."

The boy glanced about, confused.

"Where's Mom? Dad?"

"Dead."

The word was hard and flat, hitting the boy like a punch. The flashes that made up his dream crowded into his head, the world wavering as tears filled his eyes. His chest had just begun to hitch when a callused palm struck him across the face, shocking him into silence. The old man was crouching over him again.

"No time for that. Time for you to listen and do as I say, but not for that. How old are you?"

The boy stifled a sob. Touched his stinging cheek. "Huh?"

He flinched as the hand flew again, but rather than striking him, one bony finger extended to touch the tip of his nose.

"I've got more slap than you have sand, boy, believe me. Or time. Lost my horse getting you out of there yesterday. Lost some of my gear. We shook 'em, but that don't mean they can't stumble on us again. Now you best show me how it was worth losing my horse to get you out of there by *listening*, because *I* can just up and walk out of here and make it fine on my own, zombies or no. *You*, on t'other hand, may have a little more trouble. I talk. You listen. You answer. You *do*. Comprendé?"

"Yes," the boy managed, imagining for a moment being out there on his own, surrounded by the zombies that had taken his mom and dad. *Eaten* his mom and dad. It didn't seem real, though he knew it was. He looked up at the old man, fear strengthening his voice: "Yes, sir."

The finger disappeared. "Good. How old are you?"

"Fourteen."

"Seriously?"

"Last month."

"You're a tall one. I woulda taken you for sixteen, seventeen easy. Okay, now strip."

The boy blinked. "Huh?"

"Strip." The old man straightened again. "Get on your feet and out of them clothes. Hurry up."

The boy's mind flashed back to what his father had called "warnings": stories about bad things happening to children caught out by bandits and survivalists. It wasn't just young girls who had to worry about men with needs. He'd been explicit enough that Mom had left the room, and the boy'd had nightmares for a couple of days.

Fear-sweat broke out across his upper lip, and down beneath his balls. He got his hands under him and began slowly crab-walking backward on his palms and soles, his butt barely clearing the ground.

"Look, I, uh—"

He was suddenly gaping at the business end of a revolver, bullet tips peeking at him around the great staring eye of the barrel. He froze, his two eyes as unblinking as the revolver's one.

"I said we don't have *time* for this shit. God *damn* it, boy! I checked what I could last night, but I was too damn tired to fiddle with your clothes. I'm getting you out of here, but I ain't takin' a chance on you hiding sickness, then dying and turning on me in the night. You shitcan your modesty and peel off right now, and prove to me you ain't been neither bit nor scratched, or—"

The gun never wavered, rock-steady as the old man thumbed the hammer back. The boy watched as a fresh cartridge rotated into place beneath that hammer, aimed along the barrel pointing directly at his left eye.

"—I'll put a bullet through your head right now, to make sure you *won't* be getting up afterward, then set about finding me another horse."

Dark eyes gazed steadily at him over the chunk of metal death between them. One bushy eyebrow quirked.

"Are we clear?"

Silent tears ran down the boy's face as he stripped.

🐂

"We'll stop here for the night. Can you cook?"

"Some." The boy nodded. "My mom taught—"

"Good. Get to digging a fire-hole."

The boy looked about the space: a small clearing amidst a tiny copse of trees on the only high ground for quite a ways around. He dropped the saddlebags with a clank that drew a glare from the old man, then headed off sharp words with a question.

4

"Dig a hole?"

They spoke in near whispers, as they'd done all day, when not hiking in silence across the prairie. Mostly it had been silence. The boy had finally worked up the courage, by the time they'd stopped for a brief rest and a lunch of jerky and water, to ask why they were whispering.

"Shut your mouth a minute," the old man had said, as if the boy had been jabbering away all day long, "and listen."

The boy had listened for a second.

"What am I supposed to—"

"Just listen, damn it!"

So there they sat, listening to the sun shine for the better part of a minute. Then the old man leaned close.

"Y'hear it?"

"Hear what?"

"The nothing. The silence. That's what it's like being dead, boy. They ain't talking the whole day. They're quieter than any living man can be, no matter how hard we try. You're breathing. Your heart's beating. Your stomach even grumbled while we was sittin' here. You hear all that stuff all day long and just filter it out. You're used to it. It's background noise. But they ain't even got decomposition noise after the first bit passes. If they ain't shuffling along the grass, or tarmac, or whatever, then they's *silent*. Silent as the grave."

The old man nodded. "And then here come you and me, walking along, just shooting the shit. Right into all that silence. *Course* they hear us. They ain't got nothing *else* to listen to! So we got to try to be like them. Fit in, kind of like camouflage for the ears, if you take my meaning. If we don't make any noise to attract their attention, then we won't. Unless they see us. And we can see at least as well as they do."

That was the only question the old man answered all day, though he'd demanded answers to any questions *he* had, and there had been a few, whispered as he'd kept them moving along the plain at a pace just within the boy's ability to keep up. Barely.

Where had the boy and his family come from? Where were they going? What kind of guns had they had? Did the boy know how to *use* those guns? *Care* for them? Why had he hidden in the barrel? What had he planned on doing when he was found, as he, of course, had been? Had that been his first actual contact with zombies?

The boy had answered as best he could, every answer met with either silence or a snort of derision from the old cowboy.

Now, though, it was the old man's turn. He either had to explain what he meant by a "fire-hole," or dig the damn thing himself, and to be honest, the boy was so tired he wished the old man would refuse to answer.

No such luck.

"Dig a pit a foot across and two deep. Then another, 'bout a foot and a half away, big around as your arm, angled to catch the first pit near the bottom. Like the back door in a badger hole. The fire goes in the big pit, covered up with the griddle. That little hole feeds air to the fire. We keep the fire small, and we can cook us some supper without no chance of throwing off enough light to hook the zombies' attention. They can't see near as well as they can hear, but they sure as hell ain't blind. Well, most of 'em, anyway. Them's that still *have* eyes."

The boy dug and the old man prepared some kind of freeze-dried stew, mixing it thick, with the absolute minimum of water—water, the old man said as they ate, weighed more than food, but was more important.

"Out here, the only thing that'll kill you faster than thirst are those damn risen folk. It comes down to it, in an emergency or suchlike, and you have a choice between grabbing the water and the food, you grab the water. Every time."

He began dry-scrubbing the empty stewpot with fistfuls of grass, then glanced up speculatively.

"I s'pose, if it *did* come right down to it, I could always eat *you* if I had to."

He rasped a laugh, but the boy didn't see the humor. He didn't like the look in the old man's eyes: though his lips were twisted into a smile, those sharp, calculating eyes said the old man didn't really think it was funny either.

After supper the boy lay on the ground, unmindful of the dirt under his hair or the rock digging into his back. He had walked all day, saddlebags over his shoulder, and he didn't think he had ever been so tired. His eyes closed, and his mind began to wander, but it wandered into places he'd rather it not go. All day long he'd been concentrating on something or other: the old man's questions, the old man's tasks, or even just putting one foot in front of the other as he tried to keep up. Now, though, thoughts crowded into his head as if they'd just been waiting for an opening, and he lay there thinking.

Remembering.

Father's voice . . .

Mother's face . . .

Screams . . . chewing . . .

A boot thudded into his thigh, and the boy shot upright.

"Ain't time to sleep yet, boy. Still things to be done."

The boy blinked.

"What? Fill the hole?"

"Naw."

Something hard and heavy dropped into his lap, and he flinched, nearly crying out. He looked down to see one of the old man's long revolvers. He picked it up and found it empty.

"You said you cleaned your daddy's guns, and I got to find some kind of use for you. Show me."

The old man broke out a small kit of brushes, cloths, and oil, and watched as the boy cleaned the revolver. It took a little figuring, for though his father had owned a similar gun, it wasn't an exact match, and the boy had only handled the guns occasionally. The old man remained silent, merely observing as the boy worked through it.

When he was done, the old man took the weapon, broke open the cylinder and gave it a spin, flipped it closed, pulled the hammer back, and dry-fired once.

"Not bad," he said, breaking the cylinder again and slipping in cartridges. "I used these quite a bit getting you out of there yesterday. You use a gun, you clean it. Use it a lot, you make *sure* you clean it. Out here, weapon failure is *not* an option. Comprendé?"

He holstered the gun, drew the other and shook the bullets out into his palm before dropping it into the boy's lap.

"Now this one. Do it in half the time, and use a quarter the oil. What, you think I can just piss gun oil?"

He cleaned the second revolver, and then the rifle the old man had carried all day—a hunter's weapon, complete with scope—and then a third revolver that had been in one of the saddlebags. The boy was bleary-eyed with exhaustion by the time he finished the last gun. The old man watched every move, nodding when he was done.

"You'll do it faster tomorrow."

That was the last thing the boy heard before sleep overtook him, far too quickly for his mind to wander anywhere.

Feet shuffling. Many. Louder. Moving closer as he tries to muffle his sobs. He clutches at his own traitorous mouth, trying to force the noise back in, but it's like pushing a handful of water upstream in a river; the sounds rising from his hitching chest simply flow between his fingers, around his hands, until the top of the barrel is torn away—

The slap shocked the boy awake, sending him scrabbling across the grass.

"Quit that," the old man rasped. "You keep making them sounds in your sleep, you'll get us killed. I'll kill you first, if I have to."

The boy looked about the dark, confused, seeking the moon to try to guess the time.

"Your turn on watch."

"Huh?"

"Watch," the old man repeated. "What'samatter, you deaf?"

"No, I—"

8

In his confusion, the boy had spoken loudly—quite loudly—in what his mother had always called his whine. After just two syllables his mouth closed so hard and fast he nearly bit off the tip of his tongue. Iron fingers dug into his jaw as the palm cupping his chin shoved upward. The boy rocked upright, then over, his back crushing the thin grass. The old man, moving with terrifying speed, now knelt beside him, pinning his head to the earth and holding his jaw firmly closed. The boy squealed, a muffled shout escaping his nose, until two of those hard fingers gripping his face shifted slightly and pinched it shut.

Panic seized the boy as breathing ceased. He struggled, trying to writhe away from the grip, but his head seemed nailed to the ground. He arched his back, thrashed and flopped, but to no avail: the harder he fought, the more the old man leaned in, his weight pressing down painfully. The boy flailed, slapping and punching in his terror. The old man batted most of the wild swings aside, and those that made it through to strike the arm and hand holding the boy's breath hostage were undirected, ineffective things the old demon ignored.

The boy was light-headed, sparks flying across his dimming vision when he realized the old man was talking to him, whispering the same words over and over:

"Settle down, now . . . quiet . . . settle down . . . quiet now . . ."

The boy did quiet, too exhausted to struggle any more. He thought of his parents, wondered if he'd see them again when the old man had finished killing him. Unnoticed tears had streamed across his cheeks on their way to the ground; now they tickled his earlobes before dropping away. The leathery face faded . . .

The old man let go.

Air rushed into the boy in great, whooping gasps. He rolled onto his side, away from the old man, and would have run could he have gotten to his feet, but he was dizzy and sick, the dark night spinning about him. Half-digested stew clawed its way up his throat, but the old man quietly pummeled his back.

"Just breathe. Breathe and try not to puke—and if you *do*

throw your guts up, you do it *quietly*, y'hear?"

The boy forced the stew back down, swallowing hard, terrified of what would happen if the old man decided he needed to be silenced again. He crawled away, but iron fingers wrapped one ankle, hauling him back and flipping him face up on the grass. The old man loomed, a hellish scarecrow, all sharp angles and black button eyes.

"On the plain we can see 'em coming for miles. That kind of works in our favor—they can't take us by surprise. We have time, can prepare and outthink 'em, easy. In the dark, that advantage is gone. Sound still carries, though, and them zombies can still hear, and I don't aim to wake up to one of them sons of bitches gnawing on me just because you was having a bad dream, or got your feelings hurt, while one of them was passing in the night."

He helped the boy to his feet.

"Now, I'm catching some shut-eye before we have to get moving. You're on watch. I used to count on my horse to hear 'em coming in the dark, but that ain't an option no more. I got string with little bells on it wound between these three trees, about ankle high. They make it close enough to ring the bells, though, and there's more'n one or two of 'em, well, that could be trouble. You sit here, quiet and still, and you *listen*. You hear a shuffle, or a footstep, or a by-God snapping twig, then you wake me up, quiet as you can. Y'unnerstand?"

"You didn't have to choke me," the boy whispered. "You could have just *told* me."

He glared at the old man, rebelliously refusing to answer the question. The old man stared back, black eyes expressionless.

"You need to mind me, boy."

"You're not my father!"

"No, I ain't. Your daddy went and got himself killed. Got his wife killed, too. Got you stuffed in a barrel like some kind of zombie snack being saved for later."

He lunged in, suddenly face-to-face, and the boy flinched.

10

"So no, I ain't your daddy. I ain't putting you in a barrel. I'm putting you on watch."

A knife appeared in the old man's hand with all the speed of prestidigitation.

"I wake up and find you asleep, I'll hamstring you and leave you for the zombies to find. Finish the job your *daddy* started."

The knife disappeared. Those shark's eyes never wavered. "You're on watch 'til dawn. Y'unnerstand?"

The old man lay down without waiting for an answer and appeared to fall asleep instantly. The boy settled to the ground with his back to a tree, staring at the sleeping form in the dark, hating him more than a little. Wondering if he could ever manage to get one of those guns away from the old bastard.

And whenever his eyes drooped he thought of that knife, appearing in the old man's hand like a magic trick. He thought about those dark, cold eyes and those strong, choking fingers.

He was still awake when the sun brought dawn to the world.

Days passed in this manner: hiking in near silence, with muttered instruction at mealtimes, then camping on some high ground, under cover if they could find it.

"If nothing grabs their attention, if they's just wandering along," the old man explained, "they move kind of like water: downhill is easier than uphill. 'Cept for cities and towns. They congregate in towns, head for 'em like they's zombie-magnets, like they remember that's where they used to belong or something. Stick to the high ground and avoid them towns, that's my motto."

The boy had thought that first day with the old man was the hardest of his life; he later realized his mistake. Every meal the old man explained some new task, often watching the boy do it at least once, and from then on that task belonged to him. Cooking, cleaning, weapon care, stringing the emergency "alarm bells," setting snares near the occasional prairie dog town, skinning and cleaning the animals they caught *in* the snares (something that made the boy vomit the first couple of times, the old man standing over him in case he started making too much damned *noise*); the list of things the boy had to do grew all week long.

Each chore the boy took over was another thing the old man no longer did. Pretty soon it seemed that all the old man did was walk, sleep, eat, and shit—which the boy then got to bury.

The third day after the rescue, the boy noticed the pills. Several times a day the old man would fish in a pocket, pull out a small plastic bottle, and shake out a pill or two to dry-swallow. While the bottle had cotton packed in it to help keep it silent, the old man removed the packing to shake out the pills, and the bottle rattled no matter how he tried to muffle it with his hand.

Curiosity roused, the boy asked about the bottle. Twice the old man ignored the question, merely shouldering his pack and walking on. The third time, however, they were sitting around the fire-hole, a small pot of fairly fresh ground squirrel simmering on the griddle. The old man had just shaken out a pair of pills with a rattle that would have gotten the boy a hard slap and a short lecture, had the noise been his.

"Never you mind," was the harsh reply. "And get to stringing those bells. We ain't got all night."

The old man's eyes, coupled with the noise it made despite his fanaticism for quiet, told the boy that whatever it was in that bottle, the old man *needed* it.

It can't be a heart condition, not setting the pace he does, the boy thought, and try as he might he could only think of one other answer.

Terrific. Rescued from zombies to become slave labor for Colorado's last surviving drug addict.

It was also the third day after the rescue when the old man rummaged through the saddlebag after breakfast.

"I believe you said your daddy taught you how to use this?" he said, holding up the spare, third revolver.

"Yessir."

"Show me."

The gun arced through the air. The boy dropped the pot he was cleaning to fumble the weapon, bobbled it for a moment, then dropped it as well.

"Terrific."

He scowled at the old man as he scooped up the weapon. "You want me to shoot?"

"Yep."

"What about the noise?"

Bony shoulders rose in a shrug. "You let me worry 'bout that."

"Well . . . what do you want me to shoot?"

"How's about me?"

The boy stared.

"C'mon, boy. You've probably thought of doing it already. Now's your chance." He spread his arms wide, making a target of himself. "Go on. Plug me."

All those slaps and cuffs from the old man ran through the boy's head. The indignity of being strip-searched. His near suffocation. The gun came up. Rather than pointing toward the old man, however, the barrel aimed just off to the side.

"I'm over here, boy."

"I know."

"Then where the hell you pointing that thing?"

The boy was silent a moment. "My father taught me to never point a gun at a person."

"In case it goes off accidental-like?"

The boy nodded.

"I take it you ain't going to shoot me, then."

The gun lowered.

"Fine. I'm actually pretty good with that. How about that, then?" He waved a hand toward a tree, stepping aside to be far from the line of fire. "Think you can hit that?"

The boy gazed at the tree, a cottonwood only ten feet away. "Sure."

"Show me."

The boy adopted the shooting stance his father had taught him, sighted down the barrel, thumbed the hammer back, sighted again, breathed, and pulled the trigger.

Click.

The gun wasn't loaded.

"Jeeezus! You took *that* long to pull the trigger at a damn *tree*? What if that tree was coming at you, looking to chow down on some dumb kid? What if it wasn't alone? Jeeezus!"

The old man waved a hand, disgusted, then tossed the spare's gun belt and holster to the ground at the boy's feet.

"Put that on and let's get going."

The belt buckled on easily enough, though the gun felt odd and heavy on the boy's hip.

"Do I get any bullets?"

"Bullets? *Pfft.*"

The lipless mouth emitted a dry, sarcastic sound, then twisted into something approaching a smile. "When I think it might not be a waste of time, then, maybe, you'll load that thing. Now pack up and let's get to walking."

In the days that followed they practiced as they walked. The old man would hiss "Now!" from a few yards away, then move toward the boy with a measured pace. The latter would try to stop whatever woolgathering he'd been doing and get that gun out to dry-fire at the leathery scarecrow. It took half a day, and more than two dozen tries, before the gun even cleared the holster ahead of the old man's stinging slap.

"You're dead," he'd whisper into the boy's reddened face, then turn and continue on his way as if nothing had happened.

The first time the boy managed to get the revolver up and fire, he felt a second's elation before the hard palm cracked across his cheek anyway, joy becoming frustration that made him want to scream.

"I got you," he said to the old man's retreating back, "before you got me—you had no call to hit me! That wasn't fair."

The old man turned, tapping his stomach.

"You shot me *here*. That won't stop a zombie—hell, that won't even slow him down."

He walked toward the boy, one finger touching the brim of his hat.

"The body don't matter to these things, boy. It's the brain. Destroy the brain, destroy the—"

He stopped as the gun snapped up, nearly touching the end of his nose, steady in the boy's hand. His mouth twitched.

"That's good, but—"

He whipped up a hand to slap the boy's red, swollen cheek, but checked the swing at the sharp click of the revolver dry-firing in his face. His mouth twitched again.

"Good. I—"

Click-click-click—

The boy stared into his dark eyes, pulling the trigger again and again, making sure the old man heard the hammer fall every time. He stopped when he realized he'd fired eight imaginary shots from a six-shooter, and lowered the gun.

They stood, silence spinning out between them for what felt like a long time. Then that hard slash of a mouth quirked at the corners.

"Don't spray lead like that unless you can pull fresh ammo out of your ass. I know I can't. We only have what we carry."

He spun on his heel.

"Let's move."

On the fourth morning, the boy realized they were traveling in a curve. Each day they walked in a more or less straight line, following the occasional road crossing their path awhile if it was going in the right direction, but striking out cross-country again as soon as it turned the wrong way. In the morning, though, they set out in a different direction than they'd traveled the previous day: they'd been moving east, then turned northeast, then north, and were now heading almost due west. When he asked about it, all the old man would say was "Got somethin' to do," and would speak no more on the subject.

The only sign of man they saw in those four days, other than the roads, was a single car sitting alone in the middle of an eight-lane highway. The old man said he'd seen it before, but allowed the boy to make his own quick search while he swallowed a pill or two. The search turned up a Colorado Rockies cap the boy showed off triumphantly before putting it on to hopefully ameliorate the truly epic sunburn he was developing.

The house came into view in the middle of the sixth day.

They had passed another house on the fifth day, but it had been a blackened, burned-out shell. The boy had wondered about it aloud, but the old man refused to say a word. There was an extra tightness about his eyes and mouth, however, suggesting there was a story there he wasn't telling.

The house on the sixth day, though, was a *house*. White-painted walls pushing a whole-looking roof toward the unending sky; a dirt road running past the front door. They took turns gazing through the sight on the old man's rifle when the structure was more than a mile away.

"That's great!" said the boy, after one long look. "Let's go!"

He handed back the rifle as he started forward, but the old man reached past the gun to grip his forearm.

"Hold up. Ain't that easy."

He tore up a fistful of grass, letting the dry blades trickle from his fingers, watching them drift on the breeze. Without a word he set off on a diagonal to the house. The boy followed, mystified. The old man did the trick with the grass twice more, keeping an eye on the house as he moved in a wide arc. They crept along, staying low, until the house was barely a half mile away. Then the old man leaned right in to the boy's ear.

"I went through there 'bout a month ago, and t'wern't nobody there."

The raspy whisper was barely audible, despite his terrible breath tickling the boy's skin.

"Place was clean as a whistle. Looked like the folks might'a packed up and gotten out when things started to go bad, right after the rising. Probably went to the city, poor bastards. Point is, place was empty thirty days or so ago."

The boy shrugged.

"So?"

"Sniff. Sniff deep."

The boy inhaled through his nose, pulling the air down into his lungs. For the most part everything was clean and crisp. The wind gusted however, a slight breeze blowing toward them from the house, and the clean air was suddenly tinged with something that made the boy wince, flashes of a barrel and his parents' screams running through his mind.

Rot.

Decomposition.

Them.

"Last month, that place was clean. Now there's something dead in there. It may be lying-down-forever dead, but we don't know. You go running in there, all excited to sleep in a real bed or sit in a chair or something, and there's the wrong *kind* of dead in there, you just might be joining 'em. This ain't the world I was born into, boy. You neither. In *this* world you don't go running into *any* unknown situation. Not unless you're bound and determined to give up that whole living and breathing part of walking around. Y'unnerstand?"

The boy nodded, gulping, hot saliva filling his mouth at the thought of what he might have just walked into.

"We go about this careful-like. On guard, so to speak. And the good thing is, if there *are* zombies in there, the breeze carries our noise away from them just as hard as it blows their stink toward us."

He slipped the boy's revolver from its holster, quietly loading it with cartridges. He handed it back, gestured for it to be re-holstered, then handed over his machete.

"Only use the gun if you have to. Too much noise and not enough bullets."

Later on the boy was fuzzy on the details of the attack. He remembered the stink of the place, the fetid taste of rot hanging in the air. He remembered the blank eyes and shuffling gaits. The reaching hands. He clearly recalled hearing his parents, screaming amidst the shuffling feet and chattering teeth as more of the terrible, shambling *people* stumbled out of the house into the yard. His parents screamed from somewhere for him to run away. Or maybe to come to them. Or maybe find a barrel and hide in a small dark place and he'd be okay.

He remembered that: standing frozen with indecision, trying to decipher his parents' wishes, their advice, telling him what to do to make things all right. All he had to do was figure out what his parents were telling him, and everything would be all right.

He remembered that.

He remembered, too, another face, different from the others, with their blank, staring eyes, if they even *had* eyes. This face held sharp eyes. Eyes that darted about. Eyes that *saw*. And the face itself wasn't a blank, expressionless mask with a yawning, tooth-filled hole in the middle like the others. No, this face was filled with emotion, with anger, and the mouth opened and closed in a torrent of sound the boy vaguely recognized as words, though he had no time to hear them, so busy was he with puzzling out what Mom and Dad were trying to tell him as the grasping hands drew near.

A blade swung. A head rolled. Blood and other stuff, some black, some yellow, oozed from the neck-stump as the body dropped. The angry figure flitted through the slower-moving crowd like quicksilver, still spouting angry words, and where he went things fell. Arms. Legs. Heads. Bodies. Things the boy recognized, though he could not think of the names of them. Inside things, long and ropy. The angry man hurt the people, *killed* the people, and the boy began to cry.

The stink of the house grew as the people fell. Stronger. Thicker. He *felt* the smell on his skin, like he was moving through thick fog as he finally fell forward. He dropped into the darkness that swam up and around from all sides, closing him in like the curved slats of the barrel. He fell into the safety of the darkness and knew no more.

A stinging slap from a hard, calloused hand.
The boy opened his eyes.
Another slap.
He tasted blood.
Another.
Words, filled with spitting rage. "Useless." "Let you die." "Find a goddamned use for you."
The slapping hand again.
And again.
The boy felt dry ground against his cheek and realized he'd fallen. Had he been upright? He closed his eyes and took refuge in the darkness once more.

The old man walked, and the boy stumbled to keep up. He wasn't sure when they'd begun, wasn't even sure if it was the same day, though he felt the blood crusting his swollen lip and thought not. He'd woken not lying on his bedroll, or even lying down at all, but opened his eyes to find himself shambling along almost like one of *them*, only keeping the old man's back in sight because of the rope the old man held, the other end tied about the boy's neck like a dog collar.

Was I sleepwalking? he wondered. *In shock?*

These questions passed through his mind lethargically, almost at a distance. He remembered the house, but vaguely. He remembered the beating afterward, vicious slaps from a hard hand, but it was as if he'd simply watched it happen to someone else, though his aches and pains and fattened lip assured him he'd been no bystander.

"You back with us?"

He'd been recalling the quick, brutal way the old man had passed through the small zombie horde at the house, when the low voice grabbed his attention. The straight back and western hat he'd been following had stopped, so he had stopped too, drawing up behind the old man, though something made him stay out of arm's reach.

"Yeah."

"Good," the old man said without turning. "Been a whole day since the house, and you ain't been worth a tiny shit since then."

A day?

The boy understood, somewhere, that being unconscious for so long wasn't good, but the knowledge didn't worry him; it was simply something learned by rote that popped into his head.

"I . . . I'm sorry about the house," he said, dully. "I just . . . my parents—"

"I know," the old man interrupted. "You told me. More'n once. Had trouble gettin' you to shut up about it, in fact."

"I'm sor—"

"But I'm glad you're back."

He turned, and the boy flinched, more than half-expecting yet another slap, but the calloused hands remained by the old man's sides.

"I wanted you to know what's coming. What we're getting into. Dunno if you would have understood, the way you were."

"What we're . . . what do you mean?"

A thumb hooked over a bony shoulder, and the boy looked about, finally noticing where they were. As he'd stumbled along in some sort of shock, the old man had led him to the edge of a road that ended in a series of buildings. Dead ahead was the flat, open pad and canopy of a gas station. To the right of the station was a building bearing a black and orange sign: VILLAGE INN. To the left was a structure with a tall sign in the parking lot, a red square with a huge yellow M. Beyond these were more buildings, house roofs in the distance.

"A town?"

"Yup."

The boy began to shake.

"But . . . you said they . . . they *gather* in towns, don't they?"

"Yup."

"Like at the house . . . but worse?"

"Might be worse. Think it is. Ought to be, this being the only town for miles. But you want to be sure, you take a good whiff."

Though his shaking grew worse, the boy closed his eyes and sniffed a great lungful of air. They were still a ways from the town, but the breeze was moving in the right direction. Halfway through his sniff, the long inhale became a short gag.

Rot.

Decomposition.

"So, what, you want to go *in* there?"

His voice was rising, already past the limits the old man had set and getting louder.

"We can't just avoid them? Just pass by and go?"

"If they's gathered," said the old man, a calm counterpoint to the boy's welling panic, "that's the perfect time to hunt 'em."

"Hunt them?" The boy whirled, eyes wide. His voice trembled as he flailed an arm toward the buildings. "What, we're just going to walk on in there?"

"Nope."

The boy stared, but the old man's face and voice were calm and serious. Hope thrust itself into his heart.

"We're not?"

"Nope. I'm gonna carry you."

One hard fist lashed out, connecting with the boy's jaw, and the darkness swarmed up again to swallow him whole.

He woke to a bear hug, right around his chest and arms, like his father used to give him when he was small. Thin arms enveloped him, squeezing tighter than Dad ever had, lifting him off his feet in a painful embrace. Those wiry limbs *hurt*, the band of pressure running straight across his solar plexus, making it hard to breathe.

21

He opened his eyes.

The world was a carousel. The Village Inn sign flashed by. The great yellow M. The deserted gasoline pumps came into view, close but low. He looked down at his dusty boots, dangling nearly two feet off the ground. With a lurch and a painful squeeze of those wiry arms, the ground receded another eight or ten inches.

The arms, he saw, were a rope, yellow and fairly thick, wrapped twice about him, pinning his elbows to his sides.

Another squeeze and jerk and he was better than three feet from the ground and fighting for every breath. He threw his head back, craning his neck to see the rope that bound him running up over a protrusion in the canopy above, a pipe painted to match the surrounding material. The natural twist in the rope had set him slowly spinning as the rope stretched to accommodate his weight.

Part of his mind tried, uselessly, to identify the pipe. The rest of his mind wanted to know what the hell was going on, and how he'd gotten there, though the pain in his jaw from the remembered punch was a pretty good clue as to the latter.

"You're awake. Good."

The old man's voice came from somewhere over by the small, glass-fronted building sitting alongside the pumps, a red lettered sign showing KWIK-MART on a white background. The words rolled across the open lot, shockingly loud and crystal clear, with no attempt at quiet. Another jerk and rise stole his breath for a moment, and he gasped as the world spun. When he could, he hissed words in a panicked stage whisper.

"What are you doing?"

"What am I doing?" The old man actually sounded jolly, his words booming across the silent space. "I told you I'd find a use for you. Weren't you listening?"

The slow, rhythmic jerks squeezed the breath from his body again as the old man hoisted him higher and higher. Eventually the old cowboy was satisfied: the jerking stopped and the boy struggled to breathe, flexing his arms hard against the rope, trying to create some slack about his chest. After a minute, the old man strode out and stood beneath him, stretching up one hand to swat at the boots suspended above his head.

"Looks about right."

He carried something in one hand, and with a quick flip he looped a string over the right boot, hanging the object from the dangling foot, then held on to it, halting the boy's slow spin.

"Why... are you... doing this?" the boy managed, between straining breaths.

"Why? Couple of reasons. One is that there's bound to be an ammo shop in this town somewheres, and once we thin the herd a little, there's nothing to stop someone from going looking for it, if they're careful. T'other... well, I'll just keep that to myself for now."

He squinted up at his gasping prisoner.

"Sorry, boy. But this needs doin'."

He pulled something from his back pocket, a metal rod about a foot long, then reached out to thrust the rod through the open center of the thing hanging from that right boot.

A triangle of metal: an old-fashioned dinner bell.

"Come and git it!"

The yell was loud, but the boy was shocked at the volume of that ringing bell. His foot jerked as the metal rod beat the triangle, the sound drilling into his ears, filling up his head with that sharp metallic clang. Stunned by the noise, he never even saw the old man retreat to safety, but reeled in his rope prison, setting himself slowly spinning once more.

Then he saw *them.*

They passed through his vision as he spun, lurching into the far side of the parking lot, coming out of the town in response to the bell. These were the freshest of the local dead, not yet decomposed to the point where their muscles were unresponsive, and thus could still run after a fashion. Moving clumsily, but with surprising swiftness, they scuttle-staggered toward him, gray-skinned hands reaching, fingers already grasping though still dozens of yards distant. He had time to notice their jaws already working, teeth bared and chomping up and down with a machine-like rapidity, the movement indicating not a whit of intelligence, but speaking instead to a terrible, all-consuming *hunger*, before his lazy rotation took them out of his view and put them behind him.

He struggled for breath against the crushing rope, gagging as the smell of the things intensified, their putrescent fumes preceding them. Footsteps, arrhythmic and staggering, drew swiftly closer as he struggled, twisting his body to increase his spin and bring them back into view, though that view was already constricting. Every bit of air he managed was tainted with their terrible stink. He tasted rot, felt it in his mouth, the back of his throat, and he gagged. Black spots nibbled the edges of his vision, spots that grew and multiplied, blocking out the world. Familiar voices spoke in his mind, telling him to get in the barrel, to hide in the dark; that everything would be all right.

"Better lift them feet, boy! There's a couple of tall 'uns in there!"

He gasped as something struck his foot, the sudden inrush of oxygen, no matter how rancid, pushing back the darkness a bit. The blow to his boot gave him his wish, spinning him faster, though by now the rotation was irrelevant. They were all around him, reaching, grabbing, straining toward him, though only the tallest of them could manage.

The old man's voice rang out over the attack, the dead ignoring the sound in favor of the live, wiggling food hanging just in front of them.

"I told you! Lift them legs, boy! They start eating from down there, it's gonna take you a *ways* to die."

Then the old man laughed.

Something rose up in the boy, something feral and snarling. Alongside the memories of Mom and Dad telling him everything would be okay were new, powerful recollections: the old man calling him useless; cuffing him, slapping him, kicking him awake; the old man popping pills all day while the boy was a beast of burden; the old bastard hoisting him up here as live bait.

Mingling with his terror, shoving aside memories of Mom and Dad to make room, this new thing flooded the boy's awareness and rather than fighting it, he focused on it. He *hated* that old man.

More of the walking dead filled the parking lot, some older and more decrepit, unable to do more than shamble, others simply staggering in from farther away, but all of them joined the throng gathered beneath him, the only sounds their shuffling feet and champing, biting, gnashing teeth.

He hoisted his legs higher, clumsily holding the crooks of his knees with his hands when his thighs and abdomen grew tired. Groping hands flailed beneath him. One and then another of the fetid, rotting paws slapped the triangle depending from his ankle, setting him spinning faster.

He was just thanking Fate the things were too far gone to make the connection and grab the dinner bell, when one of the grasping hands went through the triangle as it circled above the crowd. The bony, greening wrist caught in one of the corners and the creature jerked mindlessly downward, simply trying to free itself. The string about his boot yanked his knees free of his grasp, stretching his leg downward. He stopped spinning, leg extended, the binding rope cutting cruelly into his torso as the creature below him, the remains of a woman, threw its full weight against the triangle.

The boy screamed in pain. The string snapped.

A hand slapped his lowered ankle, catching it in a grip like steel, though when he looked down the fingers clutching his boot were swollen, puffy-looking as rising bread dough. The boy couldn't tell which of the upturned faces the hideous hand belonged to; there was no change in any of the blank eyes, no break in the rhythm of a single set of champing teeth.

The hand began to pull.

The boy screamed again, pain ringing his torso, his knee burning like fire. More hands reached for him as he was stretched, his tortured limb pulled down toward their hungry grasp, and his scream turned into a howl of hatred and rage.

25

"Old maaaaaaaannnnnnn!"

A head exploded beneath him as a shot rang out across the lot. The gripping hand fell away with a jerk that sent him swinging, spinning once more above the crowd of dead faces and hands. The sudden fast spin coupled with the blast of stench from the burst head were finally too much for him: he vomited, raining effluvia down upon the hungry mob. They took no notice, eyes remaining open, teeth still chattering in anticipation of feasting on his flesh as the crowd surged back and forth, following his swinging form with mindless determination.

They also took no notice of the gunshots, round after round slamming home in the mob. Head after head disintegrated in gouts of meat and liquid rot, bone and brain spattering the surrounding blank faces. Several of the zombies fell, tripping on the remains of their brethren or slipping in the chunky gore now covering the tarmac. The fallen were trampled, unnoticed by those still standing, some of the older ones reduced to dragging themselves through the mess when arms and legs, brittle with their slowed decomposition, snapped beneath the horde's marching feet.

None dragged themselves far before the bullets found them, reducing them to inanimate bags of meat and muck.

The boy was sick again as this went on, the stink of the carnage burrowing its way into his sinuses, his stomach clenching like a painful fist long after it was emptied. The two- or three-dozen zombies below became a dozen, then little more than a half-dozen, shuffling tirelessly after him as his writhing maintained his back-and-forth swing. Each time his spinning brought them into view he watched them come, hating them in their mindless, unstoppable determination to have him, almost as much as he hated the old man for putting him here.

"Your turn!"

The voice startled him, so focused was he on his silent, stumbling pursuers. He craned his neck, trying to find the old man, but what with all the swinging and spinning it was impossible to make him out.

"Watch your landing, boy—you'll have to be quick on your feet."

He was swinging away from the following crowd when the rope went suddenly slack. He hit the ground boots first, dropping and rolling not so much by plan as that his legs simply gave out. Had he not already purged himself empty, rolling on the filth-covered blacktop would have made him sick; as it was he rolled clumsily to his feet, fighting to strip off the rope as he staggered away from the footsteps so close behind.

"Here you go!"

Motion caught his eye as he flipped the loops up and over his head with arms half-numb from their tight bondage. One object, then another, arced through the air to land in a clear spot by the edge of the gas station's cement pump-pad.

A revolver.

A machete.

Dead fingers brushed his collar as he momentarily lost track of his pursuers. He spun away from the grasping, reaching horror, trying not to focus overmuch on the wood-on-wood sound of the thing's teeth clacking in a grotesque parody of chewing. He ran, circling around the pad, leading the pack, the bandleader in a parade from Hell. They had him in sight, were fixed on him now; they would not stop, he knew, but would keep on coming until destroyed. He looped back, an all-out sprint putting a little distance between himself and the pack before he stooped to snatch a little bit of death from the tarmac.

He picked up the revolver.

He could tell it was loaded this time, could feel the weight of the thing, heavy in his hand. He thumbed the hammer back as he turned, backpedaling between the old fuel pumps.

On they came, slowing to force their way between the pumps, not fighting each other, simply unaware, tripping one another up as they squeezed through the bottleneck. He leveled the gun at the one in the lead; a woman, according to the dress. The weapon bellowed, bucked, and the zombie behind her fell, head a spattered ruin. The body dropped into the gap between the pumps, slowing the zombies behind it, their legs entangling in its suddenly inanimate limbs.

He avoided the female, ducking left, using the pumps to impede them again. He shot one when the range was close enough, then another, nameless stuff spraying the pumps as corpses dropped between them, further slowing the following dead. He fired three more times before the gun clicked empty, and he cast it aside as he ran to scoop up the machete.

Chest heaving, he faced his remaining hunters, two relatively fresh zombies: a male wearing a disgusting sweater who lacked more than half his face, and the female he'd missed at the pumps, torn dress still almost pretty, despite the blood from her missing right arm.

"No." The word was a sob, tears streaming down his face.

Was that why his first shot had gone wide? Had he recognized that dress even in the touch-and-go of a running gunfight, the revolver twitching aside at the last second? Had he instinctively not fired at that ugly sweater, a family joke his father had taken good-naturedly for as long as the boy could remember?

"No!"

The cry was ragged, torn from him as he backed from the staggering figures. His father tracked him awkwardly, his one remaining eye staring. His mother stumbled, ragged dress fluttering in the breeze, exposing a section of leg where there was no leg, thigh stripped to the bone, exposed muscle gnawed and raw, the leg stiff and wooden.

"That *ain't* your ma!"

He heard the words but didn't spare a glance toward the old man. He stumbled back, staring at that hand reaching for him, fingers stiffening and curling with anticipation, wondering which hand this was: the one that caressed his hair as it pushed him down into the barrel, or the one that had held the lid for him?

That one touched my hair, he decided, watching it draw closer as she staggered faster than he retreated.

"That ain't her! Your ma is *dead*, been dead for a week.

This is just something using her leftovers like a tool, a tool that *looks* like her!"

Some quiet, clinical part of the boy suspected the peak of her screaming had come when they'd done that to her leg, but that sudden stop, her awful silence . . . that had come when they took her arm.

"Take back her leftovers! Put it down, boy, take it back so we can bury her proper!"

He held the machete in a loose, two-handed grip, its tip pointed in her general direction, but this was less threat than reflex action. The blade tip bounced about as he moved, wove a looping figure eight more than a foot wide in the air, but her dead, filmed eyes didn't follow it. She was focused entirely on him, on him alone, with no evidence she even considered the weapon.

For his part, it never even occurred to him to swing. He still held the blade only because he never thought to put it down. Or perhaps there *was* some small thing of self-preservation in this; maybe that calm, clinical part of him, somewhere deep inside, was aware of her rotting flesh and champing teeth, and was afraid.

But afraid or not, he couldn't take a swing at her, *shouldn't* take a swing at her. He couldn't hurt her any more than she could hurt him. And she wouldn't hurt him. *Couldn't* hurt him. Because she was his—

"Mom?" he whispered, his feet grinding to a halt on the tarmac, left hand leaving the handle of the machete to reach out toward those straining fingers, fingers that had twined in his hair as she pushed him into the barrel. Into safety.

Right before she told him she loved him.

"Mom." He smiled, and began to take a step forward.

"*Look out!*"

Iron fingers clamped about his left bicep. A powerful yank spun him left, his right hand flying high for balance, the weight of what he'd forgotten he even carried pulling it wide, swinging it in an arc—

—that stopped when the machete's blade lodged in the side of his father's head with a wooden *chunk*.

"*No!*"

The line of the blade crossed the edge of his father's jaw, had caught it in mid-chatter, breaking it, shooting it six inches to the side like the platen on an old-fashioned typewriter. The boy reeled in horror, but his father never slowed, shambling forward, misaligned jaw waggling like a scolding finger as it tried to bite. Seeing his own hand still gripping the handle of the blade buried in what was left of his father's face shocked him, caused a change within him as, deep down, something buried even further inside than that quiet, analytical part . . . broke.

"*No!*"

He had been falling back; now he *pulled* back, twisting the handle to free the blade. He spun right as he pulled, keeping himself away from the grabbing left hand as the right hand, still tightly clamped to his upper arm, pulled the zombie off-balance. The two zombies collided, further disrupting both their pursuits. The female fell to the ground with a hollow *crack*, gnawed left leg not up to the task, but the male maintained his grip on the boy's arm. The machete rose, then fell, the blade nearly severing the zombie's arm at the elbow.

The shock knocked the clutching hand loose, but the zombie simply staggered on, closing on him with sudden speed. The boy stumbled back, feet twisting upon themselves as he tried to raise the machete for another blow, but he was too slow, *too slow*—

—and the zombie missed, the nearly severed arm dangling from the outthrust stump, hand still clutching and grabbing though only a thin strip of tissue held the remains of the elbow together. The boy sidestepped, eyes fastened to the spot just below that waggling flag of a broken jaw. The machete rose. The boy screamed.

The machete fell.

Blood flowed, thick with pus, chunks of blackened meat bumping in the weak current like the last bits of cereal floating in the bowl of milk as fluids moved lazily, without any kind of systolic pressure. The hideous sweater his dad had worn so proudly, proof of the love of a father for his young son, sopped up the gore like a woolen towel. The boy avoided looking at the round object rolling in a tight circle, bumping as the offset jaw, still waggling, tapped time in the center.

He stiffened at the *clack-clack-clack* of teeth close behind, and spun.

She lay full length upon the ground, left leg missing below the thigh. Now the boy clearly saw the gnaw marks on the stub of bone protruding from the meat, where the dead had chewed through his mother's living limb like someone starting in the middle of an ear of corn, teeth closing hard on the cob in the center, trying to suck up every last bit of sweet kernel. The chewing had weakened the bone, splintered it, so the impact of his father's body had snapped it like a rotted stick, leaving her to drag herself toward him one-armed and single-legged, in a ghastly parody of an army crawl.

Her eyes were still focused on him and only him, though now he recognized what he saw in them. It wasn't love, or caring, or even some maternal instinct mysteriously surviving death to cause a faint glimmer of recognition.

It was hunger.

Hunger drove her . . . drove *it*, to drag itself across a field of rot and gore, over the fallen body of one who had once been her husband—the love of her life—without a second glance, implacably moving toward the only food in sight: one who had been her only son, whom she had once given her life to protect.

She gave her life . . .

Long seconds passed as it clawed closer, nails splintering bloodlessly against the tarmac. The leg-stump flailed, scraping against the ground as the remaining leg kicked, leaving bits of itself behind in its unstoppable effort to reach him. Teeth clacked in mindless anticipation. Milky eyes stared.

Tears flowed, and then dried upon his cheeks.

"Goodbye, Mom."

He lifted the machete as he stepped forward.

With slow steps, the boy approached the Kwik-Mart, the last place he'd seen the old man. His eyes felt swollen and hot, though they were dry. The sound in his head wouldn't go away, a high buzz like a heat bug in the summertime. Maybe there was some water in the Kwik-Mart, something that had been missed by looters.

One could always hope.

"Nice work."

The old man stepped in front of him, blocking his search for water. He didn't carry the rifle—he'd probably run out of shells—but his revolvers sat on his hips, and his hat upon his head.

"Go away," the boy said, voice deep and raspy from crying, and thirst.

"No, I mean it. Using the terrain to slow 'em down like that. Well done! I guess you *were* listening to all my jawin'."

"Get out of my way."

The boy sidestepped. The old man slid back into his path.

"Just a minute now, just a minute. After all that, I have a question for you. That all right?"

The boy said nothing, merely raised his gaze to meet the old man's stare.

"How'd it feel?"

The old man smiled.

The boy stepped into the swing and hit the old man hard. They stood too close to use the blade, but the machete's hilt made a damn fine addition to his fist and he smashed it into that grinning face. His left hand snapped out as his right made contact, snatching a revolver from its holster as the old man staggered back. His right foot came up high then stomped into the old man's gut, pushing him away, creating room for him to swing the machete backhanded, an awkward follow-up to that roundhouse punch.

The old man flew back, blood flying from lips smashed

against breaking teeth, the wind exploding out of him. He was lighter than the boy had expected, less substantial, and much easier to move: the machete barely reached its target, slashing across ribs instead of burying itself deep in the old man's guts. The worn hat fluttered away as the rawboned old devil sprawled on his back, clutching his bloody side. The boy stepped in, stomping on one flailing arm to stop it from drawing a weapon, and aimed his captured revolver straight down at the old man's eye.

The eye was crinkled about the outer edge. Not a wince of pain, but in a smile.

"Do it."

The words were mushy, forced out between ruined lips and teeth.

"Just . . . do it. You're . . . ready now."

The words brought the boy up short, and he snorted.

What was that?

A breeze had sprung up, blowing off the plain, pushing away the stink of the parking lot carrion. He inhaled again, sniffing deep, picking up the scents of the old man: ancient body odor; coffee-powered halitosis; burnt gun oil. And under it . . . something horribly familiar.

Studying the rent in the old man's side, he used the tip of the machete to raise the tattered shirt from the skin. Beneath, just above the red gaping slice in the old flesh, a bandage wound about the lean torso, yellowed with sweat stains and stippled with the grime of long, hard travel.

Except across the ribs, where it was patinaed green and black with pus. The boy leaned down, the old man breathing hard, and sniffed. He rocked back in surprise.

Gangrene.

Rot.

Decay.

"What the hell is this?"

"T'other week. When we . . . lost the horse."

"When we . . . you mean, when you rescued me."

The old man nodded, too winded to continue. The boy shook his head, trying to make connections he *knew* were right in front of him, but the pieces wouldn't fit together in his mind.

"You got, what? Scratched?"

A head shake. "Bit."

"But then you're infected with . . ."

He trailed off, gazing at the parking lot covered with corpses that had arrived under their own power before the old man and his rifle had convinced them to finally lie down and stay there. A shaking finger pointed toward the field of meat that lay rotting in the sun.

"That was more than a week ago. You should be like—"

"Antibiotics slow the spread . . . you take enough of 'em. Won't cure it. Won't stop it. Slows it some."

The boy thought of the pills, the rattle of the old man shaking out dose after dose as the week wore on.

"But I thought those were . . . what the hell was this all about, then? You're just gonna—"

"Couldn't do it myself. Put a bullet in my brain. Not when it happened."

"But wh—"

"You'd never have made it."

The boy stared into the old man's eyes, still fierce though the leathery face was creased with pain.

"Not the way you were. Not lasted a day . . . way you were."

He lay back on the tarmac, eyes closed, breathing labored. The boy watched the ooze seeping through the filthy bandage, lost in thought.

"I'm tired."

The words, wheezed from between dry lips, brought the boy's attention up to the old man's face. His eyes were open again, bright with what looked like fever.

"I'm so tired. It's been a long damn week. I just want to rest. I just want to rest . . . and not get up."

Those shining eyes found the boy's face. Focused on his eyes.

"Think you're ready . . . to help an old man out?"

The boy held his gaze a moment, then nodded.

He thumbed the hammer back.

He tamped down the loose soil, then cast the shovel aside. It was a snow shovel he'd found in the Kwik-Mart, but it had been a far sight better than nothing. He'd dug the graves deep, deep enough to discourage any scavengers from digging them up, especially with so much meat just lying in the parking lot out in front of the little building.

"'Bout time for me to go," he said, standing at the foot of the three long humps of fresh earth. He turned and walked to where his saddlebags waited, and settled them on his shoulders, making certain not to tangle the straps on the rifle scope. Slipping the worn cowboy hat on in place of his long-lost Rockies cap, he turned back to the three graves.

"Guess this is goodbye."

Leaving the four of them behind—the mother, the father, the old man, and the boy—the man set off toward the middle of town, searching for that gun shop the old man had spoken of. He needed ammunition.

And maybe a horse.

A NIGHT AT THE SHOW

"My mom just has to check the calendar," Valerie Redfern said in school on Monday. "Once she double-checks the calendar she'll make up her mind. I know she'll let me, though. So, can you come?"

Checking the calendar seemed just silly to Hillary: what mom doesn't know her own kid's birthday? But Val came to her on Tuesday and told her it was on. The two of them, and Valerie's mom, of course, were going to the movies on Friday night for Valerie's ninth birthday.

When Friday came they went to see *Shrek 2*—not Hillary's first choice, but *she* wasn't the birthday girl—at the Palladium, the oldest theater in Spreewald. Hillary had never been to the Palladium before, and was surprised when Mrs. Redfern parked on a street with no theater in sight.

"The place is so old," said Mrs. Redfern, "there's no parking lot. You park where you can and walk the rest of the way. Come on."

Hillary was nervous for three of the four blocks they walked to the theater. The street was dirty, the sidewalk cracked, the buildings to either side old and grubby. Spray paint and boarded windows. Alleys swathed in shadow. She was pretty sure this was what her mother referred to as "the wrong part of town." She remained nervous until they rounded a corner and the Palladium came into view: even from a block away, Hillary was enchanted.

The Palladium was an ancient theater with bright lights and a brilliant marquee outside, and red carpeting and big, comfortable seats inside. The huge screen sat upon an old stage complete with an actual velvet curtain that opened to reveal the screen just before the movie, and closed after. The movie was even pretty good, both girls laughing and oohing along with each other as the story progressed. Valerie looked to be enjoying herself, while Hillary was having the time of her life.

Eventually, though, the show was over and it was time to go home. They left the theater and strolled down the street, the girls smelling of buttered popcorn, heads together, still giggling about their favorite scenes. Hillary'd had such a good time, was *still* having such a good time, she forgot all about being nervous as they walked along in the night air.

They were almost to the car when Mrs. Redfern stopped short, falling back a step to bump into the giggling girls. Peering around her, Hillary saw a big man leaning against the hood of Mrs. Redfern's car, thick arms folded over his chest like he was waiting for a bus. Hillary didn't think he was waiting for a bus, though. He was looking straight at them.

That must be the stranger Mom always warned me about, Hillary thought. *I'm glad Valerie's mom is here, she'll—*

"Uh, girls?" Mrs. Redfern turned, gripping their shoulders. "Why don't we go back to the theater and—oh!"

She stared over the girls' heads, looking at something behind them. Hillary craned about to see, and saw another man, also big, a little more than a block away. He, too, stared at them, and her heart froze when his eyes shifted to meet hers.

He smiled.

"Oh, no," whispered Valerie's mom. "No. No-no."

Hillary looked up to see Mrs. Redfern's head turning this way and that, eyes open wide, looking for help, but they were alone on the night-dark street. She saw the expression in those eyes and was shocked to realize that, grown-up or not, Mrs. Redfern was just as scared as she was. Valerie stiffened beside her.

"Mom? He's coming."

Mrs. Redfern turned back, and Hillary looked toward the car again. The man wasn't leaning any more, but walking toward them. One hand reached into a pocket and came out holding something small, something Hillary couldn't quite see, but it glittered in the light cast by the street lamps.

"Hey, lady," called the man behind them, voice rough and loud. "Where you going?"

Mrs. Redfern's fingers squeezed Hillary's shoulder as the other man laughed. She suddenly dropped into a crouch, pointing. Hillary looked, followed the finger, and saw the mouth of an alley on the far side of the street. The grip on her shoulder became a sudden, hard shove. "Run!"

They ran.

Behind them, a pair of voices shouted:

"Hey!"

"I'll go this way, you go that way! That way, *that* way!"

Hillary didn't look back, just put her head down, sprinting hard as they entered the alley, the girls leading.

"Come *on!*" Mrs. Redfern moved ahead, catching each girl by a hand. She sped up, towing them along, pulling Hillary into a speed she never could have attained on her own. Tears streamed down the girl's face, and she was already out of breath. *Strangers back there—go faster, go faster* echoed through her head as they approached the end of the alley and the relative brightness of the street beyond.

Through the sounds of their feet slapping the pavement and her own heart pounding in her ears, she heard Mrs. Redfern's voice.

"Left! We'll try to circle around to the car—go left!"

Hillary nodded with a sob, lacking the breath to say anything more. She was being pulled along, taking huge, vaulting steps, her feet only touching the ground every six or eight feet. She was absurdly reminded of her visit to the bouncy house when the fair had been in town a few months ago. That had been fun.

This was not.

A shout in the alley behind them, deep and threatening, chased all thoughts of the fair from Hillary's mind, replacing them with the wish that she could fly.

They took the corner at a dead run. The towing hand banked Hillary into a full-speed curve out onto the sidewalk, inertia swinging her wide, missing a parked car by mere inches. She wanted to shout "Look out!" but she was crying far too hard to even try.

She was no athlete, and her legs already burned with fatigue, though she dared not slow down; *couldn't* slow down. She was being helped along, but her exhausted legs were having a hard time keeping up. She urged her feet to move faster, but they wouldn't listen, feeling instead like she was wading through peanut butter. One of her sneaker-clad toes caught the sidewalk. She fell, her knees slamming to the pavement, shocking pain forcing a breathless scream. Her free hand also hit the cement, the rough surface taking skin off her palm. She fell, but did not slow. Mrs. Redfern gripped her hand hard, dragging Hillary a couple of steps before yanking her upward.

"Come on, dear, please!"

Hillary shuffled her feet under her once more and staggered on. Some dim part of her was aware of the terrible pain from her knees, but she was too terrified to pay attention right now.

"Down here!"

Mrs. Redfern jerked her sideways and then they were running down an alley Hillary hadn't even noticed, too focused on staying on her feet to keep track of her surroundings. They were passing a pair of dumpsters, the security light above them beating back the shadows that ruled the alley, when Mrs. Redfern drew up short with two hissed words. "Too late."

Hillary looked up, panting, only to wish she hadn't. A tall, dark shadow blocked the alley's far mouth. A shadow that moved toward them with an easy, confident stride. Silhouetted as he was by the lights of the street beyond, she still made out the blade sprouting from one big fist.

Hillary's head whip-snapped as Mrs. Redfern spun them all about, taking a half step back the way they had come.

"Going somewhere?"

Not ten paces away was the man who had been chasing them. His chest heaved, and he glared at them as if angry he'd been forced to run. His knife didn't glint or shine, the blade a flat black as it thrust out of his white-knuckled grip.

"It's too late," repeated Mrs. Redfern, her head swiveling as she searched the alley. Hillary looked too, but saw nothing but steel security doors and barred windows: no escape. Though the men were in shadow, silhouetted against the streets at either end of this little space, the three of them were under the security lamp, as well-lit as the two dumpsters they stood next to. Mrs. Redfern grabbed their shoulders and thrust them between the dumpsters, into a six-foot-wide cave of moist stink. She knelt before them, whispering intensely, though Hillary barely heard her over the beating of her own heart.

"Stay here, out of sight, all right? I'll try to lead them away—when they follow me, you girls *run*, you understand? Run and get somewhere safe. Find the police."

Valerie was visibly trembling, shaking her head, murmuring "No, no, no, no." Mrs. Redfern took her daughter's face in her hands.

"It'll be all right. Just stay calm, okay? You can *do* this. Just try to stay calm and quiet. For Hillary. It'll be fine, honey. We'll keep Hillary safe."

A big hand fell on Mrs. Redfern's shoulder, yanking her away from the girls. She didn't fall, but spun to her feet, stepping away from the dumpsters, out of Hillary's sight.

"I asked you a question, bitch. You going somewhere?"

"Just seeing a movie is all," came Mrs. Redfern's voice, frightened but in control. "I don't want any trouble, okay?

No trouble."

"Sorry lady," came another voice; the man who'd blocked the other end of the alley. "That's all we *got* is trouble."

Hillary listened, wide-eyed, trembling, heart still pounding in her ears. Through all that, even through the drama unfolding just out of sight around those dumpsters, she became aware of Valerie's voice. Despite her mother's admonishment to keep quiet, Valerie was standing with her head bowed and still shaking from side to side, repeating the same word with each jerk of the dark curtain of hair that hid her face from the world.

"No-no-no-no—"

Val was trembling so hard she looked like a marionette being worked by a palsied puppeteer, chest bouncing back and forth, shoulders jerking this way and that. Had Hillary ever even heard of a seizure, she would have thought of the word now. She hadn't; all she knew was the way Valerie was moving looked *wrong*, and frightened her as much as everything else that was going on. She almost called out to Valerie's mother for help, but the sound of male voices rising in anger was a forceful reminder that she needed to keep quiet. *They* needed to keep quiet.

Wanting to reassure her, Hillary reached out to Valerie. She searched for something to say that might comfort her friend, might silence her, but could think of nothing but the here and now, and the fear. She laid a gentle hand upon Valerie's twitching shoulder and the shaking and muttering stopped like a machine seizing up, the sudden stillness itself startling Hillary. She had one quick moment to think *there, I helped her, everything's gonna be okay.*

Valerie's head snapped around so fast Hillary gasped—then reeled backward, shoulders and head striking the dumpster behind her with enough force to stun, though she barely noticed the impact.

Valerie . . . wasn't Valerie.

What stared out at Hillary when the rippling barrier of hair was flung aside wasn't the familiar smiling face of her dark-eyed schoolmate: it was a monster, a demon from Hell, like she'd seen in the stained glass the few times she'd been to church.

The face—if she could call it a face—was elongated, stretched, the mouth and nose pushing forward, black lips pulled taut as the mouth widened. *Expanded.* The skin stretched and moved as things beneath it flexed and writhed. There was a series of cracks and snaps, like when the school bully had broken all her colored pencils one by one, but this was faster. Sharper.

The mouth surged forward as she watched, straining the face still further, and there was a moment where she thought *something's in there, something's in her head and it's trying to get out* before the black, flattened lips parted, spread wide, and Hillary could see what was trying to get out, what was filling that face to overflowing, forcing it to expand just to make room.

Teeth.

The lips skinned back to reveal a tangled forest of teeth, long and sharp and white against gums of red and black. So many teeth, even *that* great maw seemed crowded, packed with canines, incisors and molars. The mouth *had* to open, was *forced* to open by this terrible multitude of tooth and fang.

And she could swear they were lengthening before her eyes.

Hillary inhaled to scream, her gaze rising past the blackened, distended nose, so pushed and distorted the nostrils faced her rather than the ground. Coarse, tufted hair surrounded that mouth and nose—thickening and spreading even as she watched—to cover the cheeks, and the scream died in her throat when she found the thing's eyes.

Valerie's eyes peered out at her from that hideous mask of growing horror. Valerie's eyes: dark with anger, bright with rage, and filled with a terrible sorrow. It was that sadness, so strong it was nearly tangible, that closed Hillary's throat against the scream that welled up within her like magma from a venting volcano. The scream rose, choked off, and died, the breath leaving Hillary in a whisper, raised brows turning the quiet sound into a question.

"Valerie?"

The terrible jaw cracked open, just a touch. Air hissed through that forest of fangs, an audible intake of breath as someone might make before speaking, preparing themselves for delivering bad news or telling a hard truth. The thing's weight shifted, feet moving just a bit, as if beginning to take a step. One arm rose, half reaching toward her, and Hillary saw not a hand at the end of the arm but a claw, fingers far too long and with an extra knuckle each, tipped with talons curved like a fish hooks and just as sharp.

She saw all this in a moment; then two things happened simultaneously.

One was that Hillary took a half-step back, jerking away from that rising claw, fear slamming her against the dumpster once more, air rushing into her lungs in a mighty gasp.

The other was that a sound came from out in the alley proper, penetrating the silent bubble that had enveloped their horrid little cave, cutting through the shock fogging Hillary's mind and bringing back the drama unfolding in the alley where Mrs. Redfern was trying to save them all: the slap of flesh striking flesh and a woman's voice crying out in pain.

The thing that had been Valerie whirled to face the sound, moving so fast spittle flew from its half-open mouth, spraying the air in an arc before it. Hillary could see now just how far the thing's muzzle protruded—an inhuman profile. Dropping into a crouch, it flexed shoulders that strained the seams of Valerie's sweatshirt, thick and humped with so much muscle the head was thrust forward on its powerful neck. Those black lips, already skinned back, now peeled all the way to the dark flaring nostrils, baring fangs as long as Hillary's fingers: a full nightmare's-worth of teeth.

The thing loosed a growl, the sound reaching out to tickle the base of Hillary's spine with fingers of ice. She might have whimpered in fear, but there wasn't time. The rumble deep within its chest exploded into a roar as the thing launched itself into motion, so fluid and fast that one instant it was there, the next it was gone. Hillary caught a glimpse of its sock-clad feet, the cotton shockingly white under the bright security lamp, disappearing from view as the thing leapt out into the alley.

Distracted as she was by the black spots flicking in front of her eyes, she noticed the thing's toes had burst through the socks, just as long and taloned as those crooked fingers. She stared at the scratches the hooked claws had left in the cement; just stared and listened to the sounds of the beast roaring and men screaming, one of them fading into the distance while the other remained somewhere close by, shrieking again and again until the sound cut off with the finality of a slamming door. The scratch marks grew closer as the dumpster slid up her back, those flicking black spots multiplying until they finally blocked out the world, and she let herself fall into their embrace.

Hillary woke to a sound; a noise she knew she should recognize, but her head was filled with fog, and she couldn't quite connect the dots.

She also felt cement against her face. She pushed herself up from the ground, looking around bleary-eyed, finding nothing but dumpsters.

Dumpsters?

It all came back, a splash of cold water to the face—the movie, the men, the running . . . and then Valerie. Valerie going away and that terrible *thing* taking her place, that thing that had worn Valerie's clothes, had stood in Valerie's place like it was . . . like it was . . .

. . . like it *was* Valerie?

The last thing she remembered was the Valerie-thing leaping, the men screaming—and she suddenly recognized the sound. Somewhere nearby, a young girl was crying. Weeping like her heart was breaking in two and she wasn't sure yet whether she'd survive. Someone was murmuring quiet words of comfort. Hillary could make out nothing of the words, but recognized the voice of the girl doing the sobbing—and was surprised. It was a voice she'd heard laughing, being tough, being funny, but never crying. Not even once, no matter how mean the other kids were at school. It sounded like—

"Valerie?"

The word was a croak, her mouth too dry. She worked her tongue, trying to dredge up some moisture. The rough cement bit her palms, then her bruised and painful knees as she slowly got to her feet, her voice coming as saliva found her mouth.

"Valerie?"

Louder, but there was still no response. She looked out into the open and her eye was caught by something she hadn't noticed before: boots, large and black, lying on the tarmac. Jeans-clad legs sprouted from the boots, sprawling across the ground past the edge of one of the dumpsters sheltering her and out of sight. Her voice came a third time, a mere whisper pulled from her through reflex, unconsciously responding to her best friend's voice. Hillary stepped out into the alley. The jeans-clad legs led up to a man. She was unsteady, felt . . . disconnected. There was a soft buzzing in her ears, and the world around her was foggy. If she concentrated, though, she could make just a little bit of the world clear again.

Hillary focused, her eyes following the man's form. Knees, bent this way and that, as if he were a doll cast aside by a careless child. The jacket thrown open, shirt pulled up to expose a bulge of hairy white belly. Beside the man, one of his hands clutched the ground. She noticed the way his fingernails had shattered against the blacktop, ragged chunks of nail and skin mixing with the blood that trailed along the ground for about a half a foot before pooling beneath his ruined fingers.

That looks like it hurt, she thought. *A lot.* A part of her somewhere was trying to tell her that yes, it did hurt a lot, and it was *important*, but that part seemed far away, and she just didn't want to listen right now. The wordless torrent of sorrow sounded closer, and she could make out some of the comforting words being murmured in response.

". . . Not your fault . . . none of this . . . sorry, honey, so sorry, but . . ."

Hillary's gaze wandered higher, crossing the man's chest to

his twisted shoulders, then higher still, expecting to see a face; but her curious stare ground to a halt before getting that far, riveted by the man's throat.

Or where his throat was *supposed* to be.

Where his throat was supposed to be was a ragged open hole filled with mush, stringy things and bits, all of it reminding her of the first time she'd opened the top of a pumpkin to make a jack-o'-lantern. She'd been grossed out at the mess of *stuff* she'd seen inside, like the pumpkin was half melting, or gone bad already, with seeds and strings and *goo*, all slimy and disgusting; but this stuff here wasn't orange like the inside of a pumpkin: it was red, bright red and dark red and just red because it wasn't the inside of a *pumpkin*, but the inside of a *person* and—

This was the real Hillary doing the talking now, the part that had been trying to warn her that the splintered hand *was* important, that had started so far away but had fought its way closer every second until now it was so loud she couldn't ignore it; and though she tried not to look at the messy hole where the man's throat used to be, she *did* look, understanding what she was seeing although she wanted so much to just ignore that too, understanding that this man was dead—

She vomited: hot popcorn, soda, and the chicken she'd had for dinner (*that seemed so long ago now was it **really** just earlier tonight?*) spraying against the green dumpster with enough force to bounce off, spattering her sneakers. Her stomach clenched so hard she fell, slivers of pain driving deep into her battered knees, nearly landing in the puddle of her own mess.

"Baby, I'm so sorry."

The voice was louder, clearer now that Hillary had come back to herself and the foggy feeling had blown away. She recognized Mrs. Redfern's voice, shaking with emotion, a slight hitch in the word *sorry* stretching the two syllables into three, giving the impression the woman was crying. The pavement bit into her knees even more than the cement dumpster pad had, and the moist stink of the dumpster's contents mingled with that of the hot puddle between her hands in a way that made her stomach lurch again, the painful twitch of an already abused abdomen. She forced herself to her feet, the green metal cool beneath one hand as she leaned against it for support and turned to face the crying woman.

They sat there, at the head of the man lying torn open on the ground, Mrs. Redfern sitting tailor-fashion, Valerie in her lap. The woman was comforting her daughter, cuddling her like a toddler, rocking her back and forth as Valerie cried. Hillary watched as sobs wracked her friend, her body shuddering with such strength her mother's frame shook as well.

"I'm sorry . . . I know you tried, honey, I know . . . I'm sorry it has to be this way."

Hillary took an unsteady step. The fog might have been gone from her vision, but a touch of it remained inside her head. She could see, tottering closer, it wasn't Valerie's crying that shook her mother so, but the sobbing of the woman herself. Tears streamed down her cheeks as she consoled her daughter.

Hillary couldn't figure out what was so wrong. The bad man who'd chased them, who had hurt Valerie's mom, was dead, and that was yucky and awfully scary, but they were safe. The scary thing that had taken Valerie's place was gone—and they were *safe*! She desperately wanted to go home, but Valerie and her mom were still crying *so* much . . .

"Valerie," she said. "You okay?"

Her friend's sobbing paused, just for a second, then resumed even harder. Mrs. Redfern spoke without lifting her cheek from her daughter's hair. "She's fine, dear."

"Why is she crying? Aren't we safe now? I just . . . I just want to go home."

Mrs. Redfern's back stiffened, but she still spoke in gentle tones, still pressed her face to the side of Valerie's.

"She's crying because she's sad, Hillary. She's very, very sad."

"Because of him?" Hillary pointed toward the man, though neither of them looked at her.

"Sort of, yes. This is my fault. Just . . . all my fault. The full moon was almost here. Not quite, but close. I checked, I double-checked, I mean, everything should have been okay. Then *they* had to come along. There was too much stress, it was all too close, and she couldn't cope. She tried."

She leaned back, a hand stroking Val's small dark head, smoothing the hair back from her face. Hillary could see Mrs. Redfern in profile, could see her smiling despite her tears. Her voice lowered to a broken whisper.

"You tried so hard."

"But . . ." Hillary was confused. She didn't know what to say, what to ask.

"But," Mrs. Redfern raised her voice, addressing Hillary, though she still stared into her daughter's face. "She knows how it has to be. She tried, and she did *so* well, but she knows how things *have* to be."

"Is it the . . . that *thing*? Is that why she's crying?"

Mrs. Redfern was silent, the only sound in the alley the sobs still coming from Valerie. Quieter now, but still coming.

"That thing is gone," Hillary pointed out, starting to cry herself. She was exhausted, frightened, and she just wanted to be home in bed where her own mother would smooth her hair and tell her things would be all right. "And those guys are gone. You said we'd be safe. We're safe, right? They can't hurt us any more. Can we go home now?"

Mrs. Redfern eased her daughter off her lap, sliding her gently to the ground.

"Yes—that *thing*—that's why she's crying. I was supposed to lead those men away from you two. She tried *so* hard to stay calm. But she couldn't."

Valerie sat facing away from Hillary, shoulders shaking. Her mother rose smoothly to her feet, standing over the girl on the ground as if talking to her, though her words were still directed at Hillary.

"She was supposed to keep that thing away, but she didn't."

"But that thing saved us," Hillary said. "It was all scary and everything, but it *saved* us! They can't hurt us any more, right? Why can't we just go home?"

"Because that *thing* needs to stay secret. Needs to stay hidden. No one can know."

"But that other guy ran away, and—"

"He won't get far. And we're not worried about him right now." Mrs. Redfern finally turned to face Hillary, tears streaming unchecked down her face. "I'm so, *so* sorry, child, but we weren't trying to keep you safe . . . from them."

"But—" Hillary began, but the words stopped, breathing stopped, the whole world stopped as Hillary's eyes widened and all the fear the fog had kept at bay was unleashed all at once.

Mrs. Redfern's face . . . *changed.*

Stretched.

Pushed forward.

The breath Hillary had intended to fuel her words came out in all in a rush with a sound like a steam whistle. She stumbled back, away from the apparition that took a step toward her. Her foot slipped in the still-warm puddle of vomit and she fell, landing in the little space between the dumpsters once more, the cement biting and scratching at her hands and backside as she scrambled away from the advancing nightmare. Out in the alley Valerie continued to cry, louder now, as if trying to drown out what was going on behind her. In the mouth of the small cave formed by the dumpsters, the creature wept, tears streaming from the still-human eyes set in its misshapen, hairy nightmare face. Black lips skinned back from white teeth. Jaws cracked open and a black tongue writhed. Sounds issued forth from the terrible jaws: not growling, but four distinct sounds that might have been individual syllables had they been issued from a human throat.

No one can know.

The weeping nightmare crouched forward, crowding its bulk into the small space, easing in like a wolf into its den. Hillary began to scream.

She did not scream for long.

IN FULL MEASURE

Eva stared in wonder at the man on her front porch, the smell of Father's sickroom clinging to her clothes. She was still breathless from running down the stairs to halt the pounding that had begun and not stopped, loud enough to disturb Father even in his swoon.

Had it been, as she'd expected, some rude youth, perhaps with knocking fist still raised, she was fully prepared to offer up a sharp lesson in visiting etiquette. Yanking the door open to find an elderly dandy, barely higher than her own chin though dressed in (according to Sears and Roebuck) the very height of fashion, well, it quite took the wind out of her sails. She noticed he clutched a large, buff-colored envelope in both small hands.

Now how in the world did he pound like that with both hands full? she wondered, then noticed the muddy streaks marring the bottom of her door.

"I'll see Wilbur Clarke, if you please," the little man said, his voice high, nasal, and imperious.

Eva merely stared at his soaked and mud-covered (though still stylish) left shoe. Then at the single-horse buckboard in front of her house, right next to what had to be the only mud puddle left in the county. Then back at the marks on her door.

"Did you *kick* my door?"

"I'll *see* Wilbur Clarke, if you please."

The little old bandy cock had raised his voice, over-enunciating as if speaking to a thick-witted child; annoyance welled up in Eva, firmly pushing aside her disbelief. She spoke just as clearly as he had.

"No. You won't."

"I will," he said, stepping forward as if to actually enter the house uninvited. Rather than retreating, as he'd obviously expected, Eva stood tall and folded her arms across her chest, physically barring entry to the door-kicking little savage.

⚖

Devin nearly overbalanced, coming up on his toes to stop his forward momentum as he realized this little strumpet was *not* stepping back as she should have. He'd been thrown off-kilter by the mud puddle and had been venting his annoyance by kicking the farmhouse door when it had suddenly opened to reveal this . . . girl.

He had gotten a description of Wilbur Clarke back in town: an older man with gnarled hands, broad shoulders, and a sunbaked face both creased and leathery. He had *not* expected beautiful, honey-blond hair and flawless, sun-bronzed skin. She was such a surprise he merely gaped, his reason for being there in the first place knocked clean out of his mind. Then she inspected the mud he'd left on her door, and a strange panic struck him—a youthful, confusing feeling—and he barked out the first thing he thought of, trying to distract her.

"I'll see Wilbur Clarke, if you please."

He had to ask twice—something that had not happened for years—and then she refused.

Refused!

That slapped his confusion aside. Refused? Made to stand out in the sun by this mere slip of a girl?

Me?

He'd started forward, just as he would in any meeting, confident of compliance, knowing full well he was in charge out here in mud-flats Kansas, just as he was back in his Boston boardroom—

—and the girl had barred his way. As she drew near he detected a strange, sour odor coming from her (apparently cleanliness was *not* next to godliness out here in corn country), and when she did not move he strained to avoid touching her. He tottered back onto his heels, retreating a half step to keep his balance.

Unbelievable, he thought. *She's a pretty girl, yes, but there are* **limits,** *by God!*

Struggling to maintain his temper and at least a modicum of professionalism, something he could see these farm people sorely lacked, he drew himself up to his full height (such as it was), waved the envelope before her nose, and spoke in his most commanding tone.

"I have here certain official bank documents that Wilbur Clarke is required to see and sign. You will either lead me to him or go and fetch him, girl, but either way, you will do it at once."

"No," she said, raising an eyebrow. "I will not."

⚖

Part of Eva watched the situation developing on her doorstep with a detached pride. Following her mother's death the previous year, she had retreated from life and become nothing more than her father's daughter—a fine, God-fearing woman who cooked, read, and went to church. It had been a good arrangement: she had wanted to be taken care of in the wake of her loss, while her father had needed someone to care for and protect, as he had not been able to protect his wife from the fever that had stolen her away.

A few weeks ago, however, it was her father who had begun to require looking after, and Eva had stepped smoothly into the position, as if all she had been waiting for was the chance. She had taken more and more responsibility on the farm, and it was no mere farmer's daughter who had answered this door. Standing tall and barring entry to this old popinjay of a bank messenger, Eva reminded herself of her mother, and her heart swelled at the comparison.

Though it was also swelling with anger.

"Not that I expect a drop of sympathy, but my father lies upstairs in a sickbed, thanks in great part to your boss and his banking practices."

She heard a slight tremor in her voice, but managed to hold herself to a raised eyebrow as the only physical manifestation of her anger, looking down at this messenger-man with an imperiousness to match his own.

"I will not disturb him for one such as you. I will, however, give you a message to carry to your master."

Despite her intentions of iron control, she loomed over the small figure, her voice rising a notch in volume, her finger pointing at his nose.

"It is *his* fault you cannot deliver your missive. My father dealt with Mr. Henson for more years than I have been alive, and Mr. Henson always dealt squarely. Farming is a variable business, and sometimes there were extensions, but my father always came through; always paid him, eventually. You can ask him, if he hasn't been run out of town yet."

The old man on her doorstep shifted slightly, fanning himself with the oversized envelope still clutched in one knobby hand.

"Then he sold the bank to your Mr. Capshaw, and everything changed. All those foreclosures! Father started to worry. Little messenger-men—just like you—running about with their documents and papers, while good, hard-working people lost their land. Their homes. I don't know your Mr. Capshaw, but he's forcing people from their homes for some reason I do not understand; but understand it or not, I find it despicable."

She straightened, folding her arms once more. "My father's worked himself into a sickbed trying to bring the harvest in, trying to ward off the foreclosure he saw coming—worked harder than both our young field hands, and he is not a young man. So you take that envelope of yours and you bring it back to your Mr. Capshaw, and you tell him to bring it back *himself* if he has a mind to. I doubt he will, but if he does, then at least I'll have the chance to give *him* a piece of my mind as well."

Eva was breathing hard, her head hot with righteous anger. The messenger-man held up a palm.

"Before you go on," he said, in that irritating, nasal way of his, "please allow me to introduce myself properly."

He offered her his hand.

She stared for a moment before good manners took over, and she reached out to take it.

"Evangeline Clarke?" he said, raising an eyebrow. Startled to hear her name upon the stranger's lips, Eva gave only a quick nod. The little man tightened his grip on her fingers.

"Wonderful to meet you. My name is Devin Capshaw."

Eva froze.

⚖

Devin was pleased when his revelation shocked her into silence. Being upbraided by a woman no older than his daughters was almost more than he could bear, though he had to admit the young lady possessed a certain fire his own progeny lacked. He nearly smiled as he considered his real reason for coming out into the middle of nowhere to serve papers personally. Though he *did* want to see all the property that would soon be his, and he would never admit it to them, it was the gossip from his process servers that had really goaded him out into this world of dirt and sun and mud.

Bedroom adventures. Haybarn romps. Grateful widows and farmers' curious daughters. To overhear the men who worked for him, to listen to their talk, you'd think every farmhouse in the plains was home to at least one woman of dubious morality, if not two.

Maybe even three.

It had been enough to spark even *his* old imagination.

He'd paid little attention to her words, wondering instead what all that passion would be like when translated into action. He watched her bosom heave with barely suppressed emotion, and imagined it heaving for completely different reasons. Butterflies fluttered about in his guts. He faltered. He wondered how he could possibly dare. Then, gripping the papers that gave him legal and financial authority over this young woman, he took advantage of her stunned silence to launch into a little speech of his own, one that had been at the back of his mind each time he'd approached a door out in this godforsaken land, only to forget all about it when the door was opened by a leather-faced farmer or his even more leathery-faced wife.

This was his chance.

"My dear Evangeline," he said, showing every one of his teeth. "It is not a matter of my wanting to do ill to you and yours; it is a simple matter of the facts. Fact: you owe the bank a debt. Fact: I own said bank, so, fact: the debt you owe is mine to collect, and I am collecting—in full measure. The paperwork I have here is all aboveboard and legal, according to the laws that govern this country and separate us from the beasts of the field. Now I could be like your Mr. Henson and offer extensions left and right, but that is not my way. It has always been my practice to collect the full measure of what is mine just as soon as it *becomes* mine, and I see no reason to alter that practice today."

He tightened his grip and tugged lightly, pulling her just the slightest bit off-balance before licking his suddenly dry lips, and taking the plunge.

"Of course, you could *give* me a reason."

Her lovely eyes, blank with surprise when he'd revealed his identity, had hardened over the course of his speech. Now they went round with confusion, and just a touch of hope.

"A reason? Me? To do what, change your way of doing business? What do you mean?"

"Oh, I think you know." He hoped to God she knew. He didn't think he could bring himself to explain. "A beautiful young woman such as yourself, out here, alone, with a man."

Her eyes remained uncomprehending. He bit his mental lip and tried to smile confidently, though it felt like a weak, awkward grin.

"Come, come, Evangeline. You're a grown woman. Do I really have to spell it out for you?"

He held his breath.

Her eyes went suddenly wide with shock as the import of his words finally struck home. Reading her correctly, Devin squeezed just as she jerked back, and her hand remained trapped within his own, though he was nearly pulled from his feet.

"If your father is in the house," he said, words fueled by lust and panic tumbling out of his mouth, tripping over one another in their effort to be heard, "we can always go into the barn for privacy—I understand that's how things are done out this way?"

"Mr. Capshaw!" She tried to free herself again, but Devin hung on, desperate to keep some kind of control over the rapidly worsening situation. "But . . . you're a married man!"

Devin thought about Margaret, still back in Boston with their daughters. Never an attractive woman, even when they were younger, he'd married her for the money her father would eventually bequeath to her. She had started out homely and had only gotten older, their two children more a testament to the power of strong drink than to love. Nowadays, when she puckered up for a kiss she resembled nothing so much as a cat's backside—and was nearly as lust-inducing.

Still, the thought of the trouble he'd be in if Margaret somehow found out about this little attempted indiscretion caused his throat to constrict, his voice trembling ever so slightly.

"I won't tell her if you won't."

⚖

Eva's mind went blank for a moment when the little man with one muddy shoe introduced himself. He waited a beat, apparently letting his identity sink in, then started speaking once more. Her first coherent thought was *well, well, so this is The Banker from Boston. At least that explains why he's talking through his nose.*

Shock followed this thought, then anger at the realization that her long-wished-for confrontation had just happened, and she had effectively missed it. She felt a flicker of pride at the thought of what she had said and how she had said it, though she knew herself well enough to admit she would never have been able to make that speech had she known just whom she was making it to.

Then *his* words penetrated the emotions roiling inside her, and it all just swirled away—the shock, the anger, and the pride, like he had pulled the plug from a drain.

*Everything I said, pouring out my heart, and he simply brushes it aside! All this—the casual ruining of people's lives—it's all just **business** to him.*

The more he spoke, the more her heart filled once again with indignation, though it was tempered by the sure knowledge that nothing she said or did was going to affect him in any way. The cold emptiness in her heart moved into her stomach, and seemed to crowd out everything inside. She had a sudden and powerful urge to visit the outhouse.

Everything: all Father's hard work, all of her prayers—none of it mattered.

We're losing the farm. My God, where will we go?

"Of course," he said, "you could *give* me a reason."

Her heart fluttered in her hollow breast, a startled bird in a cage. "A reason? Me?" She reviewed his last few words in her mind, trying not to let hope push her into misapprehension. "To do what, change your way of doing business? What do you mean?"

Please, Lord, let him be as aboveboard as he claims. I don't think I could take it if this were a trick.

She more than half-expected him to laugh in her face at the suggestion he might alter his personal business practices just for her, and you could have knocked her over with a feather when, rather than laughing outright, his answer was somewhat encouraging.

"Oh, I think you know."

Evangeline had, in the privacy of her own mind, occasionally thought trousers on a woman to be a good thing, at least out here on the farm where sometimes dresses simply got in the way when one was trying to work. Today, however, and at this moment specifically, she was thankful for her ankle-length garment, as it masked the tremble that had set into her knees.

Smiling as if the expression were new to him, he offered a clue, though in her tizzy she nearly missed it, he spoke so softly.

". . . young woman such as yourself, out here, alone, with a man."

She sifted the conversation for meaning, praying this apparent chance would not be snatched from her grasp before she managed to puzzle it out, but it seemed all a muddle. People's debts. His rights. People—the Clarkes included—losing their homes. And what in the name of the Savior did her *age* have to do with anything?

Every road in her mind ran in a different direction, none of them making any connections . . . though he had said something just before mentioning her age, and though she had not quite caught it, it had sounded a little like . . .

A suspicion of what he was going on about clawed at the edges of her mind trying to get in; she could feel it, but didn't quite have it yet. The feeling that she wouldn't like it when it *did* arrive was clear as a bell, however. She was aware of him watching her as she tried to puzzle it out, when suddenly he again gave her that strange smile that seemed to have nothing to do with happiness.

"Come, come, Evangeline. You're grown woman. Do I really have to spell it out for you?"

A grown woman, she thought, pieces beginning to click into place in her mind. *A grown woman . . . alone with a man . . . can do something to change his mind?*

The pieces locked.

Oh my stars! He wants to—that's a leer, an honest-to-goodness leer! This evil little man comes out here to destroy our lives, and then says he may offer us an extension if I'll—

She tried to pull her hand away, but his grip was surprising.

"If your father is in the house," he said smoothly, his voice filled with what she now recognized as carnal intent, "we can always go into the barn for privacy—I understand that's how things are done out this way."

That last was said with a sneer, making it perfectly clear what this man from the east thought of people "out this way."

"Mr. Capshaw!"

She tried to pull away again, harder than before, but Capshaw retained her hand with compact strength, and a competence that suggested this was not his first time manhandling a woman. His other hand, the one still holding his all-important papers, flashed at her in the afternoon sun, and her eye was drawn to the shiny gold ring on his third finger. She said the first thing to pop into her head, wanting only to be rid of this horrible man.

"But . . . you're a married man!"

His eyes took on a momentary calculating expression.

"I won't tell her if you won't."

But you would know, she thought, shocked at his callous attitude. *And I would know . . . and God would know.*

That stiffened her spine. Any man who could so casually cast aside an oath made in the house of the Lord was not a man she would deal with. She straightened, glaring into his upturned face, finally snapping her hand free.

"I used to pray for you, Mr. Capshaw. I used to pray for God to find His way into your heart, to turn you from this path of moral destruction you have set yourself upon. But now, now that I've met you and seen the depths to which your soul has sunk, I can see that nothing I or anyone else can say or do will bring you back into the light."

She glared at the envelope still clutched in his hand, the legal papers that spelled out their doom, and sunlight glinted off the ring on his finger—the symbol, now, of his broken covenant with God. Any uncertainty burned away in a towering anger, unlike anything she had ever felt in her young life.

"Now, Mr. Capshaw, I only hope that God can see His way clear to giving you exactly what you deserve, whether it be striking you down or casting you out of Heaven to burn for all eternity."

She was surprised by the words even as she said them, even more so because she realized there was no exaggeration in them.

Lord, she thought, *I have never prayed ill for anyone before, no matter how angry I was, be they man, woman, or child, but I do pray to you now, God, to let this man feel your wrath and give him exactly what he deserves in full measure.*

Eva had the satisfaction of seeing Devin Capshaw's eyes widen at her harsh words, and was about to add more—she wasn't sure what yet, but she was positive it would simply shrivel his bones with its righteousness—when she saw something in the distant sky past the Boston banker's hat. Whatever she'd been about to say, the words dried up, unspoken, as she shielded her eyes to take a better look.

A cloud. Dark, like a storm cloud, it spread across the sky to the northwest.

"What is . . ." she began, but trailed off as she took an unconscious step forward, trying to see better. Capshaw stepped back, turning to look as well.

"What *is* that?" he said.

"I don't know."

It *looked* like a cloud, but it didn't *move* like a cloud. It appeared to come with the wind, but faster. And it moved . . . oddly. Wrongly. Rather than spreading evenly, as she had first thought, now that it was closer (and it *had* drawn noticeably closer, even in this short time) she saw the front edge of the dark mass thrusting forward arm-like extrusions, sparkling here and there with reflected sunlight as they snaked across the sky. She looked east and west but saw no break in this cloud, as if a curtain were being drawn across the world from horizon to horizon, leaving the earth in darkness. It flew closer as they watched, shrouding the land before them with threatening rapidity.

"What's that noise?" Capshaw's voice was tinged with fear. "Is that thunder?"

Eva heard it too, a low, humming rumble. Unlike thunder, however, this sound did not roll or fade, but grew. It grew, she realized, with the approaching cloud, riding it rather than preceding it.

"I don't know," she said, watching the line of shadow racing toward them as above the first tendrils of the cloud wound over the house, and the rumble grew into a buzzing roar.

Something fell from the sky like a stone, whirring through the air to land in the road before the house with a sharp *thack* and a puff of dirt. Another landed, farther away, but then a third came in, to light with the tiniest of thuds on the edge of the porch.

It was a locust, both longer and fatter than Eva's thumb. Eva saw it, and her heart became a solid, frozen lump in her breast.

"What the hell is *that?*" Capshaw cried, shouting to be heard over the noise.

"That, I think," Eva whispered through a mouth gone suddenly dry, "is Judgment."

She backed through the door, closing it and slipping the bolt home just before small, desperate fists began to beat upon the far side.

⚖

The Clarke woman's reaction to his suggestion was like something out of a nightmare for Devin. To be dressed down by one of his daughters' contemporaries was bad enough, but when she was actually in the right, and he knew it, it was enough to make him break out in a cold sweat. He'd wanted to interrupt her angry tirade, but she had sounded so much like Margaret he just hadn't dared.

When she'd ground to a halt, looking past him with a quizzical expression, his relief had been monumental. When she'd taken a step forward, murmuring the beginning of a question, he'd been only too happy to step aside and let her look at whatever she wanted.

Anything that distracts her from me right now, he'd thought, *is okay in my book!*

Then he saw the cloud. At least, he *thought* it was a cloud, though it was moving like no cloud he'd ever seen. The weather out here was all a mess, though—nothing like the sensible weather they had back east. He'd never seen anything like it in all his years in Boston.

"What *is* that?" he said, and heard the girl's distracted "I don't know."

He stared at the dark wall of cloud as it came, oozing over the horizon until it filled the sky. He didn't like the way it moved, surging and squirming through the air like something alive rather than a weather phenomenon. He glanced at his rented buckboard, the horse tossing its head, agitated, and felt something in his stomach. Odd . . . it felt like when he was too near those big drums they sometimes used for parades back home, though rather than a beat this was a steady feeling, like a feather twiddling deep in his guts.

Then he heard it.

"What's that noise?" he asked, the growing roar tickling his innards even more. "Is that thunder?"

"I don't know," said Evangeline, though something in her voice made him think she had a suspicion. One she did not like. He glanced back at her, but her focus was still on the strange, thrumming shadow blotting out the sky. There was a strange *whirr* behind him, and he turned to face whatever it was just in time to see something, a small stone perhaps, strike the road in a small cloud of grit. There was another thud somewhere, but before Devin could ask what was going on he heard humming, like when he riffled the pages of one of his bank's thick ledger books, and something struck the edge of the porch right in front of him.

It was a bug, brownish green and nearly the size and shape of the cigars he smoked whenever Margaret was not around. He gaped as it folded away wings nearly the span of his hand and appeared to regard him with the round, reddish eyes set to either side of its squat head.

"What the hell is *that*?"

He shouted over the growing roar of the cloud overhead,

and if he hadn't been backing toward her in gut-wrenching horror he would have missed the Clarke girl's whisper entirely. As it was, he caught only one word, but hearing it nearly unmanned him.

". . . Judgment."

The door closed behind him.

"No!"

Devin spun, the envelope containing all his proofs of power, both legal and financial, half-crumpled and forgotten in his left hand as he pounded with both fists. The door held firm. He tried the knob and found the bolt was thrown. He returned his attention to beating the thing down, though it was too stout by far to be forced by the likes of him.

Behind him, more *whirr-thud*s came, then more, gaining in intensity like increasing rain. Several struck the wooden porch, and he flinched at each hollow sound, redoubling his efforts to open the door.

"Miss Clarke, please! You can't leave me out here! What's happening?"

He heard her voice, but through the closed door and his own panic he couldn't make out her meaning. He'd just started another round of yelling when the first of the whizzing little horrors struck him in the back.

With a breathless shriek he spun, flattening himself against the too-solid door. He felt the disgusting pop of the thing clinging to his suit coat, heard the sharp crack of its carapace as he smashed his full weight against it. Before his stomach had time to rebel at the thought of the crunchy, gooey mess now coating his back, another of the things struck him in the chest. Then another. Then two came whirring in to impact his left leg.

He could see them now, falling like living hail, some swerving into a more horizontal track to come in beneath the porch overhang. More and more hurtled into him, so many that, try as he might, he could not bat them away fast enough. He swept them from his chest and legs, but for every one he knocked away, two, three, or even four replaced it.

The cloud! It's all bugs—enough to cover the sky!

Terrified thoughts of Egypt and holy plagues were interrupted as a whinny cut the air, high and terrified. He looked down and saw the buckboard he'd left in the road lurch forward several feet as the panicking horse lunged about, shaking its head furiously, dislodging a dozen or more of the huge insects from its mane.

Good God, I forgot to set the brake!

With no brake set, the only thing that had kept the horse from simply wandering away, wagon and all, during his conversation with Evangeline Clarke was its good manners; manners that were swiftly disappearing as the beast was pelted with more and more of the flying, clinging, climbing bugs.

If it fled now, he realized, he'd have no way to get to town or find cover, and the Clarke woman seemed all too happy to leave him out here in this Hell on Earth.

"Hey!" he shouted, trying to calm the horse, or at least get its attention. "He—*awwwk!*"

The locust that had flown into his open mouth scrabbled at his tongue with sharp, twig-like legs. He choked, spitting the thing out to flop, disoriented, on the porch before him. He tried to stomp on it as, retching, he started down the two steps to the front yard, but he stumbled, nearly falling as the things continued to land on him. They covered him front and back, crawling up his sleeves and pant legs, clinging to his hat and hair, their weight enough to actually slow him down as he lumbered toward the buckboard.

Devin flailed, frantic, beating at his own torso and head, but no matter what he did the number of his attackers did nothing but grow, so many of them now falling, flying, and whizzing through the air that he lost sight of the horse and wagon in the hellish blizzard. There was a new sound now, rising up to drown out the roar of billions of buzzing wings: a loud and angry hiss, reminiscent of a hard rain beating upon the ground. Terrified thoughts rolled through his head, though one idea was repeated again and again, as if the thought itself was trying to get his attention:

It's the end of the world! The end of the world!

He glanced down as he staggered toward the buckboard, his crunching feet obliterating locusts with each step, more falling every second to fill the holes he made in the squirming chitinous carpet. That buff-colored envelope, still clutched in his left hand, was half-gone now, locusts clinging determinately to the ragged upper edge of the thing, gnawing and chewing away.

They're eating it!

He stared at the insects covering the grass, at the dozens depending from his coat-front. Everywhere he looked, it was the same.

*They're eating **everything**!*

All across his chest the woolen fabric was disappearing as the army of little horrors moved about, and wherever he could see their heads those blank, alien faces were pressed firmly to him, tiny mandibles working. His head swam as more of them crawled about his ears, and the hiss grew louder, masking all other sounds but his own screams, muffled though they were; frightened to open his mouth again, he shrieked almost nonstop through clenched teeth.

Another whinny slashed the air, and he caught the hint of motion through the now nearly horizontal flow of tiny whirring bodies, and he turned toward it, one hand thrust out blindly, the other up protectively, if ineffectually, before his face.

The buckboard! It's my only chance to get ou—

The thought was interrupted as the horse suddenly erupted out of the locust swarm, eyes round and rolling in terror at the living mane of clinging, chewing insects covering its head and neck. It was panicked, running full out, thundering past Devin a mere three feet away. Realizing the danger, he tried to leap aside, but the iron-bound wheel of the trailing buckboard caught him a terrific blow to the ribs, spinning him about to land hard on his back on the locust-covered lawn.

No, *in* the lawn, as the army of already-grounded locusts washed over him like a misplaced seaside wave. He opened his mouth to scream, but somewhere along the way the wind had been knocked out of him. Two, maybe three of the marching insects tumbled into his open maw, and he gagged even as his lungs strained against their paralysis. He tried to roll onto his side, to get to his feet, to spit out the clawing, wriggling bodies filling his mouth and throat, when a sudden knife of pain stabbed through his chest, pinning him to the ground like a great railroad spike driven by the famous John Henry.

His left arm thrust skyward, stiff with pain, as his right hand beat at his breast, looking for the source. His searching fingers encountered no spike or knife, merely the tatters of his waistcoat and great swatches of skin in the places where the Hell-spawned bugs had chewed all the way through the outer garment, then the shirt beneath.

Within his breast, his terrified heart tried, but failed, to beat.

And now they will eat **me**, he thought numbly, unable to feel any more horror. As his body arched, drumming its heels upon the ground, his mind clung desperately to words and phrases he'd learned by rote back when he was in short pants, and still said every Sunday, standing next to a stiff-backed Margaret.

Our Father, who art in Heaven, hallowed be Thy name. Thy Kingdom come, Thy will be done, on Earth as it is in—

He was interrupted by blackness swallowing him as his heels slowed, then stilled, his rigid arm falling slack to the ground beside him. Stiff and spasming fingers relaxed, opened, and the last remnants of his buff-colored envelope, all the proofs of his authority, both legal and financial, were caught up by the breeze and sent fluttering into the air, where they were set upon by a dozen of the ever-chewing locusts.

In less than a minute it was as if they had never been.

⚖

Evangeline Clarke spun from the window, pressing her back to the wall and sliding down to sit on the floor, legs splayed. Sobs shook her as she stared across the room at the settee, at the fireplace mantle, at the painting of her mother above it, at *anything* but the window again. She cried, and listened to the scritter-scratch of tiny legs as they covered the porch, the roof, the entire house; the sound barely audible over the chittering hiss of their chewing and chewing.

She had watched through the window until that poor man had fallen. Watched until his body became nothing more than a hump in the crawling, writhing carpet of living insects that extended in all directions, just as far as she could see.

She had owed him that much, having called this Doom down upon him.

Long before it was over, long before he fell, she had begun to pray to God for mercy, trying to take it all back; but it was as if her Lord, so attentive to her prayers for punishment, had turned away, unable or unwilling to hear.

Lord, please, it was a terrible thought, a sin to pray for, and I do repent, but please please please take back Your plague. I prayed for punishment, and it came. I prayed for revenge, and it came. But, Lord, please . . .

She got to her knees to peer out the window, ignoring the odd hump on the lawn, carefully not seeing the black, polished, inedible shoes thrust out of one end of the squirming, man-shaped mass. She looked instead to the left and right, to the east and west, and as far as the eye could see there was nothing but locusts. Millions of them. Billions. Billions upon billions, and they were all eating. Eating *everything.*

The farm they had fought so hard to keep, that her father had worked himself nearly to death for, was gone.

Eva recalled the sky before the locusts had begun to fall, the cloud that stretched from horizon to horizon, and knew that theirs was not the only farm to be destroyed that day.

They all were. Everywhere.

She closed her eyes.

The cost is too high, Lord. Too high. I repent, Lord! It's too high!

She was sitting on the floor again, though she was unaware of it. *Our Father, who art in Heaven, hallowed be Thy name. Thy Kingdom come. Thy will be done, on Earth as it is in Heaven.*

Her hands were clapped over her ears, pressing as hard as

they could to block out the crunching, chomping hiss of those tiny little mouths, *all* those tiny little mouths, all chewing and chewing, though she no longer heard it.

Give us this day our daily bread, and forgive us our trespasses, as we forgive those who trespass against us.

She heard only her own voice, within her own head, as, rocking swiftly back and forth in that little house at the end of the world, Evangeline Clarke prayed her sanity away.

. . . forgive us our trespasses . . .

⚖

Author's note:

In July of 1874, the now extinct Rocky Mountain locust rose up to devastate the North American Plains. "The largest locust swarm in 1874, according to an 1880 U.S. Entomological Commission report, 'covered a swath equal to the combined areas of Connecticut, Delaware, Maine, Maryland, Massachusetts, New Hampshire, New Jersey, New York, Pennsylvania, Rhode Island and Vermont.'" (Lyons, "1874: The Year of the Locust," HistoryNet.com). When on the move, the swarm took more than five days to pass overhead, and when it landed it ate everything—crops in the fields, washing left out on the line, the clothesline itself, the handles from tools, even the manes and tails of horses and the wool from the backs of sheep. Witnesses compared the sound of their chewing to the roar of a hard rain or a prairie fire.

Many people thought it was the end of the world.

After eating its fill, the swarm rose up and simply dispersed, leaving the people to try to recover from its depredations: devastated crops, massive property damage, and, in many cases, financial ruin.

Then, in 1875, it happened again.

THOSE LITTLE BASTARDS

The way those little bastards look at my house usually thrills my heart, you know? I should probably be used to it by now, but it's still something to see. I watch them walking past—I know I don't see *all* of them, but I see enough—all wide eyes and anxious faces. At least when they're alone. See, that's the thing about people, kids in particular: they're all frightened when they're alone.

In groups, though, it's different. In groups they have that crowd mentality, and they're suddenly capable of much more than when they were alone. That's the bad thing about the holidays—Halloween in particular. The holidays bring people together, but Halloween brings the *children* together, and that's when things get bad, in my opinion.

I peek out the window and see them on the sidewalk. Dorothy from *The Wizard of Oz*, complete with a stuffed dog. Superman. Can you believe kids still dress as Superman? A werewolf and some sort of machete-wielding fiend in a hockey mask round out the little discussion group standing in front of my gate.

I can't hear a word, but I know what they're doing. They're daring each other to come through my gate and up the walk to knock on my door or ring the bell, then run like the chicken little bastards they are. It happens every damn year.

And this is only the beginning; the asshole appetizer, as it were. Later, after the younger kids have gone in for the night to empty out their candy bags and start eating themselves sick, the older kids come out to play. My windows have been soaped. My house and trees toilet-papered. My front porch and door have been pelted with eggs—both fresh and rotten—and occasionally smeared with what was hopefully dog feces.

I say *hopefully* because I wouldn't put anything past those little bastards, and the thought of them saving up their own leavings to brownwash my door doesn't seem completely crazy, especially after last year. Last year, they threw a rock through my pantry window, then fired some of those giant squirt guns they make nowadays through the hole in the glass. From the amount they used, and the absolutely *rancid* smell, I'd have to say they'd been saving their urine for quite some time.

It's been a year now, and the pantry still isn't what one would call *fresh*.

You'd think the police would do something, wouldn't you? You'd think, after coming here and tromping through my house and yard, after seeing all the evidence left behind, they'd put a stop to it? Maybe arrest someone?

No.

They look at everything, and talk like I'm not here, and fill out their reports, but *nothing* happens. Not. One. Thing.

And you'd think, what with the way they look at my house the rest of the year, those little jerk-offs would leave me alone tonight, too. That's what *gets* me! What happens to the fear? The respect? Gone—just *gone*—for one whole night.

And they look at the house that way, look at *me* that way, because they know. I know they know, and I know the *cops* know too. They know but they can't *prove*. That's why nothing's ever done, no matter how many times they have to come out here. They couldn't then, and they can't now.

That's why I got away with it.

And here comes the moke with the machete, opening my

gate and coming up the walk. I want to rip open the door and run out there, scare the *hell* out of him, but I don't. There's something else I want to do, have wanted to do for such a long time.

I look down at the straight razor in my hand, the light glinting along the edge as my old friend beckons me, wanting to be used again. I hear the masked idiot on the steps and move to stand at the front door, placing the razor between my teeth like some sort of pirate, freeing up both hands. He's going to knock or ring, and if I'm quick enough—and I know that I am—I can tear open the door at the first sound and grab his outstretched arm. I can snatch him in here; snatch him bald-headed as my mother used to say. Then, once he's in here, he's *mine*.

It was a long time ago, but I got away with it once. I can do it again.

I hear his footsteps, wait for the knock, the ring, my heart just *pounding* in anticipation . . . but instead of a knock or ring, the knob begins to turn.

He's coming in!

I take my old friend from between my teeth as the door edges open, slipping behind it, out of sight. I nearly laugh aloud at the quavery "Hello?" he sends into my foyer. He's not in a crowd now, and the fear is back, so big I can see his eyes right through the holes in that ridiculous mask, huge and round, as he passes the door.

I slam the door behind him as my first fluid strike takes him across the throat, cutting deep, silencing any cry. I rip two slashes—one across his chest, one on the belly—opening him before he can fall, and I drop to my knees, eyes closed, listening for the pitter-pat of hot blood spattering the hardwood floor . . .

. . . but all I hear is his boots scuffing my floor as he turns, oblivious to me, and fifty-four years of this impotent frustration—no, fifty-five now—well up inside me. I begin to sob and swing my blade in ineffectual swipes that pass harmlessly through his legs as he shouts down the walkway to his friends.

"See? I told you! There's no such thing as the ghost of Old Man Peterson!"

My God, you little bastard, I wish you were right.

I wish you were right.

MAXWELL'S SILVER HAMMER

"Damn water damage! I can't make this out—Ben, can you decipher this?"

Dr. Maxwell thrust the travel-stained note across the desk at him. Dr. Benjamin Binder took it, glancing at the weather-beaten package on the desk, its brown paper wrapping torn at the top like a Christmas present given to an excited child. He focused on the note in his hand.

"Let's see . . . you're right, this really *is* a mess."

Maxwell made an impatient gesture. "Yes, but can you *read* any of it?"

Ben held the paper up to the light.

"Well, there's a whole section right in the middle that's nothing but a blur—wait, there are a few words here. 'Powerful.' And this says 'never seen before.' Toward the end it's talking about 'controlling the heart,' and 'absolutely amazing,' and then just this last line: 'beyond our wildest dreams.'"

He held the limp note out to his mentor, who took it with a trembling hand.

"That's about what I could get out of it, too," said Dr. Maxwell, gazing into the open package. "But do I dare use it, without knowing the whole story?"

That last was a murmur, more to himself than to Ben.

"Sir," said Ben, resisting the urge to just lean over and look in the open box. "If you don't mind my asking, what's all this about?"

The old physician looked at Ben with an expression of surprise, then nodded.

"That's right, you don't know anything about this, do you? Of course, we weren't supposed to tell anyone anyway. Let's see . . . do you know Bill Harrison?"

"Dr. Harrison? Yes, I met him when I started here, but he went on sabbatical shortly after I arrived. I've never actually worked with him. Rumor is he's looking into retirement, using his sabbatical to see what it's like to not work for a while."

Dr. Maxwell waggled a hand.

"Yes and no. People came to that conclusion on their own, and I haven't dissuaded them, but it's really the opposite of that."

Ben's eyebrows climbed skyward.

"Beg pardon?"

Dr. Maxwell paused, smoothing a hand over his shock of white hair. His cheeks darkened, and Ben realized the old sawbones was actually embarrassed.

"Look, Ben . . . I know what everyone thinks of me. I'm the oldest doc on staff, and Bill's right behind me. We were in med school together, and that was back before you were born. We know everyone's just waiting for us to retire—looking forward to it, even. The thing is—" he took a deep breath, then sighed. "We don't want to."

Ben felt awkward about this conversation. Maxwell was right: the entire staff was anticipating his retirement, but Ben didn't think it politic to confirm that right now. He settled for nodding, and saying "I see."

"We both love the work. That's why neither of us ever went into administration—we wanted to stay in the field. But medicine is changing fast. Years ago, we were the hotshot young docs on the floor, but now we're falling behind the times. There's still a lot of good we can do, but not while people are treating us like a couple of broken-down horses, ready for the glue factory. We were discussing this when Bill came up with the plan."

Ben pointed to the package on the blotter. "This is part of the plan?"

"I'll get to that in a minute. Bill's idea was to try to get our edge back. New techniques come out every day; there's no way we could keep up. He wanted to go old school."

"Old school?"

"He went on sabbatical so he could travel to places where they look at medicine differently. He was hoping to find something so old it had been discounted by modern medicine, but so effective that it would look like a miracle to you young docs."

Ben pointed again. "And that would be this?"

"It's got to be—I've gotten letters, occasional phone calls, but now he's actually *sent* something!"

Maxwell reached into the box and withdrew a jar holding about a pint of pearlescent gray liquid. As the light glinted off the glass, the fluid roiled in response to Maxwell's motion. Ben thought it looked somehow organic.

"What is it?"

Maxwell shook his head, his attention fixed on the jar. "I have no idea. It's from Haiti, according to the postal markings, but it got soaked somewhere along the way. That note we can't read is the only explanation Bill sent, but it *has* to be something special! According to the note, it seems to have something to do with the heart, but I just don't know . . ."

He put the jar back into its nest, then swept the box from Haiti into a lower desk drawer. "Well, Ben, it's time. Are you ready for tonight's festivities?"

Ben smiled. Though he *had* been anticipating Dr. Maxwell's resignation sometime soon, he still admired the man's love of the job.

I hope I still look at a night working in the ER as "festivities" when I'm his age, he thought.

But all he said was "yes, sir," as the two of them walked out of Maxwell's office, and toward the emergency room.

"Her MedicAlert bracelet says she has a congenital heart defect," shouted the EMT squeezing the bag valve mask.

"How long has he been at it?" Ben gestured to the man riding the gurney side-rail as it rolled, counting aloud as he continued chest compressions.

"Six minutes!"

Dr. Maxwell looked at Ben as they rolled the woman into ER-1. "I don't know how much good we're doing, Ben. She's cyanotic. Even with help, her heart's not doing what it's supposed to."

"We'll keep working her until you call it, Doc," said the man compressing her chest. "You guys do what you have to do."

"Options?" Ben was looking at Dr. Maxwell, automatically deferring to the more experienced man.

"I have an idea," Maxwell said, turning from the dying woman and opening one of the many drawers in the ER. He withdrew a syringe, then reached into one of the voluminous pockets in his lab coat and drew forth a container of a familiar milky liquid.

"What are you doing?" Ben's voice was a shocked hiss.

"Whatever I can," Maxwell said, unscrewing the lid from the jar and thrusting both into Ben's hands. "Hold this."

"What? No!" Ben glanced at the center of the room where the team still worked.

Maxwell stripped the sterile cover from the syringe. "It's perfect! According to the note, this stuff is amazing for the heart."

"We don't know *what* that note says, remember? We don't even know what this *is*, never mind dosages, possible drug interactions—"

Maxwell thrust the tip of the syringe into the fluid and

pulled back on the plunger, drawing some into the barrel. The smell of the stuff rose up to fill Ben's nostrils. It smelled like old gym socks tinged with meat gone bad and . . . something else. It smelled somehow *warm*, although that thought made no sense to Ben. Warm, and organic, and he turned his face away before he gagged. The old doctor gave no sign the smell even registered as he continued speaking in hushed tones.

"Ben, this came from a country where they still slaughter chickens to ward off bad juju. I don't think they're too concerned with precise dosages. As for everything else, well, look at it this way: she's dying. I can't make her any worse."

He raised the syringe and gave it a flick and squirt to get rid of any air bubbles trapped in the barrel. Their eyes locked, and Ben saw determination coupled with excitement in the old doc's eyes.

"Cap that," Maxwell said, pointing at the jar with his chin, "and keep it out of sight. If anything goes wrong, I'll keep you out of it."

Without hesitation he turned and stepped to the gurney, swabbed his spot, and plunged the needle into the patient's arm. Ben screwed the cap on the jar, then put it in his pocket as they waited.

"Stop compressions," Maxwell commanded after thirty seconds. The paramedic stared at him for a moment, then leaned back and gave his arms a rest, shaking out his hands. Maxwell looked only at the EKG readout. The woman's heart beat twice, nice and strong, then jittered. The beat became irregular, the heart racing.

"Tachycardia," reported the nurse.

"I can see that," snapped Maxwell. "Just wait."

The haywire rhythm continued for a few seconds, then leveled suddenly into one long flat note.

"She's crashing!" said the paramedic, already positioning his hands to resume CPR. The watching doctor barked an order.

"Wait!"

"But she's—"

"Just wait."

Maxwell sounded commanding, his stance rigid and authoritative. Ben was the only one in the room who could see his hands locked behind his back, fingers twiddling nervously. As the seconds ticked by, Ben moved up to stand next to Dr. Maxwell. Though his eyes were on the girl who was gradually turning a lovely shade of blue, his ears caught the muttered words from the doctor next to him.

"Come on . . . come on . . ."

A nurse turned to Dr. Maxwell. "Are you going to call time of death, Doctor?" Her voice was flat.

"I—" Maxwell began, but was interrupted by the EKG bursting into a rhythm again. No stuttering transition, no slow build; one moment that horrible flatline, the next a nice, steady beat.

"Yes!" Maxwell gave a small, controlled fist pump of victory. The nurse got busy checking vitals as the EMT stepped down. They all watched the EKG bounce across the screen for almost a minute, waiting for it to falter again, but the beat remained strong and steady.

"Wow, Doc," said the paramedic. "Good call. I've never seen anything like that before. I thought she was gone."

The man gave an impressed snort, collected his partner, and walked out. Another nurse entered with an orderly in tow, the two of them preparing to move the patient to recovery, should she prove stable enough.

She did.

Maxwell ordered a battery of tests. To everyone else in the room he may have seemed merely thorough, but Ben knew what Maxwell was doing: searching for possible effects from the unknown drug with which he had injected the girl.

When Maxwell left ER-1, Ben followed, putting a hand on the older man's arm.

"That was risky as hell," he said. "What were you thinking, using that stuff?" He looked up and down the hall, making sure they were not overheard.

"Did you see that?" Maxwell's voice was filled with wonder.

"Yes," Ben said, "I saw it. I saw you using a drug that hasn't been tested or approved. Hell, we don't even know what it is!"

"But it worked!" Maxwell's eyes grew bright, almost manic. "It worked like a charm! Did you hear that man? 'Never seen anything like that before'!"

"Yes, I heard—" Ben began.

"This is just what we were looking for! It's . . . it's just what the doctor ordered!"

He grinned, oblivious to Ben's concern. He held out a hand. "Give me the jar."

"What? No!" Ben was surprised, having forgotten he now carried the jar in his pocket.

Maxwell straightened, his voice commanding again, though he still spoke in low tones.

"Yes. Give it here. I need to draw up a few syringes so next time I won't be fumbling at the back of the room. That was almost a disaster."

"You can't keep using this stuff," Ben hissed. "It's not safe!"

Maxwell was calm. "I *can* keep using it, and I'll be on my own hook if I get caught."

His stare became icy, and Ben wondered who this was, this hard uncaring man who, just an hour earlier, had been his gentle mentor in this place.

"I'll be on my own *then*, but right *now* I have an accomplice."

Ben's own heart stuttered. "What?"

"You knew what I was doing in there. You even helped fill the syringe, so you can't say you had no idea what was going on."

"But—"

"You knew—that makes you complicit. But I'm sure the disciplinary board will be lenient." Sarcasm filled his voice.

"They are *so* known for leniency. And this is *exactly* the kind of thing a young doctor wants marking his career—supposing they even let you *have* a career, after all this!"

Ben's head was whirling with horror, and he felt nauseated. Maxwell smiled and extended his hand.

"Or, you can just hand me that jar right now and keep your mouth shut. It's really up to you, Ben. Your whole future is in your hands." The grin dropped from his face. "Well? What's it going to be?"

Ben placed the jar in the waiting hand. Maxwell looked at the vessel on his palm, his fingers curled around it, caressing the glass. He looked up at Ben, and his smile returned.

"Thanks, Ben. Toddle off now, and keep your mouth shut. Let me be all I can be!"

He strode off in the direction of his office, no doubt going to measure out doses of his miracle cure. Ben watched until he turned a corner, then made his way back toward the center of the ER. He was moving slowly, in a daze.

He still felt like he was going to throw up.

Ben avoided Dr. Maxwell for most of their shift—quite a feat, considering he worked directly under the man. He kept his distance and tried to spot the old doctor using his miracle cure, but Maxwell was being cautious. Though he didn't catch him, Ben heard the glowing reports about Maxwell that night. Everywhere he went, patients stabilized, even patients the other doctors labeled as lost causes. And not just cardiac cases. Maxwell's shining moment came when they got word of a fifteen-car pileup on the freeway. The casualties were being brought to the closest trauma center: Springdale General. They didn't have long to prepare for the influx of cases, and Ben had to admit that Maxwell did an admirable job preparing the ER for a wave of nearly thirty new patients, all arriving within the span of a few minutes. He organized people and materials, implemented their Mass Casualty Triage Plan . . . then disappeared into his office for the last minute or so. Ben assumed he was filling more syringes from his little jar of miracles, and any admiration he'd felt for Maxwell dissolved like a puff of bitter smoke.

Maxwell's plan worked just as he'd hoped; by the end of the shift he was walking around the ER as the hotshot doc. People were saying he'd saved at least half the patients from the pileup himself. On his way out at the end of his twelve-hour shift, Maxwell stopped by the nurses' station where Ben was using the phone to check on a patient who'd already been moved upstairs to recovery. Maxwell didn't say anything, just gave a wink and tipped his hat as he strolled toward the exit. Ben, working a double shift, barely spared him a glance as he pressed the receiver to his ear, trying to hear over the noise of the ER. He was checking on Rebecca Stillwell.

Rebecca Stillwell was their heart patient, the first to get a dose of what he'd begun to think of as Maxwell's Miracle. The patient he himself had helped to inject with an unknown substance.

While Maxwell had run off to fill those first syringes, Ben had gone to the admissions desk to collect Rebecca's information. Maxwell was listed as the attending physician, and Ben made certain it stayed that way. He signed nothing, just found out where Rebecca was being sent for recovery and started calling the nurse's station there. Self-preservation kept him *officially* out of it, but his feelings of concern and guilt had him calling for status reports. The ER was busy, but he somehow managed a call every thirty to forty-five minutes. Four hours into the recovery, she was conscious. Six hours and she was up and about. He started to relax then, and slowed his calls to once an hour or so—good thing, too, since that was when they received the call about the freeway accident. Things got pretty busy after that.

Now, though, as Maxwell was skipping out the door, a nurse was telling Ben about Rebecca's sudden fever. There was no sign of infection, nothing that would have caused something like this. The increase in temperature registered only about fifteen minutes before Ben's call, but had climbed from 100 to 102 in that time. The patient was in bed with a saline drip while they ran tests. Ben went cold, wondering just what the hell they had done to the girl. He asked to be kept apprised of her situation, then rang off to run beside another gurney, listening to an EMT reeling off patient information. He immersed himself in the new case, focusing on the task at hand in an attempt to avoid wondering what he was going to do.

Unfortunately, fifteen minutes later he was walking out of ER-2 with nothing to think about but his predicament.

*Maxwell used that stuff on quite a few patients without my aid; hell, without my **presence**. He's on the hook alone for all those . . . but I was there for Rebecca. I **did** hold the damn jar for him. It wasn't my fault, but Maxwell's been around forever. He knows people. He won't go down alone for this, I'm **sure** he'll take me—*

"Dr. Binder?"

Ben looked toward the nurses' station.

"Line one's for you. She has some patient info for you."

Ben scuttled over and grabbed the phone.

"Yes?"

"Dr. Binder? I'm calling about Rebecca Stillwell."

"Yes?"

"I'm sorry, Doctor. Her temp spiked to one-oh-six, so we started her in a cool bath. She coded while in the bath. The resuscitation team was called, but couldn't get her back. I'm sorry, Doctor, but she's already en route to the basement."

"What?" Ben checked the clock. "It hasn't even been twenty minutes since you told me about the fever *starting!*"

"I can't explain it. Pathology will investigate, but at the moment we have no idea what went wrong."

I have an idea.

Ben hung up the phone.

All shift long Ben fielded calls for Dr. Maxwell. Wherever his patients had been sent for recovery or tests, people were calling for him, wanting to know if there was anything they should know. Most of Maxwell's patients were exhibiting sudden and apparently sourceless fevers. These fevers spiked, and no matter what measures were taken, resulted in cardiac arrest. Halfway through his shift these fevers exploded across the recovery ward, every one a victim of that freeway pileup. That's when the math became simple.

Twelve hours! Ben thought. *Twelve hours after he injects them with that stuff, they're dead. It's the same every time!*

He phoned Maxwell again and again, but got no answer. He only hoped someone else in the hospital had better luck than he was having.

At last his second shift ended. There had been an hour before dawn when everything seemed to quiet down, and it gave Ben time to think about Rebecca Stillwell, to wonder exactly what the hell had happened to her; to all of them. He felt guilt, but also, he had to admit, fear. Were they going to find out about Maxwell's potion? Chances were good. Would Maxwell absorb the blame and go down quietly, leaving Ben out of it as he'd said?

Not bloody likely.

He took his name off the On Shift board and hustled out of the ER. He was the picture of a man in a hurry to go home and get some sleep.

But he was going to the basement. To the morgue.

He knew he wasn't thinking straight. He'd been up for more than twenty-four hours; that was enough to make anyone a little fuzzy around the edges. He couldn't get the girl out of his mind—and he *had* held the jar . . .

He stumbled off the elevator into the visitor/viewing room, with the window where people came to identify the faces of loved ones. There, in the viewing room, was a woman.

He heard her before he saw her, sobbing registering on his consciousness just before he associated the sound with the figure huddled in the chair next to the door leading into the morgue itself.

"Miss? Miss, are you all right?"

*Oh, **that's** a bright question to ask her **here**! She must have just identified—*

"Rebecca," the woman sobbed into her hands. "Rebecca's dead?"

The tone was disbelieving and mournful, and the words hit him like a slap.

"Rebecca? You mean Rebecca Stillwell?"

She looked at him though the mask of her fingers. "Rebecca's dead."

"I know, I . . . we, uh—look, just wait here, I'll get Dr. Jonah, okay? Please."

He burst through the door into the morgue proper, mind whirling. "Dr. Jonah? Hello, Dr. Jonah?"

There were rows of refrigerated storage drawers, stainless steel handles gleaming under the cold fluorescents. There were gurneys, the door into the autopsy room, a desk and filing cabinet, but no sign of the pathologist. The door hissed behind him and Ben spun around, but instead of Dr. Jonah he found the woman following him. Standing, her face uncovered, she bore a striking resemblance to the girl Maxwell had injected with his potion almost a full day ago.

A sister?

"Miss? I'm sorry, but you shouldn't be in here."

As he moved to guide her back to her seat she reached toward him, and the grief etching her face nearly broke his heart.

"Rebecca's dead," she said again. "Help me, please?"

He caught her as she fell against him. Her dress was sleeveless, and as he touched her skin he was surprised at how cold she felt.

She must be in shock, he thought. *I'll have to get her to lie down. There must be a blanket somewhere—then I can call for assistance.*

"Come with me, all right? Sit down, please."

He put an arm about her shoulders to guide her, but she folded into his chest, her arms about him.

"Please, help me." Her words were muffled by his shirt, the

scrubs so thin he could feel the chill of her cheek through the material. Ben moved them toward the closest seat, a nearby gurney, in a sort of shuffling dance.

"Let's sit you down for a minute, okay? Get you a blanket, all right?"

Her arms tightened about him, fingers splayed and caressing.

"Warm," she said, as if he had not spoken. "You're so warm. Oh my God. Help me."

"Now, I'm trying to—"

She kissed his neck.

He drew in a breath, shocked, but she didn't stop there. She continued to kiss down the side of his neck as her hands caressed his back. She murmured into the hollow of his throat, her voice tickling his skin in a manner that had him standing on his toes.

"You're so warm, please help me . . . Rebecca's dead, and you're so warm . . ."

Oh my God, this is just like that Forum in Penthouse *last month, the one titled "The Doctor is In"! I thought those stories were all bullshit! No! Wait—I have to get control of this; I can't* **do** *this!*

"Now, wait! Miss? No, I—look, we can't—"

But she was all over him, kissing and caressing, somehow peeling his scrub tunic upward to expose his skin, feeling his stomach, moaning about how warm he was, and how she needed his help. Her roving hand found the bulge at the front of his scrubs, squeezing and stroking, and Ben was lost. A minute later he was up on the gurney, flat on his back with his pants about his ankles as, dress pushed up to her hips, she swayed and bucked above him.

She rose and fell on him, around him, crushing him deeper into herself with every thrust, so hard it bordered on pain. Ben just tried to ride it out, to last long enough and not get hurt. Though she had started with kisses, all softness was gone from her. Her face was twisted into a rictus of lust that was almost savage, and Ben realized he was not making love with a partner: he was being used to service her immediate need. Though that realization hurt a little, there was still a small part of him that thought *I have to write this down and send it in to Forum!*

He climaxed. There was nothing he could do to stop it, not thinking of baseball, going to his happy place, nothing. It didn't slow her down in the least—he wasn't sure she even noticed. She pounded on him with increasing ferocity, her internal friction keeping him erect and functioning. He felt teeth nipping and biting at his shoulders and throat. The combination of sharp little pains and her own frantic pleasure drove him over the edge again: his first ever double orgasm. She stiffened, hands gripping the edges of the gurney to provide leverage, bearing down with more than just her weight as she ground herself onto him, harder and harder until he felt a final crushing squeeze deep within her, her release so strong it hurt—hurt a *lot*. The battering he'd just taken coupled with his twenty-four-hour workday, and as he screamed at this sudden and unexpected pain, darkness closed over him.

He blacked out.

He awoke to a tickling near his groin, soft lips working their way down his hip. Eyes closed, he moaned softly in anticipation. The kissing lips became softly nipping teeth as they worked their way down to his thigh . . . then an explosion of pain as she bit into his leg.

His eyes popped open and he stared down to find the girl gazing up at him, her teeth buried in his thigh to the gums. His scream, for he *was* screaming, increased in volume as she jerked her head upward, savagely twisting a huge chunk out of his leg. He rolled off the gurney, on the far side from where she was standing, the hole in his flesh spraying blood across the floor.

"Jesus *Christ*!"

She shoved the gurney, sending it flying aside. Ben scrambled away as she stumbled forward, bent over to grope for him clumsily as she chewed, then swallowed.

"What the hell are you doing!"

"Waaaaarrrmmmm . . ." she replied.

She batted his ankle in an attempt to grab. Ben scooted backward, his naked butt sliding easily over the blood-slick floor. His feet were still tethered by his pushed-down pants, and somewhere he heard a banging noise. The girl staggered forward, eyes glassy, chin and chest covered with the blood from his leg like a child's bib gone horribly wrong.

He struggled to his feet, yanking up his pants despite the pain, slamming through the doors into the autopsy theater.

He stumbled around the autopsy table, tripping over something on the floor. He caught the table edge and looked down.

Dr. Jonah, lying chest down but face up, his head twisted a hundred and eighty degrees, one eye missing, bite marks covering his face. Ben screamed as he heard the theater doors open, knowing it was the girl, but he couldn't take his eyes from Dr. Jonah.

Then the pathologist sat up. Ben saw the girl coming and backed away, then watched her trip over Dr. Jonah, both of them going down in a heap. Ben lurched back out into the morgue and caught the doors as they closed, toeing down the hinged stoppers usually used to prop the portal open. It wouldn't work if they thought to *pull*, but . . .

Through the narrow inset window, he saw the blood-stained girl approach the doors, staring out as Jonah shuffled over, head on backwards. The doors strained against the stoppers' little rubber feet.

This can't be happening, he thought. *Jonah's dead, he **has** to be, and that girl . . . ohmigod, that's **Rebecca**, isn't it? But . . . that means . . .*

His gorge rose as he recalled what had happened on that gurney, but he was distracted from those thoughts by the banging. The pounding. He followed the sound to the wall of cooler drawers. There were thirty small steel doors set into the wall, and fully twenty-five of them were moving. Jouncing. The steel handles shimmied, reflecting the lights.

More than two dozen . . . *things* were trying to get out.

Ben screamed.

His mobile phone, lying on the floor by the gurney, began to chirp. He scrabbled for it; flipped it open.

"Hello?"

"Ben! Ben, my boy, where are you?"

It was Maxwell.

"Uh . . . still at the hospital, why?"

"I finally got in touch with Bill Harrison. Look, that stuff he sent me, it wasn't for use! It was something he . . . uh . . . *acquired* from some witch doctor there. Bill saw some remarkable things and sent me that sample for testing in a modern lab—but I don't have time to go into that right now! I understand that girl we dosed with the stuff didn't make it?"

Emphasis on the *we*. Ben glanced at the face staring at him from the autopsy suite.

"Yeah, she's dead." His gorge rose again.

"Look, Ben, we have to do something. I'm driving; almost there. Meet me in the morgue in five minutes, got it? No excuses!"

"I'm way ahead of you, Doctor. I'll be waiting."

He closed the phone before Maxwell could reply. He looked down at his leg, still bleeding freely, and wiped a hand across his forehead. He was sweating profusely, the fever already upon him. His leg felt strange; a numbness that did not deaden the pain radiated outward from the bite. His mind was foggy. He wondered how long he had, but decided it didn't matter.

He shuffled along, yanking open doors and pulling out drawers. Dr. Maxwell's patients rose up around him. As they tore into him he just hoped he'd have time to rise again before Maxwell arrived.

He did so want to greet the good doctor.

PHOTO FINISH

"Excuse me," said Billy.

The counterman looked up from the cardboard carton he was rummaging through, flipping a stringy gray ponytail behind his shoulder. The man was tall and wide, and with the long hair he reminded Billy of Mr. Martin, the custodian at his school. Billy discovered as he stepped up to the counter that unlike Mr. Martin, however, this man was emitting some serious body odor.

"Yeah?"

"Hi. I was wondering what you could tell me about this camera. It *is* a camera, right?"

The stinky guy just stared at the thing Billy had placed on the counter for a moment, like he didn't recognize it either.

"Where'd you find that?"

"Uh . . . back there," Billy said, pointing vaguely into the hodgepodge depths of the pawnshop. "It was on a shelf in the back, right next to that."

He indicated his best friend, Frank, who displayed a blue bag, the word POLAROID emblazoned on the side. Frank must have seen and correctly interpreted the pit stains on the man's t-shirt, and was wisely standing back from the counter, where the air was relatively fresh.

Stinky the counterman looked from the thing the boys had found, to the bag and back, then leaned toward Billy and took up the gadget. The words, "Yeah, kid, it's a camera," rode into the room on breath that stank of old cigarettes, coffee, and a complete lack of oral hygiene. Billy slid back a step, standing closer to Frank and concentrating on not wrinkling his nose or gagging.

Stinky twisted the Polaroid to see it from different angles.

"It's a camera," he repeated. "An old Polaroid One-Step Express. I forgot this was even back there. Man," he added in a whisper, "it's been a while . . ."

Frank's feet shuffled impatiently for a few seconds, then he said, "What's that slot in the front for?"

Stinky's head snapped up, eyes wide, as if he'd forgotten they were there.

"This?" He touched the slot beneath the lens. "This is where the pictures come out. Look here, kid."

His fingers, strangely dexterous for a man so large, popped open the base of the camera, just below the slot.

"Your film cartridge goes in here."

He snapped the compartment shut, then held the camera up, peering through the viewfinder.

"You take your picture—click—and the actual picture comes out of that slot. The thing develops itself once it's exposed to air or something, and wham! A minute later, you got your picture."

He placed the camera back on the counter. "So, you want it?"

"It comes with the case, right?" Billy said.

Stinky nodded.

"It's marked ten dollars. That gets me everything?"

Another nod, and Billy found himself nodding along.

"I think it sounds like fun. I guess I'll—wait a minute! How old is this thing? Can I even get film for it?"

Stinky kept nodding. "Pretty sure you can."

Frank fished in the camera bag and pulled out a pair of small rectangular boxes. "Hey, what about this? This says 'instant film.' Is this what you're looking for?"

"Cool!" Billy turned back to Stinky. "That's included, right? You said the bag was included."

Stinky shrugged. "Sure. That kind of film goes bad after a while, though. Check the box for an expiration date."

Frank looked. "August 2005."

Billy deflated. "So, it won't work?"

"It might," said Stinky. "But probably not. You can always get more film, though, right? So, you want it?"

The bell over the pawnshop door rang as Billy carried his new purchase out to the street.

■

A half hour later, Frank followed Billy out of the pharmacy and toward their bicycles.

"Dude, I can't believe that pawnshop guy ripped you off like that!"

Billy shrugged. "Maybe he didn't know."

"Oh, he knew. I *know* he knew! You heard what the lady at the photo counter said. Polaroid stopped making that film *years* ago. The new company that started making this stuff charges *twenty dollars* a pack!"

Billy would have been more angry himself, but the way Frank was carrying on kept making him smile. He unzipped the bag on his shoulder and took out the camera, unfolding it and popping the film door open as Stinky had shown them.

"What're you doing?" said Frank.

"I'm gonna try it," said Billy, sliding one of the boxes of expired film from a pouch on the side of the bag. "The lady in there said the film might work if it was properly maintained and refrigerated."

"*Might*." Frank shook his head. "It *might* work. *If* it was properly maintained and refrigerated. We found it on a shelf at the back of a pawnshop. You really think Captain Body Odor maintained it at all? He can't even use deodorant."

Billy held the camera under one arm and shook out the film

cartridge, tossing the empty box to Frank. He slid the cartridge into the slot and closed the film door with a *snick*. He almost dropped the camera when, with a grinding little whir, a black sheet extruded from the picture slot.

"See? It's all black—overexposed, right?" said Frank, pointing an accusing finger at the camera. "I told you it was too old!"

Billy pulled the black sheet loose, flipping it over to inspect both sides.

"I didn't take a picture. I think this is the top of the pack, like the camera loaded it in and opened it up. I think it's working."

"The *camera's* working," Frank pointed out. "The film might still be crap."

He sounded like he hoped it *was* crap. Maybe he was enjoying being on a tear about it. Billy flipped the camera around, peering through the viewfinder.

"Say cheese!"

Frank, unsmiling, flipped up his middle finger.

"Perfect!" Billy said.

The shutter clicked, and with another whir a square gray blur within a white frame came rolling out of the slot.

"You see that?" Frank pointed again. "Blank. You got ripped off. I knew it!"

"Just wait," said Billy. "The guy at the pawnshop said you have to wait a minute for it to develop, remember?"

So they waited, staring at the gray square . . . and slowly, an image of Frank came into view: deadpan expression, upraised finger in the foreground.

"Cool!" Billy said.

"It's all brown," Frank replied. He was right. Everything was tinted brown or tan, but it was clearly a photo of Frank giving Billy the finger. It looked antique, like something in a museum, though it was less than two minutes old.

"I like it," Billy said. "It looks kind of cool, and this pack of film works. That means I paid Stinky ten dollars for a working camera and at least twenty dollars worth of film."

He leaned forward, waggling his head and filling his voice with exaggerated cockiness. "So . . . *who* got ripped off?"

Frank nodded, smiling about the camera for the first time since they'd seen it.

"Okay, fine. It *does* look sort of cool, and you didn't get ripped off. So." The smile widened into a grin. "Can I try it?"

The ride home took more than an hour as they stopped along the way and took photos of each other. They were at the playground on the edge of their neighborhood, waiting for a picture to develop, when Frank asked, "Who's that?"

Billy looked from the developing square in his hand to the picture Frank held: Frank spinning on the little merry-go-round. The old film had turned the bright red disk of the merry-go-round a dark, reddish-brown that reminded Billy of dried blood. Frank was moving too fast for the camera as he went by, a streaky, Frank-shaped blur, trailing color behind it like the tail of a comet. He was leaning out toward the camera, and his face had lost almost all definition, though the twin dark spots of his eyes were still visible, holes in his head bleeding darkness back into the comet's tail. Beneath those holes was a larger one, dark and wide with white teeth streaking into the blur.

Frank had been laughing on the merry-go-round, but in the distorted photo, it looked like a long, terrible scream made by something no longer human, Frank's waving arm transformed into a hand thrust forth in supplication. Despite the end-of-summer warmth, it gave Billy a chill.

But Frank wasn't pointing to the hellish image of himself. His fingernail was tapping a point in the image above and behind him, just beyond the far side of the playground.

There, in the expanse of grass between the street and the woodchip-covered playground proper, small in the distance, was the figure of a man. Distinctly human-shaped but blurred, the figure strode toward them, one arm extended. His clothing was dark, and he either wore a hat or had dark hair worn loose and wild; it was hard to tell with the distance and distortion. His skin had taken on the sepia tone of the background sky, with no visible features to his face, though his posture gave him a sense of urgency.

"Well?"

Billy looked around at the playground and surrounding park and shrugged. He saw no one. Had *seen* no one. They had arrived at the park at dinnertime and had had the place to themselves.

"I dunno," Billy said. "Maybe he just went by quick and we missed him."

"Holy crap!"

Billy looked at his friend and saw that while he was examining the photo in Frank's hand, Frank was pointing at the one Billy held, eyes round. Billy held up the picture and saw it had finished developing. In it, Billy hung upside down from the horizontal ladder, holding on to one of the rungs with crooked knees, arms flapping toward the ground, his t-shirt riding up to expose his belly button. Past upside-down Billy, and his upside-down smile, was the man.

Closer this time, he was about to step onto the woodchips of the playground, just past the spring-mounted Three Little Pigs that the younger kids rode like hobbyhorses. With more clarity than in the previous photo, Billy could make out the man's long dark overcoat billowing behind him. He was hatless, his medium-length hair unkempt. Billy looked at Frank, who was already staring at him.

"So much for 'just went by quick,'" Frank said, then looked around the playground again. "I took that picture a couple of minutes after you took this one of me. Dude, I was looking. I didn't see anyone."

Billy stared at the pictures again, holding them side by side. There was the man, walking toward them. He was in the background, and with the whole picture being washed out in browns and tans, they had missed him the first time they looked at the shot of Frank. Yet to Billy, the shape also looked strangely familiar.

"Wait a second," he muttered, thrusting the two photos into Frank's hands. He sat on the ground, cross-legged, camera bag in his lap, and fished out the other pictures they had taken so far.

The schoolyard behind their school: a slightly blurry Frank riding a wheelie in front of the basketball hoops. Beyond him and to the right, the shadowy striding figure. It was farther away than in the playground photos, in the field next to the school, the distortion reducing it to a silhouette. Before, it had looked like little more than a wonky bit in the old, expired film; now that figure was obvious to Billy's eye, standing out as a familiar shape.

The picture before that: Billy riding across the basketball court, no hands, standing up on the pedals, arms spread wide like a circus performer. The figure again, farther from the camera, still in the field but off toward the trees on the far side.

Before that: a sepia-toned Billy performed a balancing act on a stack of two-by-fours in front of a house under construction, arms again spread for balance, tongue protruding in concentration. At the far side of the construction site was a low temporary fence intended to keep out pedestrians. Beyond that fence, contrasted by the backdrop of the white house on the far side of the street, was the top half of a figure, tiny, but there if one looked hard enough.

In the photos before that, Billy failed to find the figure, but his skin was already crawling. He flipped through them, pointing the figure out to Frank.

"Weird," Frank muttered, flipping through them again. "You think this guy's been following us?" He sounded nervous, and Billy didn't blame him.

"How did we miss him in these?" Frank held up the most recent pair, then scanned the playground again, looking behind them as well.

"I don't know," said Billy. Rather than looking all around the playground, he stared at where the photos said the stranger had been. He had a suspicion, but it was crazy.

Before he could think too much, he popped the camera open and took another picture, aiming across the empty park like he was taking another shot of the merry-go-round.

"What are you doing?"

"Checking something."

Billy pulled the picture loose as it whirred out of the camera. He handed it to Frank, and tucked the camera away in the bag with the already developed pictures as he led the way toward the bikes. Levering his Schwinn up from the grass, he swung a leg over the seat. Standing astride it, he took the developing photo back. Frank picked up his own bike, standing next to it, hands on the handlebars.

"Well?" Frank jerked his chin toward the picture in Billy's hand. Billy looked down at the image slowly manifesting within the white frame, and his stomach gave that little "oopsy" feeling that he got from roller coasters and some fast elevators, like some part of him was trying to throw up but the rest of him hadn't caught on yet.

"What's the matter?"

Wordlessly, Billy held out the picture.

Frank's eyes widened. "Holy *shit*." His head snapped around as he looked at the playground behind him, then swung about as he scanned the surrounding park and street beyond. Finally, his gaze returned to Billy.

"Uh . . . some kind of double exposure thing, you think?"

His voice was higher than ever and sounded tight, like he was forcing the words out. Billy knew what Frank was doing; he was doing it himself. Frank was putting everything he had into sounding cool, while inside he was anything *but*.

"No double exposure," Billy said. "The film's old, but it wasn't opened."

"Well then, what's going on?"

Billy looked at the photo in his hand, the image darkening as it developed. Clearer than ever, the man in the photo was closer, past the Three Little Pigs and halfway to the merry-go-round. Angry eyes bored out of a blurred face, and the sense of purpose in his posture was easy to see: his strong stride billowing his long dark coat, chest thrust forward, head slightly lowered, hands balled into fists.

He appeared to be marching straight toward them.

"I dunno," said Billy as he tucked the newest photo into the bag and looked out at the empty playground. "But I say we get the hell out of here."

"Fine by me."

Frank pushed his bike into motion and leapt into the seat all in one smooth maneuver, pumping his legs and gaining speed almost before his feet hit the pedals. Billy gave the park one more look before he pushed off on his own bike, standing on the pedals as he worked to catch up.

The skin on the back of his neck crawled the whole time, and he had the feeling that someone was watching him.

■

"Dinner's at six, Billy. You lose track of time?"

"Sorry, Dad." Billy had been at the foot of the stairs and moving fast when his father popped out from the door to the living room.

"Frank's not having dinner with us? I don't think he's eaten dinner at home all summer."

Billy smiled, trying to appear normal, though the truth was that Frank had turned toward his own house without a word, pedaling for all he was worth.

"Sorry, Dad. I'll tell him you missed him, though. I'll be right down. I just need to wash for dinner." He turned to run the rest of the way up the stairs, hoping to get to his room before his father noticed—

"What's that you have there?"

Slumping, Billy turned and took a few steps back down, swinging the camera bag around so it was in full view.

"It's just this old camera I got secondhand. Me and Frank were playing around with it, that's all."

"May I?"

His father held out a hand. Billy unzipped the bag and pulled out the camera, handing it over. His father held it up, a smile playing at the corners of his mouth.

"A One-Step Express," he murmured. "I haven't seen one of these in years. You know, twenty years ago *everybody* had these. The tech guys were even using them at crime scenes, before everything went digital." That last bit would have sounded odd if Billy's father hadn't been a cop.

He looked up at Billy. "So, where'd you find one of these you could afford?"

The words *at a flea market* popped into Billy's head, but his father *always* knew when he was lying. Years of being a police detective, or maybe just being a father—Billy didn't know which. He sighed.

"Eccles's Pawnshop."

His father's nostalgic smile faded. "Billy, I've told you to stay out of there. Eccles deals in stolen goods. Not everything in there, but enough. We're looking at him all the time, and if we could ever prove he knew where his stuff was coming from, we'd be all over him. Word is he does other stuff to make ends meet, too. Serious stuff, for some serious people."

Billy's father sighed. "Look, I just don't want to take a chance on you getting involved in something. I mean, what if this camera was stolen and became part of an investigation? How would that look for me, for my son to have bought stolen goods?"

"I wouldn't have known it was stolen," objected Billy. "Besides, it was way at the back of the shop, like it had been there for a long time. I mean, it was dusty, Dad."

His father digested that for a moment.

"Fine, keep the camera. But I don't want you going in there any more, okay? I know there's a lot of neat stuff in there, but please, no more. We can go to the flea market sometime, if you start feeling the need to browse."

He held the camera out to Billy, who tucked it back in the bag.

"Can I see the pictures sometime?"

"The film's old and doesn't work right," said Billy. "There were two packs, though. Maybe the other one'll work better."

Billy's father nodded.

"Okay, go wash up. Mom's waited for dinner long enough. Maybe this weekend we can see about getting you some real film for that."

After dinner, Billy retired to his room with his father's magnifying glass; he just had to remember to put it back before his father found out it had been borrowed.

Six photos formed a line across the top of Billy's desk, but he tried not to look at them. They creeped him out just being there; when he looked right at them, they scared the shit out of him. He had six of the nine pictures he and Frank had taken laid out in chronological order, numbers four through nine. The photo under the magnifying glass was number three, the first one they had taken at the house under construction.

Billy leaned over the picture, slowly scanning the temporary fence at the back of the site forming the scene's horizon. In photo number four, he'd found the figure on the far side of the fence with his naked eye. Now he scanned from right to left, from the front corner of the fence back toward where it disappeared beyond the house.

"Shit," he whispered. There he was. Farther back than in number four, as if he were walking up the street on the far side of the house. He was hard to make out at first—just the silhouette of half a man showing above the plastic fencing—but he was there. Billy slid the picture into line with the others and pulled over the picture Frank had taken in front of the pharmacy, when Billy had loaded the film. He ignored the image of himself smiling theatrically, focusing instead on the background. Using the magnifying glass to follow the sidewalk, he found the man almost at once. On the distant street corner was a tiny black figure. The distortion gave him a slightly rippled look, like he was being seen through heat coming off a street baking in the summer sun.

Billy licked dry lips with a dry tongue. He had that feeling at the back of his neck again, and he couldn't help glancing over his shoulder at his empty room, relieved to see that it was indeed empty.

Come on, he told himself. *You're fourteen—act like it! This is creepy, but you haven't believed in the boogeyman in years, and you don't believe in him now.*

Billy slid the picture to the head of the line on his desk, then pulled the last one, actually the *first* one, into place before him. He stared for a moment at the large round magnifying glass clutched in his hand. He took a breath.

Sure you don't.

It took some time, but he found it, wishing all the while he wouldn't. The figure was so small, and at such a distance, that Billy would never have seen it with his naked eye. Even then, Billy wouldn't have spotted the figure if it weren't for a strange clear spot in the old film. Sepia toned but with crystal clarity, the photo caught the man just as he was rounding the corner at the far end of the street, most of him still hidden from view.

Though Billy had eaten well at dinner, his stomach felt hollowed out and slightly nauseated. The finger that coaxed that first photo into its spot at the head of the line trembled. As he sat and scanned the line of Polaroids from left to right, oldest to newest, he felt sweat breaking out at the nape of his neck, though he was almost shivering with the chill in his skin.

No matter where he and Frank had gone that afternoon, the man had been there with them. In the pictures. Billy stared at the last image, the stranger striding across the playground toward the camera, dark eyes burning in their sockets with frightening intensity. He had *not* been there. Both boys had looked right into the playground when Billy took that picture, and there had been nothing to see but the other side of the park. But there was the man: in the picture, large as life.

Billy examined the stranger's features as best he could through the distortion. Jaw set, his forward lean imparting urgency to his motion, he seemed to stare directly into the camera, *through* the camera, at the photographer on the other side.

At Billy.

This is crazy, Billy thought. *There has to be some sort of explanation, right?*

Maybe double exposure, like Frank had said at the park. Maybe he was freaking out over nothing. Yet there was something else odd, something Billy couldn't quite put his finger on. He started to examine the photos again, but he only got to the second shot in the series when he stopped.

*Now, that's **not** possible.*

In the first picture, the man was coming around the corner down the street behind Frank. In the second, the boys had traded the camera without swapping places, but there he was on the corner behind Billy. This meant the guy had appeared in two pictures, taken a minute apart, on two different corners at opposite ends of the street!

See that? He's a double exposure or something, thought Billy. *No matter where we pointed the camera, he was in the picture, just sort of inserted into the scene. We could have taken a picture of the sky and he'd have been in it, right?*

There was another thought scrabbling about at the edges of Billy's consciousness, and he was desperately trying not to have it. Realizing he was trying to fight it, though, gave it a little opening, and it slithered into his mind like a snake, coiling on top of his brain.

*It can't be a ghost. Ghosts haunt **places**, right? All the ghost stories I've ever heard, the spook was in a haunted hotel, or a haunted room, or a haunted house. Even a haunted stretch of highway. But we went to all different places today, all across town, and he's in all the pictures. That means he can't be a ghost.*

Billy's eyes strayed across the line of photos, each bringing the stranger closer and closer to the lens. His gaze lingered on that last shot, the eyes of the man seeming to stare right at Billy, and that serpent of thought rattled its tail, letting Billy see just how dangerous a thought it was.

Unless he's haunting the camera . . .

He looked at the camera. There had been ten shots in the film pack he'd loaded that afternoon, and there were nine pictures lined up on his desk.

One shot left. He looked about his room. *One shot left, and all the others have this guy walking toward us. But they were all outside, where there was room. If I take the last picture in here and there's still a guy walking at me in the distance, then it **has** to be a double exposure or something. He won't fit into the scene.*

Billy steeled himself, then raised the camera and popped off a picture without even looking through the viewfinder. The print came out, and Billy laid it on the edge of his desk to develop. Then he got up and hustled down the hall toward the bathroom.

In the stillness of his room, alone but for that thought coiling in his head, he'd almost wet his pants when the shutter snapped.

◾

He left the door open when he returned, taking up the picture as he sat. He felt as if he were five years old again and had to go into the basement for a toy, and *knew* there was something down there that was going to eat him up.

But, just like when he was five, there was nothing there. It was a picture of his empty room, absent of any dark figure striding toward him. Tight shoulders relaxed, and he released his held breath in a relieved sigh. There. Nothing to see but his closet door, bureau, bedroom door and the window with half his bookcase showing beneath, all in shades of brown and black. It was—

Wait . . . in the photo, the dark of night had turned the glass of the window into a mirror for the flash, reflecting the bright room back on itself. But the lower window was half open to catch the night breeze, and *there*, where there was nothing but the screen to shut out the backyard, was a shape. Not a hand, exactly, but the flattened out bits one sees when pressing their hand to a pane of glass, giving the rough shape of the fingers and palm. Beyond it, just barely visible to Billy's naked eye, was a shadowed face.

The face he might have imagined; it was nothing but shapes put together, darker spots in the darkness outside the window, like seeing a puppy or a fire truck in a cloud on a summer day. Not so with the palm. The hand pressed to the screen reflected the camera's flash well, creating a light spot against the darkness. Once spotted, Billy's eye was immediately drawn to it, until it seemed not so much a photo of an empty room with a palm at the window, as a photo of the palm itself.

Billy's heart thudded in his ears, but was quickly drowned out by a rushing sound, loud and terrible, the ocean heard in a seashell bigger than the world.

The palm and the face, there at his window.

His second story window.

Suddenly his father was kneeling beside him, a hand gently shaking Billy's shoulder. The rushing sound cut off like someone had flipped a switch, and he heard his own voice calling out, shrill and odd, even to his own ears.

"Daddy!"

"Billy, are you all right? What's wrong?"

"Daddy!"

He flung his arms around his father's neck. He hadn't called his father "Daddy" in years, but right now he was less fourteen-year-old Billy than some much younger self who still lived inside him.

"He's at the window, Daddy, at the window!"

Billy was babbling but couldn't seem to stop. He realized he'd been sitting there calling for his father since seeing the hand and face in the picture, afraid to move, afraid to stay, knowing that somewhere nearby was the boogeyman, but unable to get away. Strong fingers gently pried Billy's arms loose, leaving him in the chair as his father crossed the room.

"Who's at the window?"

"I dunno. A guy, the guy who's everywhere!"

His father peered out into the dark.

"Billy, there's no one out there. We're twenty feet up. Who could be out there?"

"The guy who's everywhere!"

Billy's father wore a look of concern as he knelt by the chair again, looking his son in the eye. "It's okay, Billy. Deep breaths, all right? I need you to calm down for me so you can tell me what you're talking about."

Billy sat and breathed, and tried to shove his younger self back into his memories. His father's presence helped. The next time he spoke, he was more himself again, though he could feel his younger self prodding at the edges of his mind, propelled by fear and refusing to be put away entirely.

He told his father the whole story: buying the camera, taking the pictures, the strange discovery of the man. His father looked at each photograph, using the magnifying glass when necessary. He tapped the line of them, one by one, lingering on the last one: Billy's room and the face.

"You know there has to be some sort of explanation, right?"

From the tone of his voice, Billy thought his father was trying not so much to reassure his son as convince himself.

"It's a ghost, Dad. He's in every picture, no matter where you take it." He pointed to the camera, sitting on his desk where he'd left it. "That thing's haunted."

"You know I don't believe in that sort of thing. It's got to be . . ." Billy's father trailed off thoughtfully as he picked up the camera, popping it open into picture-taking mode and turning it over in his hands as he had before dinner.

"I see ten pictures here," Billy's father said, "and there are ten shots in a pack of film, if I remember correctly. Did you try the second pack?"

"No."

Billy's father fished the second expired pack out of the camera bag. He quickly replaced the film, and the top of the pack came rolling through the slot.

He held the camera out to Billy.

"Take a picture of your old man?"

Billy crossed his arms, stuffing his hands into his armpits. "No way."

"Come on. One picture. If it's as old as the other stuff, then chances are it won't come out anyway." He leaned forward slightly, forcing Billy to take the camera or have it dropped in his lap. "I'm right here," he said, quietly. "I won't let anything happen. Okay?"

Billy stared at the camera in his hands and muttered a short "fine." His father stepped back, struck a heroic pose with fists on hips, gave an exaggerated smile and said "Cheese!" The pose *did* make Billy smile. The camera flashed, the motor whirred, and the white square stuck out of the little machine like a tongue. Billy tugged it free and set it on the desk to develop. He handed the Polaroid off and went to sit on the bed. His father folded the camera closed and held it in one hand.

"You said this looked like it had been on the shelf for a while?"

"I had to blow dust off it. Honestly, Dad, it looked like Stinky put it there years ago, then never touched it again."

Billy's father quirked an eyebrow. "Stinky?"

Billy felt himself blush as he smiled. "That's what Frank and me were calling the guy after we left the shop. He was a big guy, and he smelled *really* bad."

"That sounds like Eccles," Billy's father said as he moved toward the desk. "The joke around the department is that Eccles was born past his expiration da—" He stopped dead, staring down at the developing photo, and spoke in a rough whisper. "What the *hell*?"

"What is it?"

Billy stood to look, but his father sidestepped into his path, scooped up the picture and held it close to his chest. Billy could see how stiff his father's posture was.

"Dad?"

"Wait. Just . . . wait. Okay?"

Time passed, during which Billy fought with himself. Most of him wanted nothing to do with whatever was in that picture, but part of him *had* to know.

"Dad?"

His father just shook his head.

"I've already seen all the others, and, I guess, technically it *is* my camera. What is it?"

His father's voice sounded far away, like he was preoccupied, but he held the photo out to his side, hanging it in Billy's view.

"I can't explain it. I mean, it's not a double exposure, not some kind of superimposition, but where . . . ?"

Billy looked at the picture, the breath catching in his throat. There stood his father in his heroic pose. The color was a little washed out, but there were no overt sepia tones like in the other pictures. It was a fairly normal-looking picture of his father—with a tall man standing beside him, staring him straight in the face.

Dad's elbows were thrust out to the sides, exaggerating his stance, but the stranger was tall enough that he could lean in over one of those elbows and get within a foot of Dad's face. The man's mouth was a tight line, the one eye visible in profile staring intensely at Billy's unseeing father. Through the space between his father's elbow and body, Billy could make out the man's arm, thrust behind his dad as if about to pat him on the back. The man's other arm obscured part of his father's shoulder and chest as the apparition pointed directly at the camera.

"Oh my God."

"Yeah," said Billy's father, a little rasp in his voice. "I don't believe in ghosts and spooks, but I really can't think of a good explanation for this." His father finally took two steps backward and didn't so much sit on the bed as allow his legs to give out. Billy joined him, and they sat side by side, staring at the new image.

"What do you think he wants?" Billy finally asked.

His father thought for a while.

"Well, he spent all that time getting closer to the camera, according to the pictures, then the first thing he does is try to point the camera out to anyone he can. I could be just thinking like a cop, but maybe he wants someone to look into that camera."

He cleared his throat and raised his voice slightly, directing his words upward into the empty air.

"First thing tomorrow morning, you and I are going down to Eccles's Pawnshop so I can ask him what's going on with this thing. Maybe it's some kind of joke, but if it is, I don't appreciate him playing it on my son."

He took a breath and stood. He went to the desk, scooped up the pictures and dumped them into the camera bag. The camera followed.

"I'll put this down in the kitchen, all right? Try not to worry about it. Watch some TV, read a book, try to take your mind off it, but don't be up too late, okay?"

"Okay. And Dad?"

His father paused in the doorway.

"Thanks."

Billy's father nodded with a tight smile and walked from the room.

■

"Eccles, where did this camera come from?" Billy's father pointed toward the camera in its case, lying on the greasy, glass-topped counter. "I know you," he continued. "You know where all your goods come from."

Eccles spread his huge hands.

"What do you want from me, Detective? I have a lot of stuff in here, and sorry, but I'm not the best record keeper out there. I mean, I could make something up to tell you, but that would be lying to an officer of the law, and that would be wrong."

False contrition was stamped thick on Eccles's face and voice.

"Come on, Roger. You sold the camera to my kid, and it's

taking weird pictures. They're freaking him out, and I don't blame him. I'm asking as a father, not a cop. What's the deal with the Polaroid? Where'd it come from? Who's the former owner? Something."

Eccles raised his hands in a slightly defensive gesture.

"Look, Detective"—he lowered his hands with a smile— "sorry. *Dad*. The camera's old. I had it so long I forgot I *had* it, and I don't remember where I got it. If the pictures are weird, well hey, I warned him about the expired film when he bought it."

He gestured toward Billy, who watched nervously.

"Ask him. I told him and his friend the pictures would come out funky if the film even worked at all."

Billy's father raised his eyebrows.

"Funky? You want to see funky?"

He unzipped the bag and pulled out the camera, set it aside and reached back in for the stack of photos. "This is a little more than funky, Roger. It's weird."

He slapped the whole stack down on the counter. The camera jumped and suddenly popped open, from storage to picture-taking mode. The sharp *clack* made them all jump.

"Look at these," Billy's father said. "Who *is* this guy?"

Eccles glanced at the photos, then did a double-take. He leaned in close, flipping through them slowly. His head was still down when he spoke, and all the cockiness seemed to have drained from his voice.

"I dunno, Detective. The . . . ah . . . the kids don't know? This looks like he was following them around—you might want to be looking for this guy, instead of asking me."

He pushed the stack away, avoiding the detective's eyes. Billy's father picked up the stack, studying Eccles, his face growing a little harder.

"But I *am* asking you, Roger, and now I'm asking as a cop. Who is this guy?"

He slapped the stack down in front of Eccles again, harder. The camera jumped, and the flash went off.

"What the hell!" Eccles shouted, startled, making Billy

jump. The detective glanced at the camera as it whirred, then turned back to Eccles. He looked back to the camera when it hummed again. The first picture fell to the countertop, pushed out of the way by a second photo.

Then a third.

It was almost comical how both men suddenly leaned down at the same time, their heads nearly knocking together as they peered closely at the small pile of pictures.

A fourth whirred into existence.

With a sudden cry Eccles bulled past Billy's father, swatting the smaller man aside as he made a break for the door. The detective, no match for Eccles's strength, was still quick. He caught up just as the fleeing man was rounding the end of the counter and kicked out, catching the side of one running foot. Eccles's leg struck its mate mid-stride, and the big man went down as if diving forward, launching all three hundred pounds of his body headfirst into the end of a shelving unit. He hit the ground, out cold. Breathing hard, Billy's father pulled the handcuffs from their case on the back of his belt.

"We *knew* you were involved in some bad stuff, but Roger," the detective said as he snapped the cuffs onto Eccles's flaccid wrists. "Looks like you *do* know our mystery man, and you're going to tell me all about him."

Billy wasn't even aware he had moved when his father looked up.

"Billy! Stay away from those pictures, son."

But Billy could not stay away. Even while Eccles was running for it, Billy had been keeping unconscious count. He knew the last picture had come grinding out of the old camera just as his father was straddling Eccles with the cuffs. From a distance, Billy had been able to see color extruding from the camera, again and again—these nine pictures had come out fully developed, instantly available.

He was drawn to them.

The pile was splayed out enough for Billy to see they were all the same picture—nine copies of the same image.

The image.

"Billy, I told you not to—"

The face, so familiar now, stared out from the photo, dark eyes wide with shock, wild hair in greater disarray. Behind and above him, Roger Eccles's face was twisted in savage glee. One of his hands gripped the stranger's shoulder, knuckles white, the other reached around in front of him holding something that sparkled in the light but was too streaked with motion to make out.

Beneath the glittering blur, the stranger's throat seemed to have grown a second, lipless mouth. Blood poured down onto the collar of the dark coat, spraying into the air in an arc cast off by the steely blur in Eccles's hand.

"You know how you said we could get more film for this camera?"

Billy's father looked up from where he squatted over the prone Eccles, punching buttons on his mobile phone, and nodded.

"Forget about it."

The bell above the door rang again as Billy walked outside. His father called after him before the door swung shut, but Billy barely heard him. He took a seat on the curb in front of the shop.

He was still there, listening to the rushing sound in his head, when the police cruiser, lights flashing blue and white in the late morning sun, jerked to a halt in front of him.

A MAN DOES WHAT'S RIGHT

Grandpa gripped Kyle's wrist so tight it hurt, long bony fingers wrapping all the way around in a handcuff of knuckles. With the other hand the old man tore open the station door, the door-closer squealing over their heads in protest; Grandpa always had a surprising amount of wiry strength, but at the moment he was what Pop would have called "crazy strong." Some of Kyle's friends might have said Grandpa had gone "full retard," but Kyle wouldn't have said that. Kyle wouldn't have even admitted to thinking his grandfather was *crazy* strong, though he was clearly out of control.

Kyle was mortified.

The sunset at their backs threw their shadows long across the bland linoleum; the silent struggle cast in ruddy light looked much more violent than the reality as Grandpa yanked him forward. The yank was unnecessary: contrary to what one might have thought, seeing just the shadow-play on the floor, Kyle wasn't struggling to get away—if anything, he was struggling to keep up. There were about a million places he'd rather be than here, but Grandpa wasn't going to let him go until he'd had his say. Kyle just wanted to get it over with so he could go home and get back to playing Minecraft. This was *so* embarrass—

"Where are the cops in this place?" Grandpa's voice was high, and normally reedy, but there was power in it tonight. "Where are the police? I came to the police station to find—"

"Can I help you, sir?"

This voice was high, too, but not reedy at all, as the cop leaned into view from behind the big charge desk. Kyle thought the man was standing on tiptoe—he couldn't see for sure behind the desk—in order to lean so far. He'd seen this officer around town—Kyle couldn't recall his name—and the man was small, barely larger than Kyle's older brother James, who was only twelve. All the kids avoided this particular cop like he had cooties—he was small, but he walked around with a chip on his shoulder bigger than he was, and every child Kyle knew could tell a bully on sight. It was how smaller kids survived on the schoolyard, after all.

"Can you *help* me?"

The tone in Grandpa's voice made Kyle's balls shrivel. It was the one he used when he said *now you listen here, sonny boy* to Pop, his I-don't-take-shit-I-give-it voice, and Kyle remembered that, as old as Grandpa was now, he'd once survived the schoolyard, too.

"I didn't come in here for you to help *me!* I came in here to help *you!*"

Oh, jeez, please don't yell at this guy, Kyle thought, picturing his grandfather behind bars as the little cop thrust his chin, already jutting aggressively, out even further, jaw muscles visible on the sides of his face. *How am I gonna tell Pop if you get arrested?*

The cop's hand came up, a finger pointing at Grandpa. Those bunched jaw muscles flexed and moved as his mouth opened, probably to shout for Grandpa to get up against the wall and spread 'em, but Grandpa beat him to the punch.

"I came in here to tell you about the Spellman boy."

The pointing finger froze in midair. The mouth hung open beneath a sharp nose and dark, angry V-shaped brows, blissfully silent. In the next instant the brows pulled up into a surprised bow, the eyes shifting sharply away from Grandpa. Kyle followed the little cop's gaze to another man in uniform coming around the corner with a hurried stride, and Kyle felt his tight muscles relax some.

"Just hold on a minute, Mr. Hickey. There's no need to shout, okay? Let's just calm down."

It was Officer Downs, Kyle's neighbor, and though he was talking to Grandpa, he was looking at the other cop, and Kyle knew he was talking to the little man, too. Officer Downs lived just two houses over from the Hickeys—Kyle went to school with his daughter, Bonnie, though she was a grade ahead—and Grandpa knew him. If Officer Downs could calm the old man, then maybe, just *maybe*, they could get out of here and head on home before Grandpa went and said something embarrassingly crazy.

"Now." Officer Downs's gaze shifted to Grandpa. "Mr. Hickey, you say you know what happened to Billy Spellman?"

Grandpa finally released Kyle's wrist and spread his hands. "Well, no. I can tell you what happened to him, but not what *happened* to him."

The cops exchanged a glance, and Kyle felt color rush into his face.

Great. Too late.

🐾

"Can I help you, sir?"

Carl Hickey heard the tone in the other man's voice before he saw him, and recognized him right off the bat. *It's that little prick, Saltz.*

He was right. There was that little prick face hanging over the intake desk. He'd had a run-in or two with Tim Saltz before, and knew *exactly* what the pint-sized officer of the law was. Well, Hickey had worked for pricks back when he'd been at the mill; he hadn't taken their shit then, and he sure wasn't going to take any from this jumped-up little public servant now. *I pay your salary, Timmy-boy!*

"Can you *help* me? I didn't come in here for you to help *me*! I came in here to help *you*!"

Hickey waited a beat, letting his own tone soak into Saltz's little doorknob head, watched the expression darken on that pinched face, then hit him with the second part of a one-two combination.

"I came in here to tell you about the Spellman boy."

The little bantam froze, and though his mouth opened, his goddamned annoying voice completely failed to fall out of it.

There! That shut you up, you little pri—

"Just hold on a minute, Mr. Hickey." Hickey turned and saw the Downs lad hustling toward them. "There's no need to shout, okay? Let's just calm down."

Thank God, Hickey thought. *I thought I was going to have to do this with just the Saltz jackoff.*

Young Officer Downs—*Joshua*, Hickey remembered—had bought the house two doors down a few years ago. He seemed a decent sort: kept a tidy lawn, a clean car, and he'd never walked his dog over to the corner of Hickey's front yard to take a shit, like that asshole Johnson across the way. Hickey swiveled away from Saltz, trying to cut him out of the conversation entirely. Honestly, if he knew that little turd was going to be here, he might have—

"Now," said Downs, shooting Saltz a glance that said *I'll handle this* before giving Hickey his full attention. "Mr. Hickey, you say you know what happened to Billy Spellman?"

"Well, no. I can tell you what happened to him, but not what *happened* to him."

Aw, shit, he thought at the cops' shared glance. *That little prick actually has me rattled.* He knew what that glance had meant: *uh-oh, Old Man Hickey's losing it.* It was bad enough that what he had to say was going to sound crazy anyway: appearing confused before he'd even started sure wasn't going to help.

"What I mean is, I can tell you what happened, but I can't tell you the *details*."

The snotty expression on Saltz's face made Hickey's teeth itch, but as the little man opened his mouth, Downs held an *I got this* hand up in his direction. "How do you know what happened, sir?"

"The boy's all torn up," said Hickey, ignoring the question. "Partly eaten, I think." Saying that last part made him feel a little sick, and he felt Kyle go absolutely still beside him, but he *really* wanted to wipe that smirk off Saltz's face. The smile *did* slip a notch, but damn it if the son of a whore didn't still look like he was enjoying this. "He's out in the woods, probably stuffed under a log somewhere. I can't tell you exactly where, but you should probably start looking near my house. That's your best bet."

Though that smirk still peeked around the corners of Timmy Saltz's mouth, Downs's face had gone flat and expressionless, and pale as milk.

"How do you know this, Mr. Hickey? Did you come across the body?"

Hickey wanted to turn and look at his grandson right then. *Needed* to. But he couldn't. He was doing this for Kyle, for his safety, and he'd needed the boy's presence to remind him of that: he might not have been able to do this otherwise. But if he looked at the boy right now it would break him. His dislike of that arrogant mouse-turd Saltz was spurring him on, keeping him going, but he'd be damned if he was going to cry in front of the man, so he *couldn't* look at the boy.

"No. I didn't come in here to report a body. I came in here to . . . to confess. I did it. I killed the boy."

Kyle gasped, and Hickey locked his neck muscles just before his head swiveled toward the sound. He stared steadfastly at Downs, who went still as a stone, nothing moving but his eyes, flicking over to Saltz and back.

"You killed the boy?"

"I did." It was an effort, but Hickey spoke these two words loud and clear, with nary a tremor in his voice, though he could feel his hands shaking. *I'm making the boy witness this.*

Might as well show him how to do this shit right.

"If you killed him," Saltz's over-loud voice interrupted Hickey's thoughts, "then maybe you'd be kind enough to show us where the body is?"

"I told you," Hickey snapped. "Weren't you listening? I don't know exactly where he is."

Downs opened his mouth, but he was moving slowly, as if dazed, and Saltz's sarcastic tone lashed out again. "Kind of an important detail, don't you think?"

"Yeah."

"But you don't know?"

"I can't remember."

"Seems to me," said Saltz, finally sidling around the desk to stand next to Downs, "killing a kid would be the kind of thing to stick in a person's mind. You trying to pull the 'confused old man' defense or something? Or are you really just confused, old man, and this is just a bunch of horseshit you made up in your own head?"

Downs held up a hand again, trying to get control of the situation, but he wasn't quite there yet. Hickey was looking straight into Saltz's sneering face—exactly where he hadn't wanted to be at the start of all this. But he was hot now, not just annoyed, and the words slipped out before he could stop.

"No, you little asshole. I can't remember because I'm . . . I'm . . ."

Aw, shit, he thought. *I've started, I'm just going to have to say it.*

He thrust out his chin, unconsciously mimicking Saltz's own belligerent stance. "I'm a goddamned werewolf."

🐾

"I'm a goddamned werewolf."

Silence fell over the police station, so thick Kyle didn't think he could have moved through it if he tried—but he *couldn't* try. He was frozen in place with horror, just as sure as if Mr. Freeze had hit him with his cold ray. *I wish this **was** a*

Batman comic, he thought. *Then maybe Mr. Freeze would just kill me, and I wouldn't have to—*

The cops looked at each other, and Kyle's horror kicked up a notch, his already shriveled balls gaining a sudden coating of ice. He knew what that shared glance meant, could read the expressions on their faces, and in his mind's eye he saw his worst fear unfolding:

"Now, you stay away from that Hickey place," Mr. Downs would tell Bonnie. *"I know old man Hickey looks harmless, but that's one crazy citizen over there. Why, he came into the station today and confessed to being a werewolf. Can you imagine that? Slap-ass crazy. So I want you to just steer clear, okay? And don't you go talking to that boy Kyle, either. You know what they say: the nut doesn't fall far from the crazy tree."*

He'd *have* to tell her. He was a cop, and her father, and he was *supposed* to tell her stuff like that, right? But the kids at school already made fun of Jennifer Powell for her crazy aunt, and that was just because the woman owned a half-dozen cats. There was no way Bonnie Downs wouldn't come into school full of stories of crazy Old Man Hickey, and his whole crazy family. Just no way.

And it *was* crazy. It *had* to be. One of James's favorite television shows was something called *Being Human,* on the SyFy channel. Kyle had watched it a couple of times, and when his mom found out she'd sat him down to talk. Yes, she'd said, it was a show with a ghost, a vampire, and a werewolf in it, but those things weren't *real.* Those were actors playing their parts, people pretending. She'd even gone online to show him the same people in different shows, where they *weren't* ghosts, and vampires, and werewolves. Mom had told him, and Dad had agreed: ghosts and vampires and werewolves *were not real.*

But here was Grandpa, flapping his arms in the middle of the police station, confessing to being a werewolf. He wasn't an actor, he was *Grandpa,* and he wasn't pretending, either. Kyle would have known just from Grandpa's grip that he wasn't kidding, never mind that they were in a *police station*, and that was as serious as you could get. And he was talking about Billy Spellman, which was weird, and Kyle would think about that later on, but he was busy now, wondering what was going to happen next. Were the cops going to slap the handcuffs on Grandpa? Or a straightjacket? And did Spreewald General have one of those rubber rooms, with the padded walls so the crazies couldn't hurt them—

"A werewolf?" said the smaller cop, his voice shockingly loud from such a small frame—so loud Officer Downs actually flinched beside him. "You crazy, old man?"

Kyle's eyes closed. There it was. Someone had said it. Grandpa was crazy. Kyle wondered for a moment about the rubber room, and for an instant how his father would take the news, but that was all crowded out by images of the pointing fingers and jeering faces of his schoolmates. Some part of him knew it was selfish, just as some other part of him was still trying to point out the stuff Grandpa had said about Billy, but he just couldn't help it. There was a slight scuffing sound, the tiniest squeak of shoe against floor, and Kyle opened his eyes, still looking toward the officers, expecting to see the little cop's sneer again.

All he saw was the back of Grandpa's grizzled head, and the surprised look on Officer Downs's face. His grandfather had closed the distance in a single stride, and now stood hunched, nose-to-nose with the little bully.

Oh, crap!

🐾

"A werewolf? You crazy, old man?"

There it was. That goddamned derisive tone—just what he knew he'd get from the prick. Hickey's knees had been practically knocking leading up to his admission, at the thought of saying it all out loud again, especially in front of the boy. *Especially* in the wake of the *last* time he'd said it all.

But that tone firmed his old legs right up. It was the same

tone Buck Townie had used more than forty years earlier, when the mill foreman had pointed to little Teddy Burgess and informed his crew that the mill paid their wages, and the day some *mill hand* like Teddy wanted to cut out after only a half-day's work, just because his wife was squeezing out their first child, that was the day that mill hand could go looking for a new job, 'cause he damn well didn't have one at the mill any more. Carl Hickey had stepped up to the foreman, looked him straight in the eye, and punched him in the jaw just as hard as he could.

He hadn't quite knocked the big man out, but he'd laid him down and put the woozy into him. Teddy had gone off to hold his missus's hand while she gave Teddy a son, and Hickey had been docked two day's pay for assaulting the company foreman. Mr. Stark, the mill owner, had considered it provoked, so he hadn't pink-slipped Hickey—or Teddy—but for the rest of the time Buck Townie worked at the mill, he walked wide around Carl Hickey. Townie had kept a civil tongue in his head, and Hickey had done as he was told, and that had been that. They'd reached an understanding.

Saltz's voice still hung in the air as Hickey took one long stride and bent to put his face right into the smaller man's. Saltz's thin-lipped mouth, still open and just starting to form a wide, smart-ass grin, snapped shut in surprise, and Hickey's clenched fists itched to smash him in it. But he wasn't that man any more—wasn't even a *man* any more, really—and he needed these cops. He needed them to listen to him, and they weren't going to do that if one of them was lying on the floor spitting out teeth.

Besides, he could feel the tail-end of the sunset, actually *feel* the scarlet light playing over his skin, and he had the sense that if he started hitting this little waste of spunk, he might not be able to stop. And the hitting might lead to clawing, and then on to biting, and then they might never get him into a cell, never mind that there were two of them, and they had guns. And he *needed* to be in a cell when the moon came up. He sensed his grandson behind him, frightened and confused. He thought about the Spellman boy, and what had happened to him—what Hickey had *done* to him—and he kept his clenched and trembling fists down at his sides, elbows locked, thumbs tight to his thighs.

"You keep a civil tongue in your head, or you and I are going to have a problem, skippy. You don't want that at the best of times. You sure don't want it now."

The sudden move shocked the grin from Saltz's face, or maybe it was the intensity in Hickey's voice, but whatever it was, the cop's cocky mask slipped. Carl Hickey found himself looking into the face of a small, scared boy; a boy who had been beaten up at school, and passed over for sports teams, and had quailed at asking girls out because he'd have been looking *up* at them to do so. That boy peeked up at Hickey with wide, frightened eyes; and in that moment, Carl Hickey understood Saltz, understood what had *made* him, and, just for that instant, he pitied him.

Then the arrogant mask slammed back into place, like one of those security grates the shop owners used in Frenchietown, to protect their front windows at night. Saltz's eyes narrowed as color flooded his face, and Hickey knew that *Saltz* knew his mask had slipped, and Hickey had seen, and he hated the older man for it. Saltz's hard slash of a mouth opened—

—and a hand slipped between them, barely fitting through the gap separating their noses, to drop, very gently, onto Hickey's chest.

"Please, sir." The Downs boy's voice wasn't quite as gentle as his touch, but it was close. Gentleness mixed with respect, and just a hint of reluctant firmness, like an honorable man doing a distasteful duty. It was this tone, more than the soft pressure of his hand, that caused Hickey to back up a step.

"That man just threatened an officer of the law!" Saltz exploded. "Get your ass in a cell, you crazy old son of a bitch, I'm—" He reached for his belt as he shouted, though whether for his gun or handcuffs, Hickey couldn't tell. The gentle hand had left his chest at the first word, though, and shot out to grab Saltz's shoulder. From the whitening of the knuckles, Hickey guessed the gentle was gone, and the angry little man froze before he could take anything from his belt.

"You're provoking him," said Downs, his tone a match for his grip. "And you know it. Just let me handle this, okay?" Though phrased as a question, it was clearly a command, and Timmy Saltz just blinked up at his partner for a moment, eyes round. Then some of the asshole crept back into his face and voice, and he jerked his shoulder away. "Fine, then. You *handle* it." He stepped halfway back around the charge desk and leaned against the wall, arms folded across his chest, sour expression on his face. Downs turned back to Hickey, gesturing toward a visitor's chair in front of one of the desks beyond the counter.

"Mr. Hickey, if you'd like to make a statement, then please take a seat. If you do intend to make a formal confession of . . . some kind, then I need to read you your rights, okay?"

The changing sunlight clung to Hickey's skin like warm syrup, but it was rapidly cooling. He glanced at the window. The rosy ambiance of the setting sun was almost gone. He didn't have much time.

"Read me my rights, boy; that's fine. I want to confess. But I want to do it in a cell. Now. I want to go to a cell *right now.*"

Saltz huffed a snort, but Downs just nodded. He took hold of Hickey's upper arm and led the way deeper into the building. It was a gentle, guiding grip, but part of Hickey's mind identified it as a *taking you into custody* grip, and something inside bellowed for the old man to break and run. Hickey swallowed hard, and stepped toward the cells.

I came here of my own free will, he thought. *This is where I want to be—for the boy's sake. For **everyone's** sake. This is where I **need** to be.*

But as the sun disappeared from the sky, and the moon's edge crested the horizon, that voice inside grew louder, the *wild* feeling stronger, and all it wanted to do was run, run, *run . . .*

And kill, of course. And kill.

🐾

Kyle's eyes were a hair's breadth from falling right out of his head. First that little bully cop had sassed off to Grandpa, and *nobody* sassed off to Grandpa, not even Pop. Not ever. But then Grandpa had gotten right up in the cop's grill, and it had looked like he was about to give the man the hard side of his hand. Grandpa never started out with the hand, like some of the kids at school did—all the time!—but he wasn't shy about taking what he called *a little corrective action,* and if Kyle had ever seen someone in need of some correcting, it was that mean cop.

But then Officer Downs had stepped in, and Grandpa had backed off—and when the cop had started to shout, wanting to arrest Grandpa, Officer Downs had made him back off as well. The little cop was still mad, and Grandpa was breathing heavy, but Officer Downs looked calm, and Kyle thought he was calling the shots at the moment.

He's the only one not mad, he thought. *If he's in charge, and he doesn't look like he's arresting Grandpa or anything, maybe we'll get out of here and go home.*

Kyle's spirits rose slightly—he might get back to his Minecraft server before all his friends had quit for the night—but the next thing he knew, Grandpa himself demanded to be put in a cell. With a heavy heart and dragging feet, the boy followed the group toward the back of the building, his insides all a jumble. He'd started out mostly worried about school, and the story of this night spreading around, but now he was more worried about what was actually happening to Grandpa. This was . . . this was *bad,* and *real.* This wasn't just his old grandfather coming down to the police station to tell them crazy stories any more. They were locking him up. Officer Downs was reading him his rights off a little card he took from his pocket, just like they did on TV. The little bully cop was following them, strolling along in front of Kyle with his thumbs hooked in his belt like some kind of gunfighter. A word popped into Kyle's head, one his father used sometimes that Kyle had never really understood, though his father had tried to explain it to him: strut.

Well, he understood it now. If this cootie-riddled, bullying, mean man of a cop wasn't strutting his way back to the cells, then Kyle thought he'd *never* understand the word.

They got to the cells, and Grandpa entered one and sat on the cot. Officer Downs turned to fetch the folding chair that leaned against the wall facing the cells, and saw Kyle bringing up the rear. He froze for a second, hand outstretched, eyes wide with surprise.

"Oh! Christ, I forgot all about Kyle." He paused a moment, then put on a more official cop voice. "Officer Saltz, can you bring young Mr. Hickey home, while I—"

"No," said Grandpa, and though he was sitting in a jail cell, there was command in his tone, like he was back home, tossing orders across the kitchen. "The boy stays. He's why I'm doing this, after all."

Mr. Downs looked at Officer Saltz, but Saltz just shrugged without turning around, like he'd known Kyle was there all along. "I say we let him stay, then. Besides." His back was still to Kyle, so the boy couldn't see the officer's expression, but his voice grew jolly, like he was almost laughing. "I don't think I want to miss this."

"Kyle."

The open cell door was right beside him, but Grandpa had chosen to thrust a hand through the restraining bars instead, leaving them separated. Kyle was shocked to see the old man looked close to tears.

Grandpa never *cries.*

This, more than anything else, left Kyle stranded in uncertainty. All thoughts of Minecraft were gone as he wondered just what was going on here, and what in the world could make Grandpa *cry*? His own eyes welled as the great mass of callused knuckles enveloped his hand. His grandfather gave a slight tug, and a little squeeze, and his voice, when it came, was as gentle as Kyle had ever heard it.

"Now, boy, don't you cry. I need you to listen, and watch, and remember, okay? I tried explaining all this to your pop, but he didn't want to listen. He was pretty clear about that. I would have tried to change his mind, but"—he cast a glance over his shoulder, at the small, wire-threaded window set in the cell wall, and shuddered—"I'm runnin' out of time awful quick here, and we Hickeys can be some stubborn assholes on occasion, so you're gonna have to do."

A tiny smile flicked across his old mouth, and was gone.

"Probably wouldn't do you any good to repeat that to your ma, though, okay?" Kyle nodded, fighting back the tears. A parade of questions marched through his head, but he daren't ask any: the intensity pouring off of his grandfather was enough to leave him tongue-tied.

"Good boy." Another hand squeeze, harder this time. "You go over in the corner and you watch, and listen. And remember." With a sudden jerk, he yanked Kyle almost nose-to-nose, and the steel crept back into his voice. "And when you get in that corner you don't come out, you hear? You *do not* come back near this cell, understand? You do and I'll tan the hide right off your backside."

At Kyle's frightened nod, the big hand pushed him, only half gently, away from the cell. Grandpa turned and took his seat on the cot again, just as Mr. Downs carried the folding chair into the cell.

"No," said Grandpa. "You sit outside. And close the door—you can hear me just fine from out there."

A snort came from Officer Saltz, leaning against the corridor wall, a derisive sound with a lot of flapping lips, but Officer Downs just swung the chair out into the corridor, pushed the cell door to without latching it, and planted himself in his seat.

"This better, sir?"

Grandpa reached out and gave the barred door a yank, closing it with a decisive *click*.

"Is now. You 'bout ready? 'Cause I'm 'bout out of time."

Officer Downs pulled out a small, gray object, about twice the size of the Zippo lighters they sold down at the corner store. He pressed a button, and a small, red light winked into existence.

"Do you mind if I record this session?"

The question was asked with the air of one who already knew the answer: Kyle had seen cops on TV and figured it didn't matter what Grandpa said, that recorder was staying on. Grandpa just flipped a hand toward the little thing.

"You can put it on a billboard up by the highway for all I care—just listen, and let me talk. I'm running out—"

"I just have the official stuff to get through, sir. One moment." Officer Downs looked at the little red light in his hand. "This is Officer Joshua Downs, of the Spreewald P.D., accompanied by Officer Timothy Saltz, also of the Spreewald P.D., and we're sitting with Mr. Carl Hickey Senior, also of Spreewald. Mr. Hickey has come to the station of his own free will to make a statement of confession, and has been informed of his rights." He looked at his watch, added the date and time, then looked up at Grandpa, holding forth the recorder like a reporter's microphone. "All set, sir, thank you for your patience. It's your show."

"It's about damn time," said Grandpa—then stopped. He looked about a moment, as if searching for words, but when his eyes fell upon Kyle he seemed to settle down, and took a deep breath.

"I been having dreams for years. Long as I can remember." His gaze swiveled from Kyle to Officer Downs. "Always during the full moon. Took me a long time to figure that out, when I was younger, but I did. Might have been that a lot of 'em were about the moon, but whatever. Three nights every month, I had these moon dreams—I called 'em moon dreams, even when they wasn't about the moon—and for the

127

longest time, they was just fine. Enjoyable. Runnin' through the fields and the woods, mostly. It wasn't like anything really *happened* in 'em, it was more the *feeling* they gave me. Woke up feeling, I don't know, just great. Relaxed and happy, like after the first time a young gal let me take her for a tumble. Three days a month I could count on waking up feeling like everything was right with the world, you understand? Been like that for 'bout as long as I can remember."

He'd begun to look almost pleased, as if just thinking about the dreams was enough to make him happy. Then he hesitated, his expression caving in on itself.

"But then, a few years ago, the dreams . . . changed. See, sometimes the running dreams were hunting dreams. Stalking little things through the woods, like rabbits. Squirrels. Stuff like that. Not every time, but enough. Enough for me to notice. I wasn't catching them, or anything. Just every once in a while I was chasing them, like it was a game, you know? Tag, or something like that. It was kind of . . . well, it was kind of beautiful."

He raised his chin as he said that last, obviously daring anyone to poke fun at him for the sentiment. Kyle waited to hear that derisive snort from Officer Saltz, but it didn't come. He glanced sideways, and found the little cop still leaning against the wall, arms folded over his chest, but for once the sneer was gone, replaced by an intense stare. Saltz didn't look at Kyle at all, watching Grandpa as if hanging on his every word.

"A few years back, though, it changed again. They wasn't *always* hunting dreams, but they was more often than not. And I started . . . I started *catching* things."

Grandpa's chin had relaxed to its usual position, but now he wasn't looking at anyone. He stared at the bars to one side of Officer Downs, but his eyes looked funny to Kyle, like he wasn't really seeing anything. Or maybe seeing stuff the rest of them *couldn't*. Like running rabbits and squirrels.

"I was catching things—still the little things I'd been

chasing before, you know, woodchuck, maybe a raccoon—and I was killing 'em. With my teeth. Like an animal."

His head swiveled, and he looked straight at Officer Downs, and Kyle thought the policeman met his eyes.

"I've hunted—near 'bout everybody 'round here does, at one time or another—and I know some guys who done that thing where you drink the blood of your first buck, supposed to bring you closer to the spirit of the deer. I never went for that shit. My daddy never told me to when I was a kid. But in these dreams, taking these little critters down like that . . . I did taste their blood."

His gaze drifted off into the middle distance again, caught up in the memories. "It was the strangest thing. I'd never really thought about it—why would I?—but the blood tasted . . . you know, *different*, depending on what it came from. I guess I'd always just thought blood was blood, but it's not. Woodchuck don't taste like rabbit don't taste like squirrel—and nothing tastes like deer. And in the dreams I liked it. I liked it all. I was always disgusted when I woke up, and started thinking of the moon dreams as nightmares. Told myself I wasn't looking forward to the full moon each month any more . . . but I was lying to myself. Part of me was always looking forward to it. But then they changed again."

Grandpa gulped, Adam's apple bobbing visibly in his skinny neck.

"I had one . . . I had one where I et what I killed." He shifted on his cot, sliding his bony shanks into a more comfortable position. "Up 'til then, the hunting dreams ended when I caught up. I'd tackle what I was chasing, or sink my teeth into it if it was a killing dream, they'd let loose this little screech, and I'd wake up right then, with the feel of the thing on my skin, or the taste of its blood still in my mouth. But it was all just a memory, you know? Like when you wake up and you're not sure whether you're still dreaming or not, but then you wake the rest of the way up and it all sort of fades away. It was like that. Then one time I didn't wake up."

He swallowed again.

"Not 'til I was done. It happened about a year ago, and that one *was* a nightmare. I—"

He broke off and looked at Kyle, his eyes showing fear for the first time since he'd started. "I'm sorry."

What? Kyle thought, then opened his mouth to voice the question, but Grandpa turned back to Officer Downs.

"I dreamed I chased Jingles, my daughter-in-law's cat. Caught it out behind the shed and drug it off into the woods."

Kyle gasped, but the old man went on like he hadn't heard.

"That's the first time I remember eating in the dreams. I woke up that morning with the taste in my mouth, and I *was* upset about that one, not just pretending. She was a crotchety old bitch, but I liked Jingles just fine. I was lying there, waiting for the taste, the memory, to fade, lying there for quite a while before I realized it wasn't going away. Then I noticed my big toe."

Kyle sniffled. Tears ran down his face, though he was trying his best to fight them. His grandfather didn't cotton to tears, 'specially not in public. *You gonna blubber,* he'd say, *you take it t'home, you hear me? 'Tisn't nobody's business but your own.* Grandpa glanced at Kyle, and his gaze stuck. When he went on, he was telling his story to Kyle, not the cops.

"My big toe was hurting something fierce, like I'd smacked it a good one, but I didn't remember doing that at all. I yanked my foot up to check it out, and that was when I saw the dirt. The bottoms of my feet were black with it—not just the usual inside-the-house dusting up, mind, but real dirt, like I'd been walking around outside. My hands, too. Palms were scratched and dirty, fingernails filthy. I realized I was wide awake, but I could still taste the blood—Jingles's blood—and I started rooting about in my mouth with my tongue."

Another throat-working swallow.

"There was blood in there, and something else, something solid, all worked down in between my teeth. I sucked a bit out and spat it in my palm, and it was fur. Like cat fur. Then I ran into the bathroom to throw up. I puked for a while, bits of stuff coming out that didn't look nothin' like the dinner I'd et the night before.

"I tried to ignore all that stuff, the fur in my teeth and my dirty feet, tried to tell myself it was just a dream and nothing more, just like it always had been. But then the cat turned up missing. Abby kept a-callin' it, and it never came. Then, two days later, the boys found the cat in the woods. Found . . . what was left of it, I mean."

Tears rolled down Kyle's face now, and to heck with that old man. Kyle remembered him and James finding Jingles half-buried under a fallen tree in the woods behind the house. The bugs had gotten to the cat by then, and between the maggots and the smell, both boys had puked their guts out in the trees. Then James had stayed to mark the spot while Kyle ran for home, crying and spitting, puke and snot running from his nose, to fetch their pop.

They had really only been able to identify her by the little tag hanging from the collar still about her neck, but Kyle would *never* forget finding the crumpled, ruined form sticking out from under that log. Grandpa said they'd found a cat, but that wasn't quite true. They'd found the front half.

Well, *most* of it.

"So now I knew," Grandpa said. "They wasn't just dreams after all. Maybe they never *had* been. I don't know. But I've heard stories of things that go bump in the night my whole life, and I been to the movies. Someone getting out to go a-killin' when the moon is full, waking up with no memory of it but some kind of jumbled dream? I ain't stupid: didn't take me but that morning of the missing cat to put two and two together and come up with werewolf."

Grandpa's forehead shone with sweat, though it was cool in the cells. He mopped his face with a sleeve.

"I did what I could. Made it almost a year. Moon dream nights, I'd head to the shed out back. Got a padlock for it, and put it on the inside, so I could lock myself in. Hang the key from a little hook, and I couldn't get out of there until I had hands to work the lock, you understand? Plus, no one could get in there *at* me, come upon me by accident, you know? I was locked in there all safe and sound for the night ten full moons runnin'.

"Then this past month, just as the sun was going down, I walked into my shed and found the hook empty and the lock gone. I looked everywhere in that shed, but I didn't find nothin', and I just ran out of time. I found out later my grandson, James, had borrowed my lock to use with his bike, but I all I knew at the time was the full moon was rising and there I was, loose. Well, I ran off into the woods just as fast as I could, getting as far away from people as I could before the change came. I'd stayed awake a few times in that shed, just to see what happened, so I knew the signs. I ran and I ran and . . . and that was all I remembered 'til morning, when I woke up with blood in my teeth and what felt like a full belly."

He wiped perspiration from his face again, unfastened the top two buttons of his shirt, then another, flapping the open neck of the shirt to cool himself.

"You all right, sir?" said Officer Downs.

"Close . . . close," Grandpa muttered, as if talking to himself. "Almost here. Gotta finish. The dream that night was so . . . my memory of it was all jumbled, but still, I kept seeing this . . . this kid, running from me. He ran, and I chased. God help me, I chased. I didn't remember the killing, or the eating, but I remembered that child, running. Screaming. I—"

He broke off, shaking his head, lips pressed tight. Kyle stared at his grandfather, cold sick coiling in his belly like a snake, feeling like he had to pee. Mom and Dad had said there was no such thing as vampires and werewolves. No such thing. But Grandpa was sitting right there, with the cops and their confession-recorder thingie, saying he changed. Saying he ate up Jingles. Chased a kid. And they *had* found a half-eaten Jingles, hadn't they? So that part was true, and if *that* part was true, then the *rest* could be—

"When they started, the moon dreams weren't nothing but that: dreams. I walked around hoping like hell it had gone back to that, at least for one night, and it hadn't been anything but a dream. I was praying it. Then, two days later, Kyle came home from school talking about a missing kid, a kid from his class what nobody'd seen since that night. The night my lock went missing. They ran the kid's picture in the paper, and that's when I knew, knew for certain. I'd seen that kid in the picture running away from me in my dream. He ran, and I chased. And that was that."

He coughed, a wet, growling bark, flinching as if in sharp, momentary pain, and his old, yellowed eyes rolled a bit in their sockets, wide with sudden fear.

"I'm out of time. I tried to tell my boy about all this—tried twice, since that last moon, so he knows about the shed now, and so it ain't safe no more. But he didn't want to hear it, this crazy talk from his old pa. He wouldn't listen."

He was standing, unbuttoning the rest of his shirt as he spoke, but he paused long enough to look at Kyle once more, and the corners of his lips twitched in an almost half-smile.

"We Hickeys can be some real stubborn assholes sometimes." His eyes shifted to Officer Downs, still seated before the cell. "So I came here, looking for you boys to take my confession and lock me up nice and safe. You'll keep me in, and people out, and figure what to do with me in the morning. But for now"—he tore the shirt off, exposing a narrow, old man's torso, long, ropy muscles still working beneath slightly sagging skin as he gestured toward Officer Downs—"you best be getting back, son."

Officer Downs turned to glance at Officer Saltz, but Kyle only had eyes for his grandfather as Bonnie's father pocketed the recorder and stood, taking the folding chair back to its spot against the wall. Grandpa stripped right down to his skivvies, folding his clothes neatly on the cot, his movements marred by occasional jerks and twitches, each accompanied by a grunt of pain. Kyle had to pee something fierce, and he wanted to run, run all the way home to use his own bathroom, so afterward he could go into his own room, and curl into his own bed, where his mom could sit next to him on the mattress and stroke his hair the way he liked, and tell him again and again that werewolves aren't real. That monsters aren't real.

But he couldn't run, couldn't move from the spot on which he stood, was pretty sure he'd still be standing there long after the pee had run down his legs like some big friggin' baby. Then Grandpa looked up at him, thrust his hands forward to grab the bars, and Kyle was pretty sure he did pee, just a little, a hot spot in the front of his Wolverine underwear.

🐾

Hickey was coming to the end of his story just in time. The sun had been down for a while, and now the moon was coming. The cells had grown uncomfortably warm, though the others didn't seem to notice, and with the heat had come the thickening, the air in the little cell congealing until it felt like water against his skin. His breaths didn't come easily any more, but required a growing effort, flowing in and out of him like the tides pulled by the moon. Sound wasn't muffled by the thick air, but instead grew sharper, more defined. He heard his own heart beating, strong, but rapid, sped up with the effort of breathing. Of talking. The itching began, every hair on his body standing to attention like there had been a lightning strike nearby, and he swore he could feel them thickening as well. *Coarsening.*

He knew from experience he'd have been itchy naked, but clothes seemed to make it a thousand times worse, as if the hair had nowhere to go and was forcing itself back *in*. He'd already opened a few buttons, but now he stood and took the shirt off, fumbling in his haste. He warned Downs away as he tore the shirt from his back, then started right on the pants, kicking off his boots and skinning the jeans down his legs. He stopped at his briefs, for now, and folded his clothes into a neat pile on the cot.

I may be a hairy, toothy killer, but damn it, my momma raised me right.

The moon was on the rise now. He could feel it. His muscles had twitched while he'd undressed, the spasms growing longer and stronger as they came. He turned and saw Kyle standing in frozen horror, like he didn't know whether to shit or go blind. He didn't blame the boy: Hickey himself was terrified, and he was a grown-ass man.

His stomach lurched, his innards rolling, muscles writhing in ways they were just not meant to move, shoving aside things within him as they heaved. As sick as Hickey felt, Kyle looked sicker, his face a shade of white that said he was about to puke or pass out. It suddenly dawned on Hickey, his abdomen twisting to the point of pain, that the boy might be too frightened to make heads or tails of what was happening, that he might not understand why Hickey had brought him along. His nose sharpened, the syrupy air carrying the scents of Ivory soap and minty toothpaste from Downs, while making it quite clear that prick, Saltz, had relied on strong coffee to wash the sleep-stink out of his mouth that morning.

Kyle gave only a bitter scent, sour and sweet and slightly acrid all at the same time, so strong it nearly stung his nose. Part of Hickey, once buried deep inside but rising with the moon, recognized that scent, and was goaded by it, surging up faster now, urging him to lash out at the scent, to bite and rend and tear and devour—to destroy the thing before him giving off the prey smell.

The boy's fear.

Hickey had to make sure Kyle understood. The cops hadn't had to come get Hickey, even when his own jackoff of a son wouldn't listen to him. He'd walked through those doors on his own. His gut cramped, worse than anything he'd experienced outside of the full moon, and he lunged forward to get a grip on the bars. The reek of piss hit him like a slap, and he knew he'd just about undone the boy, but Carl Hickey wasn't going to deliver his message from his knees.

"Remember this, boy." Something within him twisted, and when he opened his mouth he had to force aside a scream so the words could come out. "I may be a monster, but I'm also a man . . . and a man does what's right, even if it ain't easy. That's why I'm here, boy. A man does what's right."

Pain hit him hard, boring through his middle, and his hands slipped from the bars. The impact as he fell to all fours shattered his knuckles like glass within their little bags of skin, and he howled with agony. The splintered bones shifted, pulling in tight as he watched his fingers shrink through bulging eyes. His left leg broke, and started to reform, followed by his right.

Something tore loose inside him, then something else; things moved as his ribcage creaked, then cracked. Shifting. Shortening.

He moaned, unable to draw enough breath for a shriek, his lungs squeezing and reshaping, and the tone grew resonant as, with a horrible crack, his face split, lips stretching almost to bursting as his muzzle thrust forward, and his face deformed, and his teeth grew.

In seconds, two-legged Hickey was gone and only four-legged Hickey remained, pacing the wall of bars, seeking a way out of the cage. He stared out at the men, skinning back his lips in a snarl, a challenging rumble deep in his chest. The little cave stank of fear and piss and misery, and Hickey wanted to get out, to get away, into the clean night air where he could hunt under the watchful eye of the full moon.

🐾

Kyle watched what was left of his grandfather working its way back and forth in the cell. The old man crawled about on his hands and knees, nicotine-stained teeth bared as he snarled and snapped at the bars, the skid mark in the back of his drooping jockeys winking like a brown eye on every other turn. Behind him the mean cop was laughing fit to bust, giggling like a hyena until Officer Downs's stern voice ordered him to stop.

Even then, high-pitched snorts and chuckles could be heard as Kyle said, "What's going on?" He took a step toward the bars, stretching out an uncertain hand. "Grandpa?"

Quick as a thought Grandpa turned, naked teeth snapping at the extended fingers. He came up short, his forehead striking one of the bars with a clang that set Saltz to laughing again, and Officer Downs sent him out of the room. The door closed behind the cackling officer, and then Kyle felt a gentle hand on his shoulder.

"I'm sorry, Kyle. Your grandfather's pretty sick—but not in the way he thought. Your father called me about a week ago, after your grandfather talked to him, wondering what he should do. I did some research: I'm no doctor, but I think what your grandpa's got is called 'clinical lycanthropy,' and it's . . . it's a mental thing. An illness. It's . . . your grandfather's confused, Kyle. Maybe getting older has something to do with it. Maybe not; I have no idea. Like I said, I'm not a doctor. But he's delusional. All that stuff he said earlier, about the dreams, and changing into a wolf, he wasn't lying, exactly. He thought he was telling us the God's honest truth . . . and right now your grandfather really thinks he's a wolf in a cage."

The gentle hand pulled him around to face Officer Downs, but he could still hear Grandpa snarling and growling. The big police officer offered Kyle a handkerchief, and the boy wiped at his face. "What he needs right now is a special kind of doctor. We can wait 'til morning, when he stops thinking he's a wolf, and talk to him about it. But for now . . ."

"What now?" said Kyle, whose legs were already screaming at him to run away from the crawling old man behind him, to run fast and far, and if the cop hadn't been between him and the door they would have gotten their wish. "Can I go home? I want to go home."

Officer Downs looked at him with sad, brown eyes, then over Kyle's shoulder, toward Grandpa. "I understand you wanting to go home, Kyle, but there's no one here right now but me and Officer Saltz, and I"—he lowered his voice, though there was no one there to hear. "I don't really want to leave your grandpa alone with Saltz. You understand? But then, you don't really want *him* bringing you home, do you?"

Kyle thought of the sneering officer, pictured being shut up in a car with the little cootie-carrier, for even ten minutes. The man could say a lot in ten minutes. And something about being alone with him . . .

Kyle shook his head. "No. No, thanks, I don't want that." He started edging around the man, sliding toward the door. "But I know the way—it ain't far. Me and Gran—"

He stumbled over the name, hearing his grandfather moving and growling about his cell. "Uh, we walked here anyway. I can walk back. No problem, okay? I just want to go home. Okay?"

He hadn't slipped out from under that big hand yet, and for a moment it tightened against his shoulder, and he was afraid Officer Downs was going to hold him there, maybe put him in a cell right next to Grand—right next door, and tears welled again. But then the hand slipped away, the squeeze more of reassurance than restraint, and the man sighed.

"All right. It's not the best solution, but it's what we have. You hurry on home, and you send your dad down here just as soon as you get there, all right? I'll explain what's going on, and he needs to help decide what's going to happen, anyway. You just be careful, you hear me?"

"Yessir," said Kyle, sidling for the door, the words coming out all in a rush. Officer Downs said something else, but Kyle wasn't listening as he pushed through the door into the police station proper. He picked up speed crossing the big, main room with all the desks. Saltz's voice came from somewhere off to the side, but Kyle didn't hear him, didn't look left or right, just kept his eyes on the doors to the street. He was moving at a run when he hit them, and they barely slowed him down as, weeping terrified tears, he sped off into the night.

❖

Hickey Four-Legs watched as the smaller man burst back into the room outside his cage, making those man-sounds that made no sense to him.

"Jesus Christ, this is like a gift from God! Fan*tas*tic!"

"I don't like this," said the big man.

"What's not to like? You have the old fool's confession on tape, right? I mean, Jesus, he spelled the whole thing out. I noticed you never said he was in a cell or even in custody, so we can tell the chief he was in the chair out front and just got away while our backs were turned. The kid never spoke, right? Not while the tape was rolling?"

"No," said Big. "No, I don't think he did."

"So?" Little said, voice almost a squeal as he unbuttoned his shirt. "It's *perfect.*"

"I still don't like this. He's just a kid, and—"

"Says the one who killed Spellman in the first place." Little was kicking off his shoes and pawing at his belt buckle.

"That was an accident," Big said, voice rising, pointing toward Hickey Four-Legs. "It was just like he said: the kid saw me and he ran. He ran, so I chased, and things just got out of hand. We'd just spent two nights running with the pack, and you know how we get. It's hard to think for yourself; you *know* that." Big shook his head. "He shouldn't have run. God *damn* it, but he shouldn't have run."

Little waved a hand, clad only in his boxer shorts now. "Whatever you say, Josh. But it happens a lot with you. They find the Spellman kid and start searching the woods back of your house, and—"

"You have bodies there too, remember?"

"Not any more, I don't." Little pointed toward Hickey Four-Legs again. "He does. Just give me ten minutes to kill the kid, then bring old snarly-and-drooly there along to discover with the body. Bang-bang, he's dead, and we have ourselves a confessed kid-killer in the cooler downstairs when the chief gets back from Bangor."

He stepped closer, looking up into the bigger man's face.

"Look, Josh, this Spellman thing is too close to home. The chief, she's a bitch, but she's not stupid, and she's not going to let this go until she finds someone. Either we hand her this half-breed or she might find you. And me. And I am *not* down with that."

The two men stood side by side, looking into the cage at Hickey.

"You have any idea he was a 'breed?" said Little.

"Christ, no. But he's seventy if he's a day, and it sounded like he only started having the pack dreams once I moved so close. If I'd moved somewhere else, he might have just kept having the moon dreams until the day he died. Not enough wolf in him to make the change, but it's no wonder his mind snapped."

"Lucky for us." Little looked at the clock on the wall. "It's been long enough. He's away from the station, at least." He bent and stripped off the boxer shorts. "Just open that door and give me five minutes, okay?"

He bent, hunched, and a cracking like the snapping of dry sticks filled the air as his back bowed, his legs twisted, and a scent like wet dog exploded into the room.

"God," said Little, a tone of terrible longing slipping out around a mouthful of lengthening teeth, "I hope he *runs!*" Fur sprouted across his skin in widening ripples as he fell to all fours. Claws scrabbled for a moment at the hard, tiled floor, and in his cage, Hickey Four-Legs pressed himself against the wall farthest from the bars and whimpered, eyes wide.

Big stepped away from the large black wolf that stood, chest heaving, in the middle of the corridor. He pulled the door open, and with an eager growl the wolf streaked out through the police station, nostrils already flaring as it seined the air for the bitter, yellow scent of the boy's fear.

The scent of prey.

Big left the door and walked back to the bars of Hickey

Four-Legs's cage.

"I don't know if you can understand me," he said. "I hope part of you does, somewhere in there. I actually admire what you were trying to do, turning yourself in like you did. Trying to do the right thing, set an example for Kyle. And I'm . . . I'm touched by what you were telling the boy, there at the end. And I think you were right: a man does what's right."

Big bowed his head for a moment, and something within him cracked like a dry stick. His chin came up, and he looked in at Hickey Four-Legs with eyes suddenly gone red, as the wet dog smell grew stronger.

"Unfortunately for Kyle," he said, gravel and bass suddenly filling his voice, "we're not men."

Hickey Four-Legs growled at the man-wolf-thing in front of him, straining back against the wall in fear as its nonsense sounds washed over him, baring his teeth in a threat born of terror. But as he snapped and snarled and tried to raise up non-existent hackles, tears finally rolled down the old man's cheeks to spatter the floor beneath his feet.

ONE SOCK, TWO SOCKS

"Oh, for the love of God!"

Larisa flailed about uselessly with one blue sock. The rest of the laundry was already in the basket sitting atop the dryer: clothes and underwear folded neatly, socks rolled together in pairs, all but the blue sock in her hand.

She could not find its mate.

"There were *two* blue socks in there," she nearly shouted into the open dryer, bending to take yet another look into its empty drum. "I had to unroll the pair when I put them in the washer!"

She snatched up a clean, rolled pair of tube socks from the top of her basket and waved it at the open machine as if it could see and hear.

"They were rolled! A pair! What the hell do you do, eat them?"

The dryer sat motionless, not deigning to make the slightest response.

"I know it's you." She indicated the nearby washing machine. "*That* one gives back everything. *You*, on the other hand, apparently charge me something each and every time I use you!"

A part of Larisa felt pretty silly standing there yelling at an inanimate thing. The rest of her, though, was eaten up with annoyance over the missing sock.

She flung the lonesome blue sock on top of the folded clothes and snatched up the laundry basket. "I'll *prove* it's you! You can't seem to help yourself. Wait here—I'll be right back."

Larisa stomped up the stairs in a way she hadn't done since she was about six years old. A few minutes later she marched back down those stairs clutching a half-full laundry basket. She put the basket back on top of the dryer and spun the washing machine dial to *Light Wash.*

"Right! Here's the deal." She pulled a rolled pair of socks from the basket and separated them. "I have here ten pair of socks. Ten pair. That's twenty socks. I'm counting them, and washing them. Nothing but them. Let's see how many socks I get back!"

She counted each of them aloud as she dropped them into the rapidly filling washing machine. ". . . Nineteen, twenty. There: ten pair."

She backed across the laundry room toward the chair against the wall as if afraid or unwilling to take her eyes from either machine.

"There. Let's just see what happens."

Thirty minutes later, the washing machine's buzzer sounded and the machine itself shuddered to a silent halt. Larisa opened it up and started counting wet socks back into the basket.

". . . Nineteen, twenty. There, you see?" She pointed an accusing finger at the dryer as she nearly shouted. "I got back what I put in. Now let's see how *you* do!"

She counted all twenty socks into the machine, speaking aloud again, though whom she was actually talking to was a mystery, even to herself. She slapped the front of the dryer closed and gave the knob a somewhat savage twist, choosing a twenty-minute timed dry. She backed toward her chair once more, eyes glued to the quietly roaring machine. She stayed that way, nearly unblinking, for the entire cycle.

When the dryer's buzzer went off, Larisa was yanking the front of the machine open before the internal drum had even come to a halt. She put the basket on the floor next to the open door and began counting warm, dry socks into it.

". . . Eighteen, nineteen—son of a *bitch!*"

She stared into the empty dryer, looking for sock number twenty, but saw nothing but the white enameled surface. She dumped the socks out onto the top of the dryer and recounted them into the basket, just in case she had miscounted.

Nineteen.

"Son of a *bitch!*" she repeated, standing helplessly for a few seconds, then her jaw muscles bunched as she clenched her teeth in frustration.

"No way. It *has* to be in there somewhere. It's just not *possible!*"

Bending low, she thrust her head and shoulders into the open machine. She swept her hands about the rear of the dryer, checking that nothing was stuck to the back of the three agitator vanes built into the drum. Her voice sounded hollow inside the round metal box.

"This is impossible. It *has* to be in here. They *all* do! I'm going to find out where they go, even if I have to take you apart!"

At her words the drum suddenly went into motion, spinning a half revolution clockwise; since Larisa was bracing her hands on the inside of the drum for balance, she spun, too. As her upper half twisted around, her legs followed suit until she fell, landing on her side on the inside of the open dryer door. The drum gave a kind of lurch, and seemed to Larisa to lengthen and gain depth. At the same time the door beneath her hips gave a sudden heave upward, causing her feet to actually leave the floor. She felt herself slide further into the machine, further than she thought possible, the edge of the opening actually catching her at the back of the knees.

She inhaled to scream and almost choked on the air as the

back of the drum opened right before her eyes. What was revealed was *not* the wall behind the dryer, but instead what looked like a tube or tunnel, sloping downward and out of sight. The drum gave another *lurch*, the door gave another *heave*, and Larisa found herself bodily sliding down that tunnel. It was a pinkish-red, and to her hands it felt warm, wet, and slippery . . . and resembled nothing so much as a huge throat. There was another shuddering lurch and her headfirst slide picked up speed. Her breath finally came out in its intended scream, but it was far too late.

The dryer door closed behind her.

From the top of the stairs, her husband's voice floated down.

"Hey, honey? Have you seen my other blue sock? I can only find one here. Honey?"

MUTES

Tape begins:
Test, test, is this thing on? Okay. Right. Okay . . . where to start? I found this old tape deck, and I have one tape. I need to get this told, just in case, but I have to hurry. I don't know how much time I have. Granny McCalloum was right. She always said—wait, I'm getting ahead of myself.

My name is Scott St. Armond. I'm making this recording in my apartment, and I swear I'm of sound mind. I swear to God.

I'm from Slaughter, Louisiana, population about 1,000. My Granny McCalloum is the local hoodoo woman there. She used to claim I have the sight, too. But I wasn't like her. Not then.

Anyway, I came to the big city when I turned eighteen, trained up and got work as an EMT. That's when shit got weird. I'm not sure exactly when it started, but the first time I noticed anything was at this car wreck my partner and I responded to out on Route 18.

Oh, hang on—

I just checked the window, and there's too many to count. Jesus, this is bad.

Okay, Route 18. Some kid out speeding around lost control of his car and went off the road, into a tree. The driver was banged up, but walked away. His girlfriend, though, wasn't

147

wearing a seat belt and was thrown from the vehicle into another tree. We found her at the base of an old pine, in rough shape. She'd been impaled by more than a dozen branches, some of them as thick as my two thumbs together. She'd rolled to the ground with snapped-off pine stakes sticking out of her torso, legs, and one eye.

She was still conscious. We found her by following the screams.

Another crew showed up for the driver while we went for the girl. We strapped her to the stretcher, branches sticking out of her this way and that, and started carrying her up to the road. I'm a pretty big guy, lots bigger than Jerry, and I had a hard time carrying her over the uneven ground in the dark. I don't know how he managed.

We jostled her a little, and that got her screaming again. Now I was still green, and this was easily the worst thing I'd ever seen. You can watch videos and movies, even real stuff like the surgery network, but it's nothing compared to up close and personal. Especially the screaming. I was freaked out.

So when I looked up from watching for rocks and holes and saw five dark silhouettes backlit by our ambulance strobes standing not ten feet away, I reacted badly. I caught a whiff of a sweet licorice smell. I thought *Sambuca* and figured they were drunk.

I yelled, "What the hell are you doing? This isn't your fucking entertainment! Back away; get back to your cars! Go on now!" But they just stood there.

Behind me, Jerry yelled, "Scott! What the hell are you doing, man?"

I glanced back at Jerry and shouted over the girl's crying.

"What the hell's it look like?" I said, "I'm telling these looky-loos to—"

I stopped dead and the stretcher gouged my lower back. The night was clear with a good moon, but when I turned back to them, they were gone. The field between us and the road was empty, not a soul in sight.

Jerry struggled not to drop the stretcher, and yelled at me to move my ass.

We got the girl into our bus and Jerry started us rolling while I tried to stabilize her. Jerry waited until we'd left the ER to ask what the hell I was doing out there.

"Didn't you see the people?" I said. "The people in the field?"

He just squinted at me and said, "I didn't see anybody but you. Yelling at a field."

Jerry had worked there a couple of years already, so it was practically part of his job to rib me as the newbie. He walked around for a while saying I'd already cracked from the strain, but that wasn't it.

That was the first time I saw the Mutes.

The next time was the night of my accident.

I guess it was about a month after we pulled Tree Girl out of that field when we got called to the warehouse. One of the eighteen-wheelers had been pulling into the warehouse when the big rolling security door let go. That heavy steel door came down in its track like an axe, chopping right into the windshield. The driver was unconscious, steering wheel bent right down into his chest. The truck was still rumbling out diesel fumes as it idled with that massive door propped on the hood.

I ran into the warehouse, and some of the guys helped me stack a couple of spare eighteen-wheeler tires next to the truck, like a platform to work on. Jerry was more experienced, and would fit in the cab better than me. I stayed on the ground, ready to hand up anything Jerry might need. I didn't actually see what happened. Jerry told me about it later.

Jerry jacked up the steering wheel, but the driver was also bound up in his seat belt's shoulder harness. Jerry cut the belt and the driver collapsed sideways onto the gearshift. Suddenly the idling truck was dropped into reverse without the benefit of a clutch. I know the truck jumped backward with the sound of tearing metal. It knocked me and the stacked tires to the ground, and then that huge steel door came crashing down. I'd landed on my back when the tires cut my legs out, and I saw that door coming down at me like the Hammer of God. I didn't even have time to scream.

I'm told that it came down on me and, luckily, the big tire that had knocked me down. The tire compressed, then bounced the door back up to a height of about eighteen inches. Before the door bounced, though, it came low enough to hit me right across the chest, cracking my sternum and stopping my heart.

Now, here's the thing with *commotio cordis*, or cardiac arrest due to impact trauma: it's quick. There's no buildup, no arrhythmia, no moving pain or shortness of breath; there's no time. Your heart is beating, and then it stops.

Period.

And it hurts. A lot.

My chest hurt more than I'd ever imagined anything could hurt. I'd both heard and felt the crack, and I knew it was bad. I'm told it was only about ten seconds before I passed out, but time sort of . . . stretched out for me.

Jerry was screaming, but I wasn't sure what he was saying. Everything sounded all drawn out, like slow motion in the movies. I couldn't move, all I could do was stare up at the distant warehouse ceiling—and then they were there.

Angels.

That's what I thought at first. A half-dozen faces leaned into view, moving just as slow as everything else, and they were smiling. I mean smiling *big*. Like it was the happiest day of their lives. Their skin and hair were paper white, their lips and teeth making big white grins. They wore jeans and jackets in regular colors, not white robes, and as they leaned closer I saw their eyes had color, too. They were red. Not bloodshot. Solid liquid red, like their sockets were full of fresh blood, but it was their eyes.

That's when I started thinking maybe they weren't angels.

I finally managed to draw a shallow breath, but as it came in all I smelled was licorice, so sweet and strong I would have choked on it if I wasn't already busy dying. The little breath caused the pain in my chest, already immense, to grow. As it did, the grins on the faces widened, and those eyes of blood closed, as faces screwed up in what looked like ecstasy.

Suddenly there were warehouse workers mixed into the crowd above me. These guys looked scared, all talking, yelling, but it was all stretched out like everything else and I couldn't understand it. The shard of pain in my chest suddenly shattered, exploded, and everything went white.

Then black.

I woke to the harsh lights and stinging smells of a hospital room. Jerry was there, thank God. At least there was something familiar to hold onto, because I was disoriented as hell. I had strange memories: white light and kind-eyed, faceless beings looking down at me from above, and the feeling of a vast void. I'd always laughed at people who told stories of dying and seeing Heaven, only to find out later they were just hazy memories of the emergency room. But the feeling that I'd been dead was so strong it was almost funny. It was kind of spooky when Jerry said, "Welcome back to the land of the living, partner," and asked if I was planning to hang around for a while.

When I tried to answer, my mouth and throat were too dry, and the pain in my chest flared when I pushed at the words. Jerry saw I was having trouble, and stopped asking questions. Instead, he gave me some ice chips for my thirst, and brought me up to date. That last flash of pain back at the warehouse had been Jerry pulling me out from under that door.

"I'm sorry. I had to," he said.

One of the guys inside had yelled that I was alive, but he couldn't find a pulse, and had no way to lift that door. That's when Jerry told me about that tire that kept the door from cutting me in half. He told me, "Even with the tire, the damn thing killed you."

A second ambulance had arrived, but I died as they were loading me in. No pulse, no respiration, pupils fixed and dilated. My heart had stopped when the door hit me, but apparently it took a minute for the rest of me to catch on to the idea.

"So," I asked, "I was . . . dead?"

Jerry said "as a doornail," which almost made me laugh. He told me about resuscitating me on the ride, but then described how I woke up just as we were getting into the ER.

"You started talking in spite of your chest, spouting off about angels with eyes of blood. Spooky shit! You scared the hell out of that new ER nurse. Man, you sounded awful!"

—I just checked the window again. There's more of them, and they look like they're organizing. They were just milling about before, but now they're in little groups. Christ, I hope I have time to finish this. Where was I?

Oh, right. Angels with eyes of blood. That's when I remembered the weird stuff from before I died in the ambulance.

Spooky shit is right, I thought, *those "angels" seemed more like demons to me.* My thoughts must have shown on my face, because Jerry asked if I was okay and went to get a nurse. Which I guess he was supposed to do as soon as I woke up.

As the door swung shut behind him, a woman in street clothes walked by, peeking in as she passed. I only saw her for a second, but what I saw chilled me despite my no doubt heavy medication. She had hair and skin the color of typing paper and her eyes were one solid color: no whites, no pupils, just the bright red of a Crayola crayon, fresh from the box.

An angel with eyes of blood.

Once the nurse was gone again I asked Jerry if he'd seen anything strange back at the warehouse.

He said, "I saw you lying there with a one-ton door on your chest."

I remembered the ribbing he'd given me after Tree Girl, calling me crazy; what would he say now? That I was seeing things? I decided to keep my mouth shut.

A couple of days later, when I was up to taking a few steps, I shuffled slowly to my room door, held onto the frame, and peeked out. I saw what I thought was a husband and wife having a conversation, with one of these albinos, a woman, leaning right down in between them. They just kept talking like the pale figure wasn't there, within kissing distance of the bandage covering the wife's eye. A man with an external fixator was wheeled by. It looked like he had a birdcage bolted around his leg. The orderly pushing his chair paid no attention to the two white shapes pacing them, who were smiling and bending over to . . . well, it looked like they were smelling the guy. One of the nurses saw me hanging onto the door, and I guess she misread the look in my face, like Jerry had, and came to help me back to bed. I just had to ask about the girl with the couple.

She looked where I was pointing, and said "What girl?" She saw the couple, even told me their names, then started looking around for the girl I was talking about. I told her to never mind, trying to sound natural, though I had ice water trickling down my spine. The albino was still there, grinning, almost nose-to-nose with the woman, but the woman and my nurse—they couldn't see.

Granny McCalloum always claimed I had the sight, and I had ignored her, but I guess dying changes a person. Now it was different. I kept seeing these . . . things. *Everywhere.*

I took to wandering about the corridors and public areas of the ward. I saw doctors and nurses working with people, talking to people, these red-eyed freaks right there, but no one ever acknowledged them.

I didn't either, but sometimes it was so hard.

The nurses acted all impressed that I was exercising, "trying so hard to get well," they said, but all I really wanted to do was keep an eye on the ward. I was also terrified one of those things might come into my room and I'd be trapped, with nowhere to run.

So I watched them in secret. They were so silent, never speaking, that I thought for a while I might be seeing ghosts, but what I saw made me eventually decide differently.

As far as I could tell these albino mutes were stealthy, but couldn't pass through walls. Someone would enter a room and one or two pale figures would slip through before the door closed. I don't know if they couldn't open doors or if they just didn't want it showing up on the security tapes. They could touch the doors: a couple of times I saw them knock on a door lightly, attracting enough attention that a passerby would check it out, and the Mutes used the opportunity to slip through.

Then there was the smell I'd noticed at the warehouse: these things reeked of licorice. That made me realize what I'd seen back at Tree Girl's accident. Those silent watchers had been Mutes. I hadn't been able to see their skin and eyes in the dark, backlit by the ambulance, but I had smelled their sickly sweet scent.

I used to like Good-N-Plenty candy. Now I can't open a box without the smell reminding me of those things.

I don't eat Good-N-Plenty anymore.

Another thing. Once my meds stopped dulling my mind, the pain came back, and this scared me most of all. The Mutes seemed to gather whenever someone was in a lot of pain. They always hung around fresh post-ops, or during physical therapy. Remember that guy with the external fixator on his leg? Every day when the nurses cleansed the pins holding the fixator to the bones, the Mutes formed a crowd. I sometimes heard him crying out during the procedure. The Mutes were enjoying people's pain. Maybe . . . feeding on it, somehow. That thought really scared me, and I knew I had been right not to attract their attention.

I spent three weeks in that hell, ignoring those silent parasites. I wasn't sure how many of them I saw. With their white skin and red eyes, they all tended to look alike from a distance, only the hair showing that one might be a woman.

After three weeks I left the recovery ward, and I spent five weeks here in my apartment before I was ready to go back to work. Emergency medical services work is pretty physical, and until I could move and lift a stretcher without pain again, I was no use to anyone out there. For five weeks, when I wasn't exercising, I was sitting in the chair by my front window that overlooks the street, keeping an eye out for Mutes. In five weeks I didn't see a one.

Then I went back to work.

Jerry had picked up a temporary partner in my absence, a new guy named Mark. No big deal, we'd just run a three-man team for a while. Happens all the time. We piled in the truck and were off.

Our first call of the night was some guy who had passed out at a company party. Jerry was behind the wheel and I was riding shotgun, nervous as hell, as we rolled on in to pick the guy up.

When we got to the restaurant, Jerry wanted me to check the guy out.

"Naw," I said. "I wanna see what the rookie can do."

That wasn't it. I really wanted to stand back and look for Mutes. I was sure they were going to be gathered around the injured, smiling obscenely at his wounds, lapping up his pain, or whatever they do, and filling the air with their nasty sweet smell.

There weren't any. Not around the guy lying on the floor; not in the crowd of concerned co-workers; not even mingled in amongst the other diners. I scanned the place twice, but there were no white faces, no blood red eyes, and not the faintest hint of licorice. I started to relax until I noticed Jerry staring at me. Down on one knee, helping Mark get the patient ready for transport, he kept giving me long looks while Mark was talking.

Tape ends, Side A.

Tape begins, Side B:

I just checked the window again, and there don't seem to be any more of them than before. They might come soon. I don't know. They seem to be gathering around one particular Mute. If they have a leader, I guess that's him.

Anyway, Jerry waited until we had the guy in the ambulance and we were en route to the ER before asking me what the hell I'd been doing back there in the restaurant. I told him it was nothing, I was just checking out the new guy, but he didn't believe me.

He kept his voice low, so Mark wouldn't hear, but he said "You didn't look at the new guy once. You were looking all over, but you barely looked at us, or even the pickup. What the hell were you looking for?"

I tried to think of something smooth, but I've never been good at that shit. I just looked away and said I was watching, but it sounded lame, even to me.

"Look," he said, "I don't mean to be a hardass here. I know the door thing was bad—I was there, and it was bad for me, too. But if you're not up to the job yet then you have to take more time. You can't freeze like that. Not on this job, man. People will die. You understand me?"

He was right, and I nodded, but his eyes were on the traffic. He glanced at me, a risky move at that speed, and asked me again.

I said, "Yeah, I understand."

We pulled into County General, where up on the fifth floor recovery ward I knew the Mutes would be wandering about and grinning. I forced that thought from my mind as we climbed out of the truck.

Jerry opened the rear doors to the vehicle and told me to help transport the guy.

I nodded and took the foot of the stretcher. We dropped the wheels and started rolling. We burst into the ER and one of the docs came and paced us, directing us to take our patient to ER-2 while Mark gave her the rundown. I just pushed the stretcher, concentrating on putting one foot in front of the other, trying not to stare. Or scream.

The Mutes were there.

It wasn't like up on five, where there were just a couple at a time—three or four at most. In the hubbub of the ER, they seemed to be everywhere.

Next to us in ER-1 was a woman who looked like she'd gone through the windshield of a car. The side of her face looked like hamburger from sliding along on the macadam—what motorcyclists call road rash. She had little cubes of safety glass in her hair and ground into what used to be her skin. The blood running down her cheek on the abraded side of her face hinted that some of those little cubes were even lodged in her eye. Every movement and twitch of her optic muscles were grinding that eye to jelly. The doctor and two nurses slid, unknowing, in and out of a ring of almost a dozen red-eyed demons. The Mutes showed white teeth and red tongues as they silently laughed whenever the girl made a sound of pain. The whole thing had a strange grace, like some macabre dance.

Mutes crowded around the patient in ER-3 so tightly I couldn't even see what was wrong.

Everywhere I looked, there they were—except in ER-2. We wheeled the patient in and helped transition him from our stretcher to the hospital gurney, and as far as I could tell, not one of them even looked our way. I looked at the guy we'd brought in, trying to avoid staring at the Mutes and going stark raving mad right there. I was trying to figure out why they weren't swarming in here for the fresh meat when it hit me.

Our guy was unconscious, and he wasn't in any pain. He hadn't even hit his head when he fainted. There was nothing here for them, so they were ignoring him.

We trooped back out to our ride, and I brought up the rear, avoiding any conversation until we were outside. I tried to focus on Mark and Jerry, ignoring what only I could see around us, but we passed some folks waiting to be seen, and there were Mutes waiting with them. One guy's hand looked like he'd caught it in a machine, fingers sticking out at every angle but the right ones, blood leaking from several places where the bone had poked through the skin. He was holding it elevated, sobbing in pain; there were two Mutes bending down to inhale dreamily over the ruined hand like they were sniffing a bouquet of flowers.

I struggled not to cry.

We took up our positions again, Jerry driving with me riding shotgun. Mark and Jerry kept up a constant stream of conversation, but I was mostly silent as we cruised for about a half hour without a call. I started to hope it would be quiet night, which would have been fine with me; I needed some down time to try to assimilate what I'd seen in the ER and figure out what the hell I was going to do. But then the call came in, and like that one that sent us to the warehouse, this one wound up being a life-changer.

There was a fire. A big one. Just thinking of it now still makes me want to scream.

Burn victims go through more pain than any other trauma victim. It's supposedly the most painful way to die. This wasn't going to be some businessman fainting quietly at a company party. I had never been to a big fire before, but I figured I knew what to expect. Even with the Mutes.

I had no idea.

Jesus. I checked on them again and they were all looking at my window. They weren't moving around or anything. The leader guy was in the front. I—I don't think I have much more time.

Anyway, the tenement was what firemen refer to as "fully involved." Flame roiled out of windows on all four floors, reaching for the sky—the building was a lost cause. Hoses were aimed at the surrounding buildings to keep the fire from spreading, and toward the front door of the inferno in case any more tenants were able to escape. There were people still in there. The fire roared like a wounded giant but there were still occasional shrieks, the mindless sounds of someone driven mad by pain or fear, barely heard over the din.

Jerry told us to stop gawking and start working, and gave us the plan. We would split up and triage whomever we could on the scene. Anyone who needed an immediate ride to County would go with two of us while the third stayed to keep working triage.

Mark tore his eyes away from the fire and said "got it, boss," in a voice that didn't sound at all convinced it was going to be that easy. I just nodded at Jerry, not trusting myself to speak. I hadn't been staring at the fire.

I was staring at the Mutes.

Dozens of them. Maybe a hundred of them—it was hard to tell in the flickering firelight and all the rescue personnel running about. The Mutes seemed to ring the entire structure, probably in as close as they could get and still bear the heat. Each time there was a shriek from the flames the whole ring of them swayed, leaning in and out, the faces I could see twisting with obscene pleasure. Their grinning, bone-white faces were bathed in the rippling red firelight as they seemed almost to dance.

In my nightmares, it's what Hell looks like.

I picked my way through the milling people, looking for wounded to take care of. I heard "Hey, big guy! Little help here!" and saw one of the firemen trying to flag me down.

He was carrying a blanket-wrapped bundle in both arms, and it was moving. There were three Mutes trailing him, two male and one female, all grinning and nodding. I ignored them as best I could and pulled my kit around so I could get at it. He flipped the edge of the blanket back, and I saw her.

She was maybe six or seven. Hard to tell in the blankets, and she might have looked younger with her hair burned off like that.

This was bad.

All I could see was her head and face, but I barely kept from screaming. The left side of her face was untouched, and perfect. Tears of pain streamed from her left eye, round and staring, open wide enough that I could see the white all the way around, like a maddened horse. That side of her nose was straight and strong, leading the way down to her mouth, which was open as she panted, wheezing sounds coming from a throat made raw by smoke and heat.

The right side of her face was a ruin.

What skin remained had the blackened look of burnt meat. There was an amoeboid splash of lighter color where the fluid from her eye had landed when it burst, boiling in its socket. Teeth were clearly visible where her upper lip had burned away, shockingly white in this darkened field of burnt flesh. Even the bone poking through her cooked cheek had a scorched, blasted look to it.

The fireman was crying. So was I. I gently pulled back more of the blanket, trying to see the extent of the damage. A high, breathy keening came from her ruined throat, and I saw something stuck to the pulling fabric. Something black and shriveled, but also glistening with fresh blood.

Along with the blanket, I had peeled away her ruined ear.

My stomach leapt into my throat as I choked on a sob and turned my face away—nothing in the world could have prepared me for this—and came face-to-face with the Mutes again.

One of the males and the one female were all over each other like hormonal teenagers. They were kissing passionately, hands all over each other, groping, squeezing and unbuttoning. The whole time their eyes were wide open, focused on the shape huddled in the fireman's blanket. The other male was closer to the girl than the other two, staring at her. Red eyes reflecting the firelight, his mouth was slack and open, tongue protruding slightly. He had one hand shoved down the front of his undone pants, unashamedly working himself as he took in the girl's pain.

They were all turned on by her agony.

It was more than I could bear. My rage overcame my fear of the things, of letting them know I could see them. I started yelling. "Get the fuck out of here, you goddamned ghouls!"

I stepped forward and put myself between them and the small, tortured girl. Their licorice stink overpowered even the soot and smoke of the fire, and I fought not to gag.

They didn't stop what they were doing, though they suddenly . . . well, they flickered just for an instant, like they were part of an old movie. When the flickering stopped, they were dimmed. That's the only way I can describe it. Like a filter had been clicked into place that affected only them. Their colors were suddenly muted, shadowy; and they were harder to see.

Other than that, they had no reaction. The one with his

hand in his pants leaned slightly to the side to look around me and his hand kept working, right up until I grabbed him.

I may have mentioned that I'm a pretty big guy, and I work out. I bunched my fists in the material of his light jacket and lifted him right off the ground.

I shouted "Get the fuck out of here!" again, and his eyes opened wide in surprise, probably shocked that I could see him, never mind touch him. From the corner of my eye I saw the couple spring away from each other as I prepared to throw the one I was holding to the ground. Before I could send the pale sadist flying through the air, he ripped his hand free of his pants and thrust it at me, his flattened palm stopping inches from my shirt.

My chest exploded in solid, unbelievable pain. Pain I knew and still haunted my dreams—the pain of a suddenly stopped heart. I fell to my knees and let go of the Mute. He dropped to his feet and looked over his shoulder at the couple, who were looking at me, wide-eyed. Those weird, blood-red eyes were hard to read, but their silent expressions were afraid. I could hear my pulse pounding in my ears, the thud-thud drowning out everything else, so my heart hadn't stopped, but the pain . . .

The other two nodded, and stepped toward me, each bringing up a palm. The male thrust his hand forward and suddenly my pain grew, multiplied, as a line of fire traced itself down the center of my chest.

My sternum.

The female reached toward me, and my left forearm exploded in pain, exactly like the time I broke it playing football in high school.

It was pain upon pain, all distinct and yet complementing each other; each individual, yet multiplying.

A high-pitched keening penetrated the thudding of my heart, much like the sound the girl had made as her ear peeled away. It was *me*, though, and I had been making that sound since the first Mute had extended his hand toward me. It had only been seconds, though it felt like forever, and I was running out of breath. The sound petered out, my lungs emptied entirely, and though I strained to draw a breath, nothing happened.

That's when I blacked out.

I came to in the recovery ward again. They'd given me the full workup, but they hadn't found any damage, and no one could say what had happened to me. Hours later Jerry shambled in, plopped into the visitor's chair, dirty, exhausted, smelling of smoke and blood, and asked what the hell happened.

I had been pondering this very question since I woke up, and it was while I was sitting there thinking that I noticed something different about the ward.

There were Mutes wandering about, just like before, but before they had ignored me. Now, despite the fact that I was in no pain, every Mute on the floor was watching me. Looking at me as they passed my door, staring at me as I walked down the hall.

They knew I was aware of them, and they were very, very aware of me.

I was terrified. Still am.

I had no answer for Jerry. I couldn't tell him about the Mutes. Not while they were watching. Would he even have believed me?

He said, "That's terrific. What I heard is you pulled back the blanket, got one good look at that girl, and you lost your shit. Started yelling about having to get away from her, then just screamed and passed out. That sound familiar at all?"

I had to admit that it did.

He said, "I told you that if you weren't up to the job to take more time," and ordered me to go home and call him in a week.

I agreed, and when I was discharged a couple of days ago, I did as he said. I came home.

The problem is, they followed me.

I went to the store this morning, and when I got back everything in my apartment looked untouched, but the rooms reeked of licorice. Opening some windows to air the place out, I spotted one of them, hanging out across the street from my building. I thought it a little funny that he was sitting on the curb, dressed as a homeless guy.

Weird, I thought. *Why does he need a disguise when no one can see him?*

Then my stomach clenched. *No one but me.*

He was there keeping an eye on me.

So I kept an eye on him, peeking through the curtains every now and then.

And then there were three of them.

Then seven.

They've been trickling in all day, gathering in the street below. By afternoon there were almost fifty. By evening there were too many for me to count milling about down there. Passersby don't notice them. Motorists don't see them.

But I do. And they know it.

I've been thinking about what happened at the fire. They feed on pain, drink it in, eat it like candy. But I guess they can spit it back out, too. Give back your pain. Force-feed it to you. Three of them dropped me the other day. There are close to a hundred of them outside right now.

So I've been thinking. How much pain can a person stand before they just . . . die?

That guy in the ER, his hand was a mess, but he was just sitting there. Tree Girl was impaled in a dozen places, but she was still screaming. That little girl . . . half her face burned away, her ear peeling off . . . and she was still alive. Still kicking.

There's no damage with what they do. So how much pain do you think they can give me before my body just . . . gives out?

How much?

Shit, I just checked the window, and they're gone. I don't hear anything—hang on . . . shit! I can't hear anything but their fucking smell is coming from outside the front door, the front hall, so strong it chokes me. God, I think they're—

Tape ends.

ON CATS AND CRAZY LADIES

"Tell me again why we're doing this?"

Billy crouched in the bushes, staring through the greenery toward the huge house: three stories of white walls, old-fashioned gingerbread trim, and wide windows, all capped by a vast, peaked roof and surrounded by a fair expanse of lawn. He didn't like the look of the place. Big houses like that, way out here on the edge of town, usually sported high-tech alarm systems. Alarm systems meant cops. Cops meant jail.

Billy really didn't want to go to fucking jail.

He turned to see Dagner staring at him around a shrub, eyes huge behind his thick, horn-rimmed glasses.

"What?" Dag whispered. "Now?"

"Humor me," said Billy. "What, you got something better to do until the old bitch leaves? Tell it to me again."

The little man sighed. "Fine." He indicated the house and its detached garage. "Great big mansion, way out from town. No neighbors. Cop response time, not so great—for them, anyway. For us, it's pretty good. Rich old lady living all alone, goes out every day to buy food and shit. She goes out, we go in and find the cash she has stashed in the house. We can't find it, we wait until she gets home, then make her *give* it to us. We find a bunch of sweet lookin' stuff we could hawk for cash, we wait 'til we get her wrapped up, then pull that"—he threw a thumb over his shoulder toward the van parked amidst the tallest of the bushes—"up to the door and load in everything we can. Then we drive off, leaving the old lady tied to a chair for the mailman to find or something."

He brushed his gloved hands together, as if dusting off after a job well done. "Easy-fucking-peasy."

Billy looked at the big old house again, eyeballing the wrought iron fence surrounding the property, sunlight actually glinting off the spikes along its top. "What about alarms? Mansions like that usually have electric eye beams and shit."

"Can't be." Dag grinned. "She's one of them crazy cat ladies. Got like fifteen, twenty cats walking around in there— I'm not sure, exactly. I peeked through the windows with some binocs, but they keep moving around and fucking up the count. But that many cats, shit, you can't have electric eyes, motion sensors, nothin' like that. Especially this broad. Looks like she gives 'em the run of the place. And if you look around—"

A single finger stabbed toward the house, at targets *there*, *there*, and *there*, but at this distance Billy couldn't tell *what* the fuck he was pointing at.

"—you can see she don't have no security cameras or nothin'."

"How do we know she even *has* money?" said Billy, trying to poke holes in the plan *before* they were in handcuffs. "I've seen a couple of them crazy cat ladies back home. Bag ladies in flowered hats, talking to cats like they were people. Acting like the cats talked back."

"The cats again. She goes out every day to buy food for two dozen cats, and she ain't buying the cheap shit. I'm telling you, Billy, those cats in there eat better than me."

Billy eyeballed the smaller man's spindly frame and didn't doubt it.

"How do we know she even has—"

"I watched her in the market three days running, and she always paid with cash," Dagner said, anticipating the question.

"Never a bank card or nothin'. She got gas in that big car of hers with cash, too. I asked around, from some people who would know, and they say Agatha Harper *has* a bank account, but she don't never use it. Maybe like once a year, if that. So whatever she's using to feed her and all those cats, it's in there, right now, just waiting for us."

"Yeah," said Billy, fidgeting nervously. "If we can even get in there."

"I told you, the cats have a—oh, shit! There she goes!"

Billy whipped toward the house again, and a scarecrow stood on the front porch. Tall and skinny, with flyaway gray hair and a shapeless brown bag of a dress, she slowly pulled the door closed, speaking in the sing-song tones some people used when talking to babies, though she was too far away for Billy to make out the words. Three small, dark shapes squirted out through the closing door and began twining about her bent-stick legs, like clinging smoke. Billy hated the way cats did that, but Agatha Harper didn't seem to mind, just stepped carefully out of the tiny tangle of legs and tails and made her way, with a slightly skipping gait, to the detached garage, entering through a side door Billy couldn't see. In a minute, the big bay door levered itself open. There was a cough, then a low, powerful rumble, and a shiny black car rolled out . . . and out . . . and out.

"Holy *Christ*," whispered Billy. "What the hell *is* that thing? It's longer than our fucking van!"

"1975 Rolls Royce Phantom," said Dagner, and Billy could hear the smile in his voice despite the snooty accent he'd assumed. "At twenty feet long, you are correct, sir; it's two and a half feet longer than our van." He dropped the accent. "I looked it up. And there ain't a spot of rust or rot on her. I checked while the old biddy was shopping."

He gave Billy a gentle chuck to the shoulder.

"Whaddaya think? Still wondering if she got money?"

Billy just watched the shiny black ark of a car pause in the driveway to let electric motors crank the gate back. The Phantom rolled smoothly into motion once more, turning toward town and gaining speed like the shadow of an avalanche, the gate shuddering closed behind it.

"Holy *Christ*," he whispered again, and then Dagner was tugging on his arm.

"Come on, man, we gotta get in there before old Aggie gets back."

They sprinted over the thick grass to the black iron fence, eight feet high, the top foot and a half canted outward to make scaling more difficult. Billy squinted up at the points, seeing them up close for the first time.

"Jesus, you weren't kidding about them being sharp."

Dagner just grunted as he tossed up first one padded moving blanket, then another. It was time to do something physical, and Billy knew this was why Dag had asked him along. Dag thought of himself as the brains of the operation—he thought he was the brains of *every* operation—and that worried him: Billy was one of the people who understood Dagner's nickname.

When Valentine DuBois had decided to run with the rough crowd, he was smart enough to know a little guy named Valentine wasn't going to cut it. Having "Danger" tattooed across his left bicep to help bolster his contention that "Danger is my middle name" might not have been the smartest thing to do, but going to a shitfaced tattoo artist while shitfaced himself was even worse. He hadn't even noticed the tattoo was misspelled until he was already showing it off, and by then it was too late: Valentine "Dagner" DuBois was forever stuck with the moniker, and a permanent reminder that Val DuBois was a fuck-up.

Billy looked at his partner and had to refrain from shaking his head. At five foot two, and a buck twenty if he was wearing a heavy coat and boots, Dagner DuBois almost could have walked right between the bars, but there was no way he was getting over them without help—not even if he had a ladder. But he'd draped the packing blankets over a section of the fence to help Billy avoid being skewered, and was, even now, leaning into the fence, bracing himself the way Billy had taught him.

"You ready?"

Dag nodded, and Billy went up and over him, stepping on a thin thigh and narrow shoulder on his way to the top of the fence, where, using the padding and one of the fence posts, he went up and over the spikes as well. He turned to find Dag wincing, rubbing the stepped-on shoulder.

"You ready?" he said again, then stuck his own knee and shoulder through the bars. He had to stick an arm through, too, and help boost the small man, telling him where to put his hands and feet, but eventually a hard-breathing Dagner DuBois stood inside the fence with him.

"Thank God we're going out through the front gate," Dag said, hands on knees. "I don't think I could get back over that thing, even *with* your help."

"Out's easy," Billy said. "You just have to—"

"No time," said Dagner, tugging the blankets down. "The fence took longer than I thought, and we got to get into the house before she gets home."

They made their way to the rear of the house, where an overgrown and weedy garden took the place of a backyard. When they reached the back door, Dagner pulled a ski mask over his face and threw himself down onto his back. He lay on the doormat for a moment, tried to look up at Billy, then started yanking on his mask, lining up the eyeholes with the glasses beneath. When he could finally see, he looked up at Billy, still breathing hard.

"If there's any kind of alarm panel," he said as Billy slipped his own mask into place, "or the door looks wired or something, I'll holler to you and you hide—out by the front of the house, if you can. I'll nab her when she comes in, *after* she punches in the alarm code. Got it?"

"Yeah, I guess s—" Billy started, but Dag had already pushed the pet flap open, and begun to work his way through. He lead with one hand, and had his head and shoulders inside the house before something occurred to Billy.

"Hey." He crouched beside Dagner's writhing body, stage-whispering through the opening. "This looks awfully big for a cat flap. Are you sure—"

"That's . . . because . . . it's a dog flap," Dag said between grunts of effort, pulling his other arm through and twisting to get his hips lined up on the diagonal.

"She has a *dog?*" Billy was suddenly assailed by visions of skinny legs kicking spasmodically as Dag screamed, caught halfway through the door and unable to even flee as a rottweiler or a German shepherd ate his face. "Why didn't you *tell* me she has a dog?"

It hit him like a slap that, what with a doggy door, there was no guarantee the dog was even *inside* the house. It *could* be—

He leapt to his feet, spinning in midair to land facing the yard, leather gloved hands ready to fend off a powerful, thrusting muzzle, feet *more* than ready to try their luck at racing a guard dog to the fence. Dagner said something, but muffled by the door, Billy couldn't make it out.

"Whuzzat?"

There was no answer. He glanced downward—and found Dag's legs gone, the pet flap swinging out, then in, then out, then still.

Oh, shit. Did the dog get him?

He hunkered next to the flap. "Dag?" he whispered. "Buddy? You all right?"

Nothing. Billy leaned closer. "Dagner?" He stretched forth a finger to poke open the flap, steeling himself to peek in, when, with a sharp click, the door swung suddenly into the house. Billy jerked back so hard he overbalanced from his squat, and his ass thudded onto the mat.

"No alarm panel," said Dagner, looking down at him through the open door. "No wires I can see. It wasn't even locked. Who knew?" With the ski mask covering his head, Billy couldn't see the grin on his friend's face, but he sure could hear it in his voice. "If you're done sitting on your ass, you wanna come give me a hand?"

Billy scrambled to his feet. "What about the dog?"

"I just told you." Dagner stepped back, inviting Billy in. "She don't have no dog, but she's got one great big cat around here somewheres. I seen him sittin' on the windowsill a couple of times, catching some sun. Huge fucker. Now c'mon."

They entered a kitchen like Billy had only seen in the movies: huge and spacious, with a big old stove and lots of counter space. Above a stand-alone central butcher-block workstation hung a huge rack, from which dangled, as far as Billy was concerned, every pot and pan known to man. "Jesus *Christ*," he said pointing. "That fridge is bigger than my whole fucking *apartment* . . . oh my God, what is that *smell?*" The pointing hand clamped across his lower face, pinching his nostrils shut through his mask, and he was glad for the layer of material filtering the air before it got anywhere near his nose. "Is there a body somewhere or something?"

"Cat box," said Dagner. He hadn't reacted to the odor filling the kitchen, but Billy could tell he was mouth breathing. "Or, cat *boxes*, I guess, unless she's got the granddaddy of all litter boxes stowed away somewhere. I told you, she's got like twenty cats in here, and one of 'em's a doozy." He looked sideways at Billy as they made their way across the kitchen, deeper into the house. "S'matter, didn't you never have a cat?"

"No." Billy adopted Dag's mouth-breathing trick. "Don't like 'em. They kind of creep me out, tell you the truth."

"Really?" The grin was back in Dagner's voice. "Then you're gonna *love* this place."

They hadn't even crossed the kitchen before they found the cats—or, more accurately, the cats found them. Four of the little beasts came through the door at a trot, followed by a fifth, smaller cat, all apparently curious about the noise, or maybe expecting the old lady to be back from her food run; Billy didn't know. The straggler hung back a bit, but the four never hesitated, approaching the strangers without fear, rubbing on and about the men's shins. Billy tripped, stumbled, then came to a halt, the back of his neck crawling at the smooth, slithery feel of their little bodies against his legs.

"Aw, Christ, Dag. What do I do?"

The little man had bent at the waist to scratch his own two assailants about the ears for a moment, before scooping each aside without actually picking them up. "Just nudge 'em with your foot and keep walking." Then, to Billy's surprise, Dagner loosed a hearty laugh. "Jesus, Billy! Relax. They're cats: they ain't gonna hurt you."

Dagner strode confidently into the next room, deftly avoiding the smaller cat—maybe it was still a kitten, Billy thought—that batted at his shoelaces as they went by. Billy awkwardly toed the cats aside, four of them now that Dagner was gone, but they simply surged back, writhing against each other as well as his feet. Eventually, recalling the high-stepping technique he'd seen the old woman employ out front, he followed Dagner in an exaggerated, cartoon-style tiptoe.

"Wait up, damn it!"

He caught up with the little housebreaker in the next room, the dining room, according to the central table and surrounding chairs. Dagner DuBois was standing statue-still, arms spread slightly. "And here he is."

"Here *who* is?" Billy said, stepped around Dagner—and then he, too, froze, as his friend's body no longer obscured what lay atop the dark wood table.

"What," he whispered, "the *fuck* is *that?*"

"It's a cat, stupid," said Dagner, still not looking at him. "Maybe one of them Maine coon cats, but I dunno. I told you I seen him on the windowsills, through the binocs, but he's, uh, he's a lot bigger in person."

Big was an understatement, in Billy's opinion: the thing lying in the center of the dining room table was *enormous*. Easily four or five times the size of any cat Billy had ever seen. The fluffy orange beast stared at them with wide, golden eyes, head erect and obviously unafraid at being approached by two strangers. But for the bushy tail lazily lashing back and forth, the great feline was perfectly immobile: Billy couldn't even see it breathing.

One of the tall, tufted ears twitched, and Billy flinched at the quick movement. His attention drawn to those ears, Billy suddenly realized what the cat reminded him of: a show he'd seen on the Animal Channel, or the Nature Network or something, a year or two back, about bobcats. Part of the show had been a video of a bobcat attacking a fox, and the red-furred canine never stood a chance. Billy had thought it almost funny at the time—a cat finally kicking some ass on a dog—but he didn't find it funny now.

No wonder the pet flap's so big, he thought. *Christ, that thing's bigger than most of the dogs in my neighborhood. If he couldn't get out through the flap, he might just knock down the whole d—*

The huge cat yawned suddenly, mouth apparently unhinging like a snake's, and for a moment all Billy could see was a ring of yellow-white teeth, fangs that looked nearly as long as his fingers.

"Holy shit," whispered Dagner, followed by a low-sung, "nice kitty." He edged around the room, trying to pass the table without getting any closer to it. Billy edged after him as the yawn ended and the big cat resumed his stare, though Billy was now aware of the tips of two great fangs poking out to overlap the lower lip slightly, as if they just wouldn't fit into the huge mouth. Focused on those protruding teeth, he was halfway around the room before a slow movement caught his eye, and he glanced toward one of the chairs surrounding the table.

It held a cat. They *all* held cats, he realized, each just as still as the monster lying on the table. White, black, calico; their much smaller heads swiveling to watch the men was the only motion they made, and Billy's skin prickled beneath their bright, unblinking gazes.

In the hall beyond the dining room, Billy realized he'd been holding his breath, and little black dots were beginning to invade the edges of his vision. The air rushed out of him in an explosive "*Fuuuuuuck!*"

"I know, right?" said Dagner, a little breathless himself. "I almost pissed myself when I saw him lying there." He adjusted his glasses beneath the mask, then checked his watch. "We don't got a lot of time. Let's see if we can't find Aggie's bankroll."

They moved through the house, checking rooms as they went, looking for likely spots for an old whackbag like Agatha Harper to store a big wad of cash. They searched a desk in what looked to be a den, pulling out all the drawers and dumping them out on the floor. They did the same with the one in the library—Billy found himself awed by the library, he'd only seen that in movies—and the two hall tables, as well as the breakfront by the front door.

The work might have gone faster if they'd split up, searching two rooms at a time; Billy considered it but never suggested it. He assumed Dagner had rejected the idea for the same reason as Billy: the fucking cats.

There were cats in every room, at least four, often a half dozen, lying on the floor, on the windowsills, on the furniture. White cats, black cats, tabbies and toms, all calmly twitching tails and wide staring eyes. Not one of the felines ran from the intruders, nor seemed the least bit disconcerted at being approached. Unless physically shooed away, the cats remained where they were, one or two watching calmly from barely a foot away as Billy searched the desk or side table they lay upon.

"They got to keep staring like that?" Billy finally said, trying to ignore the lambent green eyes observing him from atop a small writing desk; he could *feel* the gaze on the back of his neck as he bent to paw through the drawer.

"Yeah." Dagner was pulling books off a small bookshelf in the corner, quickly riffling pages before tossing each aside. "They do that. It's kind of a cat thing."

"It's fucking unnerving." Billy slammed the drawer, hoping to elicit some response from the gray-and-white patterned cat sitting tall atop the desk, tail curving around the front of its primly placed feet; the very tip of that tail twitched, but that was all. "It's like they never blink."

Which was true. As far as Billy could tell, once the eyes were upon them, they never closed or turned away. Even the few he and Dagner had come upon that had looked asleep—and how an animal could sleep with its head held upright rather than resting its chin on its paws was something Billy had wondered anew each time—once the animal opened its unsurprised eyes, they hadn't closed again, not even to blink the sleep away. They just opened their eyes and stared, like some kind of furry little watching machines.

"Yeah, they do that too," said Dag, riffling, and dropping another book. "Don't try staring back. It won't do nothing but lose you a staring contest, trust me."

Billy wrenched his gaze from the cat's, glancing guiltily at Dagner's back as the little man picked up yet another book. He looked around at the six—no, make that *seven*, he hadn't seen the one on the windowsill, behind the curtains—cats in this room alone, and another question popped into his head.

"And I thought you said there were like a dozen cats, maybe fifteen."

"I said fifteen, maybe twenty. Why?"

Billy realized he'd stopped searching and just stood there whining at Dagner, but he couldn't help it. The room was done, but for Dag's bookcase, but Billy'd be damned before he'd move on to another room all alone.

"Because I haven't been counting or anything, but I'm pretty sure we've seen like thirty of the little bastards. Maybe more."

Dagner tossed the last book aside and stood straight. "I told you, they're hard to count: they move around."

"I haven't seen any of 'em moving *anywhere* since that little greeting party in the kitchen." Billy followed Dag back out into the hall. "They're there when we get there, and they don't move unless—"

He stopped as Dagner strode into the doorway across the hall and stiffened suddenly. "Son of a bitch," the little man whispered, then stepped aside with a sweep of his arm, offering Billy the door. "You were saying?"

Billy looked past his friend, his gaze following the pointing arm, and a single word hissed from between tight lips.

"*Motherfucker.*"

It seemed to be a front parlor, with a pair of breakfronts against the walls to the left and right, each bracketed by sitting chairs, also against the wall. A pair of easy chairs faced each other across a low coffee table in the center of the room, while a long couch sat against the far wall, spanning one of the wide front windows of the house.

The fluffy orange goliath from the dining room lay along the top of the couch, bathing in the sunlight pouring through the window. Billy squinted against the sudden brightness, but the big cat sat with its huge eyes open wide and fixed, unerringly, on Billy. It looked for all the world like it had lain there all morning, but there was just no way Billy was going to believe there were *two* such cats in the big old house. If there were two, there could be three, or even more, and Billy denied *that* thought before it could get a decent toehold. It was that or run from the house right now, clamber up and over the damned spiky fence and let Dagner figure the rest of the thing out for himself.

Sunlight flashed off the cat's chest, and Billy caught sight of a shiny disc nestled in the creature's ruff, like the ID tags that usually hung from dogs' collars. He tore his gaze from the golden oval to look at the beast's calm, expressionless face, opening his mouth to suggest they go search another room—and close the door to this one, leaving the huge feline locked inside to enjoy his sunshine—when movement beyond the big, orange head caught his eye. He looked past the cat, through the window . . . and saw the gate at the end of the driveway sliding open, silent at this distance, the sleek bulk of the Rolls Royce Phantom waiting at the widening gap.

"She's home," he said, with something approaching relief: people, he could deal with. He turned from the parlor, motioning for Dagner to lead the way. "Let's get to the front door."

As Dag turned to go, though, a sudden thought stopped Billy in his tracks. He looked into the room, at the huge cat lying motionless on the couch, then leaned in to grasp the door knob. He gave it a quick jerk, shoving the doorstop out of the way (a ceramic cat, go figure), and swung the door closed, latching it firmly, with a sharp click.

There, let's see you sneak around now, you big fucker, he thought, hurrying after Dagner to welcome the crazy cat lady home.

It wasn't his fault. It was the damn cats.

Agatha Harper had entered the house trilling like a character from a Disney flick, singing out "Hey, babies, Mommy's home!" Then she'd seen the mess left by the search of the table in the front hall, and two masked men coming toward her, but it had already been too late. For everyone.

Her voice had cut off with a little *urk*, eyes going comically wide. She'd turned, groping for the door again, but Billy was already there, gripping her thin shoulders in his big hands and spinning her to face him. She'd come around with one hand raised in a claw, and it had only been the thick weave of his ski mask that kept her nails from gouging deep into his face. As it was, her swipe had come to within an inch of hooking a finger into his left eye, and he'd reeled back in surprise.

That had been a mistake on his part, that backward step. In response to her call, cats were already flowing into the hall in a furry flood. Dagner had been hollering something behind him, a warning about the cats, most likely, but Billy had been too busy with the woman to pay attention. He'd not yet seen the cats crowding in, so was shocked when his back-stepping foot came down on something soft, almost soiled himself at the earsplitting screech that came from the floor, and had stumbled back still further in panic.

That had been Agatha's chance, that second stumble: he was too far away to grab her, his weight moving in the wrong direction for a quick dive after her, had she simply spun and fled through the door. But with a scream to rival that of the stepped-on feline, the cat lady had attacked, extended fingers driving for his eyes again. Billy had managed to ward off her first blows, but had been distracted by what he could see of the floor—or *couldn't* see of it, now that he was looking. Everywhere, little heads and backs moved, upthrust tails following along like fuzzy, crook-topped sharks' fins; there didn't seem to be a square foot of open space to step into.

And the noise! Every cat announced itself, even as they rubbed up against his shins in that creepily familiar fashion, the chorus of meows rising as more of the damned little things packed into the small hall, and Agatha Harper screamed *Don't you hurt my babies!* again and again.

With the cacophony of wailing cats and screeching woman, nowhere to step as little bodies packed in closer, and Agatha's long, scarecrow arms moving in a constant, flailing attack, Billy had felt claustrophobic and panicky, and he didn't know what else to do . . . so he'd popped the old lady one.

Some part of him had registered that, up close and personal, Agatha Harper looked like a bundle of thin sticks held together with string, and at the last instant he'd pulled his punch, turning his frightened blow into more of a jab than a haymaker. It had been enough, though. Her eyes had gone wonky, and Billy'd been obliged to catch her as she sagged toward the floor; they'd wound up standing like a couple in some old movie poster, Billy leaned over her, one arm beneath her, as Agatha swooned backward, fingers nearly touching the carpet.

"Way to go, Mike Tyson." Dagner had beckoned from the doorway, shaking his head. "C'mon, bring her in here."

And that was how they'd wound up standing around in the kitchen, waiting for the old woman to come around so she could answer their questions. Billy stood beside Agatha, holding a steak from the fridge to the woman's eye, as Dagner finished zip-tying her wrists and elbows to the straight-backed wooden chair she sat in.

"Don't make 'em too tight," Billy warned. "We don't want to cut off her circulation. Old folks have trouble with that anyway, right?"

"Says the guy who clocked her in the eye," said Dagner, squinting up from his squat beside the chair. "They have that osteo-whatsis brittle bone thingy, too, and what's she weigh, about ninety pounds? Christ, you coulda killed her, big guy."

A retort sprang to Billy's lips, but he saw that even as he cracked wise, Dag was checking the thin plastic strips around Agatha's left arm, making sure they weren't too tight.

"What are you doing in my house?"

The scratchy, old voice wasn't loud, but still surprised Billy so badly he nearly dropped the steak. He fumbled with it as Agatha Harper tilted her face up toward him, eyes fluttering open, though still a little unfocused, and one already swelling. He reached to put the meat on the counter, but flinched when he saw the countertop was lined with small feline bodies. He glanced about, for the first time not distracted by the woman's eye, and saw that the whole crowd from the front hall had followed them deeper into the house, and now sat all around them, staring with their bright, flat eyes.

"Jesus," he whispered. "Dag, look at all the cats."

But Dagner was busy answering the woman's question.

"Your money, you crazy old woman! We're here for your money!"

He was leaning close, shouting into her face like some B-movie villain. Billy figured he was trying to make up for the fact that, when the woman was standing, Dagner wasn't quite up to her shoulder. He was taking control of the situation, being the bad guy he'd probably always wanted to be: large and in charge. But the situation, in Billy's opinion, was rapidly growing weird; Dagner was just too busy to notice.

"What money?" Agatha shouted, only half-cowed by Dagner's antics. "What are you talking about?"

"Uh, Dag?" said Billy.

"The cash," said Dagner, ignoring Billy. "That green stuff you keep using to buy cat food. I seen you. Always cash. Where is it?"

"That's not *my* money," Agatha said. "That belongs to them."

"*Them?*" Dagner stood straight in his confusion, barely taller than her, though she remained seated. "Who the fuck is *them?*"

"Dag?" Billy said again, not looking at Dagner and the woman, but aware of both in his peripheral vision.

"Them." Agatha Harper twitched a shoulder, reflexively trying to gesture with a bound hand, then jerked a chin toward the kitchen around them, but Dagner didn't take his eyes from hers. "The cats. It's their money—I just use it for them. They can't very well just go to the store themselves, can they?"

"Holy shit," said Dagner. "You really *are* crazy."

"*Dag!*" Billy finally reached out a groping hand and grasped Dagner's arm, *hard*, unable to take his eyes from the rest of the kitchen, his voice a strangled half-shout; he *had* to break Dagner's focus, but he wanted, very badly, not to draw any other attention to himself. Dagner's arm jerked from the grip as the little man turned to face him.

"What? What do you—oh!" Billy heard air hissing in through clenched teeth, then a whispered "Holy *shit*."

There were two things Dagner could have been reacting to, but Billy wasn't sure which of them had made the tiny tough guy sound like he's just been punched in the gut.

The first thing, what Billy had spent the past minute or so trying to get Dagner's attention over, was the cats—no, the *cats*. Billy had thought all the cats had been in the front hall with them when he'd popped the old lady, but that had been a narrow hall, a much smaller space than the vast kitchen. There had been fifteen or twenty packed into that hall with them, but there were easily four times that many, maybe five, sitting and staring at them from the surrounding kitchen. And they were *still* coming, strolling through the door in twos and threes, occasional loners loping along solo. Counters, table, chairs; everywhere he looked, Billy saw furry little bodies, of every color he'd ever seen on a feline. There were short-haired cats, and fluffy cats—even a couple of those hairless things that looked like tiny, wrinkled aliens—all sitting statue-like, lashing tails all stilled.

And they were silent. While the cats greeting the old woman in the hall had filled the air with noise, packing more purring, meowing cat-chatter into that hallway than Billy had thought possible, they were closing on a hundred cats in that kitchen, not one of them making so much as a sound. They paid no attention to each other, but came in the door, chose a spot amongst the crowd, and either sat or lay down, all their unblinking attention fixed on the three-person tableaux before them. Everywhere Billy looked, he found silent, staring eyes.

It was fucking unnerving.

The second thing Dagner may have been reacting to, the thing that had spurred Billy to reach out and grab his partner—would have given him a shake to get his attention, a slap if necessary—was the huge, orange, goliath of a cat stalking toward them from the open door. As they watched, the big beast reached the edge of the expanding circle of sitting, staring cats about them, and the dense carpet of furry bodies parted before it, cats shuffling or rolling aside to make way for the newcomer, then sliding back to fill the space behind it as it moved on. Not one of them challenged the big cat, nor even looked its way, but moved as if responding to instinct, or some inaudible command.

For an instant, Billy thought it must be a different mammoth feline. Hard on the heels of that thought, though, came the same one that had occurred to him when they'd happened upon the orange monster lying across the back of the couch: there was no way there were two of those things in the whole world, never mind within the walls of a single house.

It had to be the same one.

"But," said Dagner, "I thought you locked him in the—"

"I did." The words were a dry-throated rasp.

"Well then how . . ."

"I have no fucking idea."

The great cat reached the far side of the butcher-block centerpiece and leapt up without a sound. A scattering of thuds marked the half dozen or so cats that *had* occupied that perch dropping to the floor, silently taking up new positions as the felines about them made room.

It's like he's their king, Billy thought, watching the cats redistribute themselves as the big boss cat made his stately way to the front of the block and sat, back straight, head high, boxing-glove shaped paws practically dangling off into space. His huge, fluffy tail curved in from the side, wrapping about in front, covering the paws, and then the big cat went just as still as the rest of them.

"Oh, no," came the whisper, and it took Billy a moment to realize it was the woman, not Dagner, who had spoken. He tore his eyes from the cat—made even more impressive by the height of his perch, for sitting up on the block brought his eyes to a level higher than Dagner's—to take in the other two people in the room. Agatha Harper looked haggard, long, withered features drawn into an expression Billy might not have identified, but for her eyes, staring at him and bright with fear. Dagner's expression was also unreadable, thanks to the mask, but his magnified eyes were busy, darting here and there about the room. The voice that finally seeped through the mask was an awed whisper.

"Holy *shit!*"

"I know," Billy whispered, still trying not to attract attention, though they were clearly the focus of the room; all of those bright, expressionless eyes fixed in his direction gave him the feeling his skin was crawling around on him. "Why don't we—"

"Look at them all," said Dagner, as if Billy hadn't spoken. He sounded dazed. "You feed . . . all of these, without . . . without going to the bank? Paying in cash?"

"Just wait, buddy," said Agatha, her voice low, but still the only one above a whisper.

"*All* of them?" Dag's voice rose now as well. "Billy, do you have any idea how much that would *cost?*"

"Huh?" said Billy, not really tracking the conversation as his eyes swung toward the huge orange cat again. Sunlight glinted off the beast's broad chest, and Billy caught sight of that golden disc dangling from some collar or chain buried in the thick orange fur.

"There has to be ten grand in this house," said Dagner, and Billy winced at his sudden volume in the big, silent room. "Maybe more. *Where is it?*"

This last was a ragged scream. Billy whirled to see Dagner, nose-to-nose with Agatha, little fists bunching the front of her brown-sack dress, spitting the words in her face. He'd been trying to intimidate her before, but this . . . this was something different. His partner's words rolled through Billy's head, and delayed comprehension followed.

Ten grand? he thought. *He was only talking about a couple thousand before. Ten would be his biggest score **ever**. No wonder he's losing it.*

"Buddy," said Agatha Harper, her voice straining for calm, "leave it alone. I'll handle it."

"Handle what?" said Dagner. "You'll hand it over, is what you'll handle."

"I told you." She turned from Dagner's wild eyes, looking in Billy's direction. "It's not my money to give. It's the cats'."

"Well, let's talk to one of *them* then!"

Moving with athletic speed and surety he could never have managed if he'd thought about it, Dagner snapped out a gloved hand, snatching one of the cats from the nearby countertop. As Dag spun back to the old woman, Billy caught a ripple of motion from the corner of his eye.

He looked at the small sea of cats surrounding them, expecting that Dag's sudden fast movement had spooked their furry audience. As his gaze swept the kitchen, however, he didn't think any of them had moved an inch, and it took him a moment to recognize what was different: though not one of them had taken a step, all their heads were down now, little triangular chins almost touching the floor, their eyes, unless he was mistaken, fixed on Dagner.

"Dag . . ." he murmured, something about the cats touching a nerve, some instinct buried within him, from way back when man was not at the top of the food chain. Earlier, the mob of little animals had given him the creeps; now they seemed to exude an air of menace, and the primitive urge to back down into the safety of a hole and pull something over it welled up, almost strong enough to drown him. Agatha Harper wailed, tearing Billy's eyes back her way. Dagner faced her, a small black cat in one hand. Despite the claws from three feline feet being buried in his wrist, he'd managed to get a grip on one forelimb, and now held it stretched straight out from the little black body.

"Buddy, please! They don't understand!"

"Oh, I know *they* don't understand." Dagner thrust the little ball of fur and claws toward her face, forcing her to see it. "That's why I'm asking *you*. I'm counting to three, and if you're not already tits-deep in telling me where the cash is, I'm snapping this leg like a fucking matchstick. One."

"Hey, Dag!" Billy said in protest, but he could see it was no use: with the money in his head, Dagner's world had shrunk down to just him and Agatha Harper. He wasn't even hearing Billy any more.

"Don't!" shouted Agatha. "I—I—" Her head whipped to the side, her eyes spearing Billy again. "Buddy!" Billy stiffened at the woman's obvious plea for help, his longing for this to just all be over warring with his almost physical need to flee.

"Two." Dagner set his shoulders, obvious in his intention to follow through with his threat and snap the little cat like a schoolyard bully breaking a pencil. Agatha shifted her head to the side, then further, leaning as much as her bonds would allow . . . and that was when Billy realized she wasn't looking *at* him, but *past* him.

Wait! He spun to look at the huge orange cat behind him, sitting high and watching the proceedings almost regally. *Buddy?* The golden disc flashed again, an errant bit of sunlight dancing across its surface. Billy leaned in closer, fearful of putting his face within reach of the beast's undoubtedly huge claws, but with a burst of insight it was suddenly vastly important that he *know.* The tag, or whatever it was, lay flat across the broad chest, thrust forward by the thick ruff beneath it, and as Billy squinted slightly, the engraved lettering became clear:

BUDDIKSHASA

"Buddikshasa," Billy whispered, and with the word something about the cat changed. That feeling that he should run, should run *right now*, swelled to monstrous proportions. His gaze darted up to the big cat's eyes—

—and was captured, as he realized what had changed. Since entering the kitchen, the big cat's attention had been on the woman in the chair—and maybe the little man threatening her—but not Billy. Just as the woman had looked past Billy to see the cat, so Buddikshasa had looked past him to see the woman. At the mention of his name, though, his *full* name, the great orange animal's attention had shifted, and was now wholly on Billy.

The eyes staring straight into Billy's were wide, and golden, and beautiful, but they were also cold, and alien, and somehow merciless, and Billy felt the world shift as he met them, like the jounce at the end of a fast elevator ride. He nearly lost his balance, but though his body wanted to take a steadying step, *tried* to take a step, his feet refused to move. His bowels tightened, then loosened, as the sensation that the shit was hitting the fan washed over him.

"Three," said Dagner, and Billy wanted desperately to spin and tell the little man to stop, stop what he was doing right fucking *now*, to forget about the money and just run. He *knew* the little man was doing it again, thinking he was *so* smart but was too caught up in what he was doing to see the world around him, to *feel* that it had all gone wrong, gone *so* wrong, and Billy desperately wanted to tell his friend to drop it, cut his losses, and they could just *go.*

But he didn't. *Couldn't.* Couldn't look away from those beautiful, terrible eyes, as the bushy, orange tail lifted toward the ceiling as if drawn by a string. In his peripheral vision, Billy saw shadows shift across furry backs and haunches as feline muscles flexed and bunched, and the tension in the air was suddenly thick, and electric. The room was silent, but for Agatha's quiet sobbing, so Billy clearly heard the voice of the small cat clasped in Dagner's gloved hands: not a sound of pain, but of fear and confusion.

A request for help.

Buddikshasa's mouth cracked open, and as his tail fell to the butcher's block with a thump, he loosed a low, rumbling cry: *Mraaaaw!*

The room about them exploded into motion and sound. A hundred tiny throats spat out a hundred terrible moans, sounds he'd never heard from the cats on television, like the wailing of lost souls falling into Hell. Though he couldn't tear his eyes from those of Buddikshasa, all around the edges of the butcher's block table he detected flickering motion, little kitty bodies flowing forward like water through a burst dam. They brushed his legs again, but rather than twining about his lower limbs like warm and purring climbing ivy, they sinuously slipped past his shins and ankles. He was standing in the flow of small forms darting by without pause, only brushing against him because that took them along the straightest path between where they'd begun and—

Dagner cried out: first in surprise, and then in pain, and finally he screamed in terror.

"Billy! Jesus fuck—stop 'em! Billy! Help!"

Words degenerated into another brittle scream, and then thudding footsteps mingled with the soft, rolling thunder of hundreds of paws and those terrible yowls. The screams and footsteps moved as Dagner made his way across the big kitchen, and the light in the room changed as the back door opened, then slammed.

No! Billy thought. *Dag, please, man, take me with you!* **Please!**

Though he strained to call out to his partner, wanting with all his heart to turn and follow the fleeing man out into the world, away from this crazy lady and all of her cats, Billy stood silent and still, staring into the wide and faintly glowing eyes of Buddikshasa. Screams faded into the distance, and the doggy door flap-flap-flapped as the cats flowed right on through to continue their pursuit. Buddikshasa's eyes grew, widening until Billy saw nothing *but* those eyes, alien, and merciless, and though his body made not a sound, Billy's mind screamed and wept as it tipped and fell into those utterly bottomless eyes.

". . . And you didn't see the man trying to scale the fence?" said Detective Shaun Gantry, breathing shallowly, and through his mouth; the smell in this house was enough to knock a man down. Beneath the table, he nudged a small, feline body away with one foot.

"No, Officer," said the older woman with the shapeless brown dress and flyaway hair. The demotion stung, but he knew it was unintentional, and the woman had been through a lot. He let it go. "I was tied to the chair, like I told you."

"Until Billy"—he checked his notes, the flipping pages attracting the paw-swinging attention of the kitten in the chair beside him—"Spavington, here, released you." Gantry pointed his pen toward the large man sitting next to Agatha Harper, but the man didn't react.

"Like I told you," the woman repeated.

"And he's your live-in helper and handyman, is that right?"

"Like I told you."

Through the window behind them, Gantry could see the medical examiner's team hoisting the body off the spikes along the top of the fence, three cats supervising from the grass. They'd identified the man as Valentine DuBois, and though he hadn't known Valentine, the way he'd died made Gantry suppress a shudder.

"And you have no idea how the man wound up, uh, on your fence?"

"I told you, Officer, I was—"

"Tied to the chair," he finished for her. "Yes. So you said." Gantry eyed the man, who sat staring silently back. There was something . . . *off* about William Spavington. He'd been here when the police arrived, but the woman had done all the talking. She'd explained that Mr. Spavington didn't speak, and when Gantry had asked the man for some ID, Ms. Harper had helped him get it from his wallet. It looked to Gantry like the man had never even *seen* a wallet before.

And there was something else, Gantry realized. They had all sat down while Gantry did his incident interview, and while he had flipped pages in his notebook and jotted things down, and Ms. Harper had fidgeted about, fussily arranging and rearranging her dress, occasionally trying to smooth her wild hair, William Spavington had sat still as a statue, head erect, strange golden eyes open the entire time. And when he thought back on it—and he *was* thinking back on it now, *hard*—Gantry couldn't recall the man even blinking, though it had been more than ten minutes.

A flash of gold at the man's chest caught the detective's attention, some kind of oval pendant peeking out from Billy's open collar. There was an inscription of some kind, a single long word scrawled across the surface, but before Gantry could lean forward to try to make it out, the old woman spoke, drawing his eyes away.

"Is there anything more, Officer? I'm exhausted, and I'd like to go lie down, if you don't mind."

"Of course not, ma'am," the detective said, rising. "If we need anything more, we'll be in touch." He held out a card. "And if you think of anything more, please, don't hesitate to call me. I can see myself out."

Agatha Harper took the card with an "I will, thank you," and turned to make her way across the kitchen. Gantry looked down at Billy Spavington just in time to see the big man rise with sudden, sinuous grace, and without offering a handshake or a nod, turn to follow his mistress.

And though the cats scattered about the floor flocked to the old woman, writhing and twining about her legs as she walked, wherever the man with the golden eyes stalked, little bodies moved out of his way, slipping and rolling aside before him, only to flow closed behind him as he passed, as if responding to instinct, or some inaudible command.

MA LIANG'S CRAYONS

The house was filled with people. Black suits, dark skirts, and solemn voices. People sipping from clear plastic cups, or carefully holding undersized paper plates to their chests, trying not to make a mess with the pasta salad, or let little deli meatballs roll off onto their shirts and ties. She didn't even know half the people currently occupying her living room, and most of those she *did* know, she hadn't seen in years. Especially not the *past* year, when she could most have used some help, or even just a shoulder to—

"When's Daddy coming home?"

Julie looked down, surprised. Pearl stood in the kitchen doorway, looking strangely adult in her formal dress, a string of faux pearls around her tiny neck. *Pearls for the Pearl,* Connor had said, making the little girl laugh when he'd given them to her. He'd always been a hit with Pearl, always been the fun uncle. And that had helped: someone else to distract Pearl when Danny had gotten sick. Someone else to shore her up when Danny had taken a turn for the worse, and Julie had needed to focus on caring for her hus—

"Mommy?" The voice was small, but insistent. "When's Daddy coming home?" Julie heard things in her daughter's voice, things that shouldn't *be* in the voice of a six-year-old.

There was fear in that voice, and sadness, and confusion, and an impending sense of loss, but on top of it all was the tone—the over-careful enunciation—of a young woman trying to ignore all that, and act as if everything was fine, just spiffy, tip-top, business as usual.

As if a little girl burying her father could ever be *usual*.

Julie heard these things in her daughter's voice, and knew that her heart should have broken to hear them—shattered like a wine glass assaulted by a high C. And it would have, had it not already *been* broken. She looked over Pearl's head once again, to the people out in the living room, the strangers, and friends so recently in absentia, who had come to eat her food and celebrate the life of her husband, though not one of them had been willing to help him though its ending, the cancer consuming friendships as readily as it had consumed Danny himself, only faster.

She glanced back down at the little girl standing in the doorway, the woeful child demanding an answer. Pearl deserved an answer, Julie knew, but what was she to say? This was her daughter—*their* daughter—and she'd been through a lot, even more than she understood yet. Julie should be helping Pearl to understand what was happening, what had been happening for the past year—and more—and console the little girl in her grief. She knew she should do this. She *knew*.

But the words wouldn't come from her dishrag heart, wrung out with saying goodbye to Danny after so long, and her head was filled with confusion about Connor, missing for the past ten months, and not even making it to his own brother's funeral. And so her answer, poorly chosen for nothing but its honesty, came out flat, and matter-of-fact.

"Never, Pearl. Your daddy's never coming home again."

The words took a moment to register on the small face, but when they did, the oddly adult expression, the rigid mask Pearl wore to help hide her fear and uncertainty, crumbled like a house of cards tumbling down. Disbelief flashed across her daughter's countenance, almost too fast to see, before her soft little features settled into an expression of sorrow so deep it almost frightened Julie. Sorrow, tinged with something Julie couldn't quite recognize—at least until Pearl spun away, wailing as she pelted across the packed living room.

"I *hate* you!"

Shrill words degenerated into sobs as she ran, colliding blindly with some people, clumsily avoiding others, until she disappeared into the hallway. The slamming bedroom door cut off the sounds of her sorrow, leaving the crowded room filled with awkward looks and silence.

"You all should go now." Julie's voice was quiet, but none of her guests had difficulty hearing her, and her tone brooked no hesitation or rebuttal. A muted murmur rose as plates and cups found perches about the room, and coats were collected, but the voices never rose up into intrusiveness as the people, those she didn't know and those she did, filed out without offering their goodbyes.

The package arrived two days later.

Julie had spent the intervening day trying to make up with her daughter, to patch the rift she had torn between them with her thoughtless words. She'd been a kind of automaton after sending everyone from her house after the funeral, numbly cleaning up in the wake of the reception. Putting away the food—and there was plenty left over—collecting and disposing of plates and cups, wiping everything down, even breaking out the vacuum cleaner; it all gave her something mindless to do that she, nonetheless, put her mind to. Focusing on making the house cleaner than it had ever been—this allowed her to push all of her terrible emotions into the background, and kept her from having to think about what had gone on that day. And the day before that. And the day before that . . .

She had woken the next morning with a kind of emotional hangover, pounded by her own grief and sorrow, but horrified at the way she had handled Pearl's. The girl hadn't spoken when Julie had gone in to put her to bed the night before, merely faced the wall, either asleep or shamming; Julie hadn't cared which.

The next morning, though, Pearl's last words to her had rung through Julie's head as she approached the bedroom door.

I hate you.

Pearl had woken unsmiling and remained that way through breakfast: peanut butter pancakes slathered with Cool Whip, and chocolate milk, her absolute, number one favorite. Julie had kept a light tone and a smile on her face, but it took an effort. They had spent the day on the couch together, watching Pearl's movies (Julie was sick to death of *My Little Pony: The Movie*, and *The Care Bears Adventure in Wonderland*, but watched every scene as if rapt), eating Pearl's favorite foods for lunch and dinner, and watching Pearl's preferred nighttime TV. Julie had remained bright and smiling all day, though her heart shriveled, slowly but surely, as her daughter's expression remained unswervingly grim.

*She **has** been through a lot,* she'd thought, putting Pearl to bed that night—not perfunctorily this time, but with all the back-pats and cheek-kisses she could fit in. *And I wasn't any help. If anything, I made it worse.* She'd paused at the doorway to look at Pearl, curled against the wall and offering her back to her mother once more, rather than making her usual pleas to stay up for just five more minutes. *But if I give her time, she'll come around, right? I mean, I can't **make** her forgive me. But, God, I do miss her smile . . .*

The next morning the postman arrived with an express package for Pearl. Julie signed for it, then carried the cigar-box-sized, brown-paper-wrapped parcel back toward the kitchen, marveling at the sheer number of foreign postage and border stamps, most of them in illegible script and eastern characters, though she recognized the words Hong Kong, Cairo, and Mumbai.

"Hmm," she muttered. "Express, by way of *everywhere*."

She ground to a halt in the kitchen doorway as, seeing past the road grime and official ink, she took note of the handwritten address for the first time. Suddenly all the foreign border markings made sense.

Connor.

Ten months ago, just as Danny was starting what was to be his last downhill slide, his brother, Connor, had come charging into their house, fit to bursting.

"The brush," he'd said. "It's the answer. You get it? The brush—I can't understand why I didn't think of it before!"

Julie had tried to get the story out of him, but the man was nearly unintelligible in his excitement. As always when it was her uncle Connor, Pearl had gotten caught up in his emotion, dancing after him as he bounced about the house like a pinball, words spilling from him in a confusing flood. There was something about a brush, and a trip, and then he'd been holding Pearl by the hands and saying, "When I get back we can use it on your father, Pearl. Won't that be great? The brush'll make him just as good as new," and that was when Julie's heart fell.

Connor was a minor archaeologist who saw himself as Indiana Jones, traveling to the far corners of the world to find items thought lost—though he hadn't actually found one yet. The problem wasn't that he lacked smarts, or drive, in Julie's opinion: he lacked sense. While his Hollywood hero, Indiana Jones, had been portrayed as a skeptic, locating things mentioned in ancient scholarly writings, her brother-in-law was a *believer*, who chased after things found only in legends and folktales.

The blade of the shovel Hercules used to clean the Augean stables—that turned out to be made in Taiwan. The wooden wheel from Thor's goat cart—that actually started life attached to a milk wagon in Scotland. The Sword of Attila—somehow forged from 220 stainless steel, smelted right in good old Detroit. If Miss Cleo had been an historian too, instead of just a fraudulent psychic with a 1-800 number, she could have made a bundle off Connor.

And now here he'd been, running off on some wild goose chase after the Caduceus of Hermes, or Hippocrates' stethoscope, maybe a tongue depressor made from a splinter of Christ's cross, some kind of magical doodad from antiquity that was probably "handmade by monks" in a factory in Boston. They'd just gotten the word that Danny was in the home stretch—but not because he was cured and coming home. Medicine had failed: he was heading to a hospice, not home, and there would be no happily ever after. This was going to be the hardest part, for herself and for Pearl—and for Connor, too, she understood that—when they all should have been leaning on each other, helping each other get through this thing. But Connor had dashed about making promises to Pearl, promises the girl would take as gospel, Julie knew, but that he just wasn't going to keep, and then run out the door.

"I'll see you in a month," he'd called over his shoulder. "Two, tops!"

And then he'd just dropped off the face of the earth. She'd sent a few letters, mainly outlining Danny's decline, because she knew Con was having his mail forwarded, but she hadn't known where it was forwarded to, and there had been no reply. Not for ten months.

Not until now.

Swallowing her anger at the man, knowing the almost worshipful way Pearl felt about her uncle, she held out the package to the small, slumped back sitting at the kitchen table. "Pearl, this is for you. Looks like an early birthday present from Uncle Connor."

The effect was immediate, and all Julie could have hoped for. The little back straightened in surprise, and the face that turned her way bore a bright, broad grin.

"Really? Where? Can I have it?"

"Here," Julie said. "Just be careful, we don't know—"

But it was too late. Pearl was already sitting on the floor, tearing at the brown paper wrapping like it was Christmas morning. Which made sense, when Julie thought about it: after ten months, she wondered whether Pearl remembered her uncle at all, or if she merely thought of him as someone akin to Santa Claus, who showed up occasionally, bringing her cool presents from around the world. She had a shelf of them in her room, and knew where each of them had come from: the doll from Nicaragua, the top from Botswana, and a half-dozen others. Those things would now be joined by . . .

"Cool!"

It was a hinged wooden coffer, about the size of a cigar box. The light wood had a dark pattern inlaid in the lid, some kind of eastern characters Julie couldn't read, and the whole thing was polished to an almost mirror-like sheen.

"Oh, that's *beautiful*," Julie murmured. "Honey, let me try—"

She was again too late: Pearl's clever little fingers had found the simple catch, and she was levering the box open. As the lid rose, it pulled with it an internal layer, cleverly designed to unfold into an upright rack within the box, a rack containing—

"Crayons!" The girl rocked on her little bottom in excitement, though, to tell the truth, Julie was more impressed with the box than its contents.

It doesn't look like there are any metal parts at all, and that moving rack is beautiful. That is some serious craftsmanship—seems a little silly to do all that work just to hold a set of Crayolas.

But as she got a closer look at the crayons Pearl was pulling from their holders, she saw she was mistaken. These weren't Crayolas at all—not unless the company had drastically changed their labeling policies. For one thing, the wrappers for each crayon were blank, without the familiar logo; for another the wrappers themselves were unlike anything Julie had ever seen. She couldn't tell what color they were, as each looked different depending on what angle she saw it at. A wrapper might appear blue, but then, as Pearl twisted and turned her new toys, that same wrapper would shift to green, or even red. A couple of them flashed white. Julie thought there must be some sort of metallic wrap, or maybe one of those holographic films, but when she bent to touch one she found it soft, almost like cotton cloth.

Jesus Christ, she thought, *this paper feels handmade. And the colors! Between this and the box, these must be worth a fortune.*

"Pearl, honey?" Julie looked up to find herself alone on the floor. She'd been so engrossed in the toy in her hand, she'd been blind to Pearl's collecting the rest of her present and bringing it to the table, where she now sat, crayon poised over a piece of paper.

"Oh, honey, wait." Julie scrambled to her feet, cradling the special crayon as if it were made of glass. Pearl's wide smile faltered before she'd made it halfway up, and Julie realized she was making another thoughtless blunder. Smiling wide, she threw as much cheer into her voice as she could muster. "Sweetheart, these are from Uncle Connor, and you know what that means: he always brings you something special. Before you start wearing them down, why don't we put them in your room with the rest of your special things? That way they'll still be new and pretty when your uncle gets here to tell you where they're from, all right? I bet he'd like that."

Just the thought of her special uncle describing the exotic locale where he'd found her new present put a smile back on Pearl's face. Julie puffed a mental sigh of relief, considering this a disaster narrowly averted. The two of them put all the crayons carefully back in their slots and closed the box, then Julie followed Pearl into the little girl's room. Pearl placed the wooden box on the shelf with her other treasures, right in front where she could see it easily, then spun back to her mother with an excited grin.

"I'm going to draw Uncle Connor a doggy," she said, clapping her hands lightly. "A special doggy, with my special crayons!"

"Okay." Julie was just happy to have her smiling girl back again: keeping her from using the expensive crayons was a worry for when Connor came back. *If* he came back. "That's great! What kind of doggy?"

Julie spent the rest of the day hearing about the masterpiece her daughter was planning for Connor. In Pearl's telling, the dog became a princess, then a bird, a horse, her father, a unicorn, her father *riding* a unicorn, and finally a dog again, each with its own embellishments along the way. Julie smiled at each new twist in the plan, not so much listening to the words as enjoying her daughter's happy smile, not caring that it had taken her absentee uncle to put it there. Pearl was happy, and, in the manner of all six-year-olds, her anger toward her mother appeared forgotten. As far as Julie was concerned, that was all that mattered.

The dog in the sketch was yellow, with a black nose and fluffy tail, and he stood in the middle of a green expanse—Pearl's version of their kitchen floor. Scattered about the drawing were several crayons in special paper tubes that seemed to be all colors at once, and the open wooden box lay, half empty, in the center of the kitchen table. Small fingers were just reaching for another crayon as Julie came into the kitchen, slippered feet *whisking* over the floor, still sleep-groggy and in the throes of a serious case of pillow-hair.

"What are you doing?"

The words came out more harshly than Julie had intended, and the little fingers flinched, sending the crayon rolling across the table. The eyes her daughter turned her way were filled with guilt.

"I'm drawing a doggy for Uncle Connor," she said. There was a touch of defiance in her voice, but most of what Julie heard was fear: Pearl had done something wrong, and knew it. But Julie remembered the smile that had broken out on her daughter's face at the gift, as well as the day she had just spent wishing for that smile's return, and made the very conscious decision that wherever this set of crayons had come from, whatever they had cost, it was worth it. She let out a breath that blew away her first reaction to her daughter's willfulness, then took another.

"Well, they're your crayons now, I guess you can use them if you want—especially to draw something so special for Uncle Connor." She pointed to the yellow dog on the page. "That's really good, honey. I'm sure Connor's going to love it." Pearl's smile returned, though it was a tentative thing, as if unsure of its welcome.

Julie touched her daughter's soft hair, then kissed the top of her head. "Can you put them away long enough to have breakfast, though?" She twitched the picture off the table by a pinched corner. "I'll put this on the fridge for now, okay? Keep it safe until Uncle Connor can see it."

"Okay, Mommy."

Pearl began to gather the scattered crayons together as Julie tucked the picture under a pair of refrigerator magnets, Dora the Explorer and her friend Boots the monkey holding the paper securely by the corners.

After her shower, Julie returned to the kitchen for her second surprise of the morning.

"Where did *he* come from?"

Pearl looked up from where she knelt, hands buried in thick, golden fur. The dog, a retriever, Julie thought, merely wagged his tail, thoroughly enjoying the little fingers scratching beneath his jaw. "He was crying at the front door," said Pearl. "Can we keep him? Can we, Mommy? Please?"

Unease began to seep through Julie's surprise. "Oh, honey, I don't know. He must belong to someone."

"He doesn't have a collar." Pearl's voice held a wheedling lilt. "If he doesn't have a collar, he can't belong to anybody, right?"

"Now, that's not necessarily true . . ."

Julie's gaze was drawn to the refrigerator door, and the crayon sketch hanging there. Her eyes flicked from the drawing to the scene in the kitchen, then back. Even with the addition of her daughter clinging to their visitor's neck, the resemblance between the two was obvious, right down to the expanse of green floor.

Christ, she thought, *that's almost creepy.*

"Are you *sure* you don't know where this guy came from?" she said, thinking Pearl may have seen the dog in a neighbor's yard, and incorporated it into the drawing for her uncle.

"The porch."

"No, honey, I mean do you know who he belongs to?"

"He doesn't have a collar, Mommy. He doesn't belong to anybody."

"No, honey, I mean . . . what's this?"

Distracted by the dog, she hadn't seen the crayon set, open and scattered about the table again, another drawing lying haphazardly beneath the mess.

"What did you do, pull that out again as soon as I went to take a shower?"

"Huh?"

Focused on the retriever, Pearl wasn't really listening. Julie looked at the dog closely for the first time. He appeared well nourished, and clean, and was obviously used to children: definitely someone's family pet. It occurred to her that, as well cared-for as he looked, no one had as yet vouched for his house training. She looked out the window to check that the back gate was closed and saw the yard was secure.

"Why don't you take him out into the backyard while we figure out what to do with him."

"Okay."

Julie held the door while Pearl led her new charge out to the grass, then turned to packing away the crayons again. Rather than putting them back in Pearl's room, where they would be a constant temptation, she slipped the wooden box up on the refrigerator, tucked out of sight, toward the back. She scooped the new drawing from the table and stuck it on the fridge door, next to the dog.

She looked closely at the pooch in the sketch.

*Wow, that really **does** look like that dog in the yard,* she thought. *That is the **strangest** coincidence!*

She glanced at the new picture, some kind of big green bird with a red forehead and a big, black, threatening-looking beak, and shook her head with a smile. Pearl was really going to some colorful lengths to impress her uncle. Wherever he was. She turned toward the window over the sink, the one overlooking the yard, intending to check on Pearl and Dog—and froze.

Perched on the windowsill, head twisted sideways to better stare in at her with one round, black eye, was a big, green bird. Almost a foot high, from its great black talons to the scarlet splotch on the crest of its head, the bird stood motionless, nothing but that dark eye twitching as it scanned the kitchen, the hooked, black beak—nearly as long as Julie's finger—actually touching the glass.

Julie whirled to look at the drawing on the fridge: big green bird, red splotch, hooked black beak. She spun back to the window: big green bird, red splotch, hooked black beak.

That's impossible!

Without thinking, Julie lunged toward the window, wanting a closer look at this strange, new visitor. But the bird at the window was not a drawing, and her sudden motion sparked an explosive flurry of feathers, and the window was empty when she arrived. She touched the glass, the pad of her middle finger coming to rest on the spot where the great beak had so recently rested.

"What the hell is goi—"

The door burst open beside her, nearly stopping her heart as a shrieking six-year-old thundered into the house. "My bird! Did you see my bird? Mommy, I saw my bird!"

"Honey," Julie began, a little dazed from seeing the bird herself, but an abrupt commotion from the front hall startled her into silence. Sharp knocking rapidly progressed to frantic pounding, and Julie peered into the front hall to see the solid oak front door actually shuddering in its frame. She reached for the phone, thinking a 9-1-1 call might be in order, when a shout came from the front porch in a voice she recognized.

"Julie? Julie, are you in there? Pearl, honey? For Christ's sake, is anybody home?"

Swinging away from the phone, Julie marched down the hall, flipped open the deadbolt, and flung the door open, revealing a tall man in travel-stained khakis, a worn leather jacket, and a slightly ridiculous wide-brimmed fedora, which she knew—*knew*—he thought made him look like Harrison Ford. She opened her mouth to speak, but from behind her came yet another shriek, adding to the confusion roiling in her head.

"Uncle Connor!"

Julie was nearly bowled over as Pearl pushed past her, cannoning into the tall man's legs, wrapping herself about one of them in a hug worthy of the most amorous of canines. A hand reached to pat the child's back, but the tall man's focus was entirely on Julie, staring at her with intense, fear-stricken eyes.

"Has it arrived?" he said. "Did I beat it here? *Did the box get here yet?*"

Catching her balance, Julie ignored the tall man's questions, instead finally finishing one of her own.

"Connor, just what the *hell* is going on?"

"I was trying to get here before the damn box even arrived," said Connor, pacing about Danny's den, ignoring Julie's instruction to take a chair. Julie perched on the edge of Danny's desk, arms folded over her chest, counterpoint to Connor's wildly swinging limbs. It had taken them over a half hour to get Pearl to leave her uncle alone and go in her room to play. Julie finally had to invoke the words, "We have some grown-up stuff to discuss," and Pearl unhappily tottered toward her room, allowing the adults to retire to the den, closing the door for privacy.

"Well, you didn't make it," said Julie. "Missed it by a day, actually. Just like you missed your own brother's funeral. What the hell were you—"

"Where are they? In her room? Does she have them now?" He was already moving toward the door, with the obvious intention of fetching the box. "Has she used them? The crayons? Has she draw—"

"They're on top of the refrigerator for safekeeping, and I'm not answering another damn thing until you tell me where the hell you've been for the past ten months, Con!" Her shout brought him up short, surprise sloughing the fear and intensity from his features for a moment. "You said you'd be back soon, then left for *almost a year*. Danny was circling the drain, and you ran off on one of your stupid treasure hunts. I needed you. *Pearl* needed you. And Danny was asking for you, there at the end."

Connor's hands were up, patting the air between them in a placating gesture, words still tumbling from him in a torrent.

"I know. You're right. I know. I was horrified when I got your letters—the mail didn't reach me where I was, and I got a whole bunch all at once when I got back to the city. By the time I was reading them, Danny was dead, and I wasn't going to make it back in time. I haven't had a cell phone in months, and when I realized what was happening I put everything I had into a plane ticket home, and—look, I'm sorry, Julie, sorrier than I can say, but we really need to focus on fixing what's going on here and now, okay?"

"That's what I've been asking." Her frustration was palpable. "What the hell is going on, Connor? Explain. Now."

The last two words were said in the same tone she'd used on the night of the funeral reception, and now, as then, they brooked no hesitation or rebuttal.

"I went to China," said Connor.

"China."

"Yes. It occurred to me that the brush was the answer, so I had to—"

"What brush?"

"Ma Liang's paintbrush. Do you know the legend of Ma Liang and his magic paintbrush?"

She sighed. "No."

Connor took a breath, gathering his thoughts. "There's a folktale in China, about a young man named Ma Liang who acquired a magic paintbrush. How doesn't matter. But according to the legend, whatever Ma Liang painted with the brush would come true: animals came to life, food could be eaten, he even created an island in the sea. Other people tried to use the brush, but it would only work for Ma Liang."

"What does this *fable* have to do with—" Julie began, but Connor's voice rose, and did not stop.

"'Wow,' I thought, 'if only someone else had ever been able to use the brush, that would be just the thing to save Danny: paint him healthy, and he'd be healthy.' It was the way the brush worked for Ma Liang, and no one else—*that* bugged me. So I did some research, made some phone calls, and looked into some databases I wasn't supposed to. I managed to get a look at the most accurate renditions of the legend—not the watered down, Americanized version you might be familiar with—and I came up with a theory."

"I told you, I'm not fam—"

"I discovered that while the Americanized versions all referred to Ma Liang as a young man, the ancient scrolls mention him as a *youth*. As in a *boy*. And what's the biggest difference between children and adults?"

"Connor . . ."

"That's right! *Belief!* Kids believe in everything! Santa Claus, the Easter Bunny . . . just *everything!* Grown-ups don't believe in anything. You have to prove things to us. Even when we *want* to believe in something—God, Satan, infomercials— there's a little part of us that's holding back, hoping not to be disappointed, because, like it or not, we don't *believe*. Not like children do, wholeheartedly and without reservation. And if belief was a factor in the magic . . . I went back through the records, looking for *everyone* who might have given Ma Liang's paintbrush a try: adults, every one.

"It needed to be a child. All I had to do was find the brush and get it back here for Pearl, and she could save her father. It was perfect! It . . . just took longer than I expected."

"No shit?"

"I—look, I finally tracked the brush to a little village in China, a tiny place a million miles from nowhere. Of course they didn't want to give it to me, so that . . . slowed the process again."

"What, you mean they didn't want to just hand over this

miracle? Even if it *was* all bullshit, if it had *any* historical value at all—how did you talk them into it, anyway?"

Connor looked at the floor. "I, uh . . . I didn't."

"What do you mean you didn—" her arms came off her chest, practically levitating to her feet as realization came. "Oh my God. You *didn't*! You *stole* the damn thing?"

"It was the only way I was going to get it out of there. But it took me a while to figure out how to do it—even in a small village, they have the law, and it's not like I'm a master criminal or anything."

"Master *bonehead* is more like it! What the hell did you do?"

"It's a long story, and we don't have time. I got the brush out of there, and mailed it to you; let's leave it at that."

"Mailed it to us? Well then this is your lucky day, Connor. We never got a brush. All we got were some crayons—they're these gorgeous foreign crayons and all, and it's a terrific box, but no brush. Sorry."

"That was it. That was the brush."

"I just told you—"

"I had to get the thing out of the temple, then the village, then the *region* . . . look, when the thing went missing, don't you think they'd search anyone who stood out? I was the only white man in the village. You want to talk about a sore thumb? I had to disguise the brush, or alter it somehow. Figuring that out was part of what took so long. Then I had to have the box made. See, when I found the brush it was nothing but a handle; the bristles—probably hair from some animal—had long since turned to dust. But the wooden handle was pristine, not rotted or desiccated at all. They claimed this thing was over a thousand years old, but it looked like it had just come from the factory."

"It probably had," said Julie. "I remember that time—"

Connor waved a hand. "Just listen. The magic of the brush was in the handle, not the bristles, and when I got it out of the temple, I needed to change it to something they'd not recognize. You understand? And making paper isn't really that hard, once you have some pulp to work with, so I ground up the handle—"

"You what?"

"Listen! I ground up the handle and mixed it with some other pulp and made a sheet of paper out of it. I was pretty sure the magic was intact, because, well, you've seen the crayons, right?"

Julie remembered colors shimmering along paper tubes, and suddenly Connor didn't seem quite as silly as he had a minute ago. She nodded.

"I used the paper to make new wrappers for some Crayolas I'd bought for Pearl, and sent the whole thing back here for her. The magic of the handle flowed through the bristles, so I figured the magic of the wrappers would flow through the wax . . . and I was right."

He suddenly straightened, looking about.

"Has Pearl drawn anything yet? Anything at all?"

Julie's mouth had suddenly gone dry. "A dog. This morning she drew a dog. It's on the fridge."

"And did anything happen?"

She brought him to the window: pressed close to the glass, looking at a sharp angle, they could see a good slice of the backyard. As they watched, the golden retriever wandered through their field of view.

"He showed up less than an hour later," she said. "I thought he was just from a neighbor's house, but now—"

They both flinched as, with a flapping tumult, a foot-tall green parrot landed on the sill, black claws scrabbling for a grip, neck twisting to peer in at them with one huge eye.

"Oh, yeah." Julie sounded flat, and felt dazed. "She drew a bird, too." She pointed to their finely feathered Peeping Tom. "That one, I guess."

"Not exactly," said Connor, leaning in slowly, so as not to spook the parrot. "Look at his foot. See that band?"

Julie did look, and saw a cuff about the bird's left ankle, metal dull from weather and wear.

"What's that?"

"That," said Connor, straightening, "is an ID tag, probably

from a pet store or zoo. Given the size of that parrot, I'm betting a zoo. And you were right: Pearl's new dog probably *did* escape from a neighbor somewhere. Has she drawn anything else?"

"No, that's it—and the crayons are hidden on top of the refrigerator, like I said. What do you mean 'it's from a zoo'? I thought the crayons were magic?"

"Not the crayons. Their wrappers. And I might have done something I hadn't counted on, here. Maybe in changing the shape of the item, I changed the magic. Maybe it's that each crayon only has one sixty-fifth of the power of the handle. I don't know. But it . . . well, the crayons don't work exactly like I thought.

"Two days after I got the brush from the temple, I mailed the crayons out to you, but I had just a touch too much paper. I needed sixty-five crayons, but there were only sixty-four in the box. I had just enough paper left to wrap around a pencil and give it to a local street kid to try out for me. He—look, I don't have time to go over everything right now, but the boy wanted sweets to rain from the sky, so he drew that. Later that day, a truck lost its brakes and shot off the road. It smashed straight through the front window of a local sweet shop. The driver, shop owner, and two customers were killed, but the impact threw a bunch of the shop's stock into the air, and for a few seconds, it rained sweets in the street."

Julie's hand covered her mouth. "Oh my God."

"There were other things that happened before I got the pencil away from the boy, but they were all like that. Instead of creating things from scratch, like the legends say Ma Liang did, the pencil was making things come true, but using what was available to do it. It was just after that I got your final letter."

Connor finally took the seat Julie had directed him to when they'd come into the den. "When I ran off to China, I was thinking that all Pearl had to do was draw her dad looking healthy, you know? In the pink. The magic would have taken over, and Danny would have been cured. Now, though, he's dead, not sick. And Pearl's not some fantastic artist: she's six.

She was good enough to hook a neighborhood dog, and a bird from the zoo, but if she drew a picture of her father *now*, I think—"

"Jesus Christ!" Julie felt sick. "Yesterday, Pearl was planning to draw you something special with her special crayons. She couldn't make up her mind. Had a whole list. But on that list were a dog, and a bird—and her father. It might have been him riding a unicorn, but it was going to be Danny." Part of her wanted to shout that this was crazy, that this couldn't be happening, but, then, there was that bird . . .

Connor puffed out air. "Wow. Are you sure the crayons are somewhere safe?"

"She doesn't know they're on top of the fridge, but you're right, we should put them somewhere safer." She tapped a fingertip to the desk blotter. "This desk locks. Let's put them in here, until we figure out what to do."

"Good idea," said Connor, already on his feet and heading for the door. Julie followed him down the hall, until he stopped, back stiff, in the kitchen doorway.

"We may have a problem."

Julie scooted around the tall man, then froze when she saw the kitchen . . . and the chair pulled up next to the counter beside the refrigerator. The refrigerator with the now-empty space on top.

"Oh, shit." They exchanged a glance. "I *thought* she didn't know it was up there."

"You don't think she's . . ." Connor began, but they were already moving toward Pearl's bedroom. They were halfway there when the slow, heavy knock came from the front door. They froze for a beat, then hurried whispers burst from each of them.

"That can't be him, it's broad dayli—"

"Doesn't matter to the brush, it doesn't—"

"But people would see—"

"He hasn't been in the ground very long, right? He might look perfectly—"

"You weren't here in the end, you son of a bitch! The cancer ate him alive. Danny weighed all of eighty pounds when he died—half of what people saw during the viewing was putty and pancake makeup, stuck onto a goddamn skeleton. Danny couldn't have walked the street while he was *alive* without attracting attention. Now . . ."

The knock came again, louder, though no faster, the beats as evenly spaced as roadside telephone poles: *knock . . . knock . . . knock . . .*

"Look," said Connor. "We don't even know if it's him. It could be just a Jehovah's Witness or something. Why don't you go look through the peephole and—"

"Jesus Christ, I'm not going *near* that door! *You* go look!"

Connor took a breath, then nodded and crept toward the front door. Julie followed him to that end of the hall, but would go no farther. Connor hesitated, then slipped into the dining room to peek out through a window overlooking the front porch from the side.

"Well?

"I can't see the face, but he's wearing a suit," Connor whispered. "How are we going to know whether—"

"*Julie?*"

Her hand clamped over her lower face, but the voice from the front porch forced a whimper through her fingers. The whimper became a strange, high, gurgling noise, almost a shriek, almost a giggle, when the doorknob began to jiggle back and forth.

"*Julie? I can't find my key. Julie?*"

It was Danny's voice—*Danny's*—but breathy, and distorted, like the words weren't coming out quite right.

The undertaker ran a wire under his skin, she thought, words skittering through her head like frightened spiders. *A wire, from one corner of his mouth, up over his nose, and down to the other—it's how they get that peaceful smile. Must be hard to talk with a wire in your face like that.*

Connor scrambled toward her, flapping his hands like

someone chasing away pigeons in the park. "Go," he said, not bothering to whisper. "Pearl must have drawn this—make her draw something else!" His eyes, though terrified, brightened at a thought. "Make her draw him in a coffin! Go!"

Julie burst into the bedroom. Pearl looked up from her place on the floor, sketch paper in front of her, eyes wide with fear. Again she had done something wrong, and knew it, and was babbling an apology even as her gaze shot wildly from the empty box, to the scattered and rainbow-wrapped Crayolas, then back to her mother, looking for something to say to make it better.

"What did you do?" Julie snatched the drawing from the floor, recognizing it easily: Danny coming home from work. It was something Pearl had drawn many times before Danny was diagnosed, and after, when he'd continued to work as long as he could. She stared at the scarecrow man in the boxy suit standing on a rough porch, hand on the doorknob.

She's even got the smile, she thought, remembering the mushy speech and the wire. She wondered what would happen if she just tore the drawing, ripped it to bits. Would that destroy what was in the picture, or would the magic do something else, something completely different? Worse?

"Julie," Connor's voice came up the hall. "Hurry!"

With a convulsive jerk, Julie tore the picture in two, and Pearl cried out, heartbroken. She tore it again. Then again—

Then the breathy, distorted, *un*-Danny voice came floating up the hall. "*Connor, I told you, I can't find my key. Just open the door so I can come see Pearl. I need to see Pearl!*"

Pearl was on her feet and staring at the ruined artwork in her mother's hands, eyes already spilling tears. Julie cast the shredded drawing aside and gripped the girl's small shoulder. She fell to her knees, pulling Pearl down with her, and started scooping the scattered crayons toward her daughter.

"You have to draw Daddy again, okay? I want you to draw Daddy again. Draw him in a coffin. In a box. Right now." The girl sputtered, sobbing, pointing toward what was left of her first sketch, but Julie dialed for that voice she had, that voice that was never disobeyed. It came out quivering around the edges and tainted by fear. "Just do it, Pearl! Do it now, and don't give me any backtalk!"

Pearl settled to the floor. Julie went back to the bedroom door and pushed it almost closed, peering out and down the hall, though she couldn't see the front door. She could hear what sounded like an argument, two voices in a back-and-forth, hurried on one side, slower and more plodding on the other, though she couldn't make out any actual words until one of the voices rose to a shout.

"Hurry *up*, please!" Connor sounded panicked. "Julie, what the hell are you *doing* in there?"

Julie slammed the door, leaning back against the wood, bracing herself as much as it. She looked to the floor, where Pearl was hard at work, making straight lines and corners: the edges of the coffin. The words *hurry up, faster!* flowed through her mind, but she pressed her lips tight together: in her terror, if she started screaming at Pearl, she might never stop.

"Julie! What's going—wait—no, *no!*"

Connor screamed as the other voice—the *un*-Danny voice—bellowed a hollow, almost two-toned note, something both more and less than human. There was the thud of something striking the wall, hard enough to shake the house. Connor screamed again, rising toward a throat-tearing pitch— but was cut off like someone had flipped a switch. In the silence that followed, Julie leaned on the door, staring at nothing, focused only on *listening*, listening so hard it almost hurt.

Then she heard it.

Slow, unsteady footsteps, making their way closer to the bedroom.

"Jesus Christ," she hissed, looking down at Pearl. "What did you do? What did you—"

She saw the drawing, pinned to the floor by tiny fingers. Angles and corners, the shape hastily scrawled, but easily recognizable. The squarish box at one end, for the thumb and forefinger to pinch. The straight spine. The row of jagged teeth. It would be hard *not* to recognize this crude sketch for what it was.

A key.

Julie's eyes shot up to meet her daughter's, and found them steady, hard, and frighteningly adult; she realized with a terrible start that Pearl had not *known* where the crayons were; she had *overheard*. Maybe not everything, but *enough*.

"But, Pearl, honey, you don't understand—"

From just to the other side of the door, the *un*-Danny spoke, the nearness of that voice making the back of Julie's neck crawl.

"Julie? I must have lost my keys, but I found yours on the porch. Is everything all right? Is Pearl all right?"

"You said Daddy was never coming home," said Pearl, her voice flat and emotionless, her words horribly familiar. "And you yelled at me. I want my daddy."

"Is Pearl all right?" the *un*-Danny repeated, as the doorknob turned. Julie shook her head in denial, locking her legs to jam the portal closed with everything she had.

"Is something wrong?"

Pearl pushed the drawing aside and bounced to her feet, smiling toward the door in anticipation. Julie strained, but her feet slid on the floor, yielding to the inexorable pressure from behind. The door opened, just a crack, before her sneakers regained purchase on the carpet. Through the thin opening the voice rode in on air that smelled of chemicals and dirt.

"Juuulliiieeeee . . ."

As Julie began to scream, the edges of her sanity collapsed under the strain. With a fluttering commotion at the window, the great green parrot settled onto the sill, watching the scene unfold with one round, black eye.

WENDIGO

Nearly four thousand pounds of bronco-bucking aircraft aluminum and safety glass, two tons of fuel and fear, whirl across the sky like a leaf tossed in a breeze. Maggie's hand squeezes mine, well-manicured fingernails digging into my flesh, and just for a second I don't hear her panicked cries, or see her eyes—huge, blue, and round with terror—staring into mine. Instead I have a flash of memory: a woman I do not know, small and dark, probably Filipino. Her name tag reads SUE. She holds Maggie's hand aloft, twisting it this way and that to showcase clear nails tipped with white, something I have just learned are called "French tips."

"You like?" she says, and Maggie nods, smiling, stretching her other arm to its fullest extent to examine that hand at a distance.

Strange, the things your mind latches onto when you think you're going to die.

"Mayday, Mayday." The pilot's voice snaps me back into the present, tense and loud enough to carry clearly over the engine noise and the storm pummeling the little plane. "This is Piper N-two-eight-seven-nine-D, en route from Fargo to Saskatoon. We've taken damage to the engine. We've lost altitude and the wings are icing. I need to make an emergency landing. Please advise!"

I tear my eyes from Maggie's to look out the window. This is my mother we're going to visit, and I've made this flight before, and I know what I *should* see: treetops, all the way to the horizon, greedy green fingers thrusting skyward from the thick, white snow that marks the Canadian winter. All I see now is white, the snow not lying prettily on the ground like some sort of picture postcard, but whirling through the air, clawing at the window like a hungry animal as the wind howls and buffets the small aircraft.

"Mayday! Mayday!" shouts the pilot again. He has a name, and I know that I know it, but it won't come to me. Before he can shout a third "Mayday," my stomach flips as the plane dips, those greedy green fingers suddenly rising through the kaleidoscope of white, much closer than I have ever seen them, closer than they have any right to be, to poke the Piper in the belly.

The pilot (*Bill*, a part of my mind says, far too calm for the situation, *his name is Bill*) bellows into the radio again, but Maggie's shriek drowns him out as more trees strike the plane, harder this time, and then I am screaming. My scream goes on, the only sound I hear until the final, terrific *cruuuump* of some great ancient trunk shearing off the wing outside my window. The world barrel rolls, flinging me hard against my seat belt, knocking the wind out of me. Hot piss stings my lap, and that part of me that knew the pilot's name has an instant to feel embarrassed—to hope that, when we get out of this, no one notices my soiled pants—before there is an earth-shaking *crack* and an instant of pain before everything spins away into blackness.

I open my eyes slowly—they're sleep-sticky, like I have a bad cold—and Maggie's face swims into focus in the dim light. Something doesn't look quite right, but I'm not fully awake yet, and I can't put my finger on it. I open my mouth to ask if she's all right, but what spills from my lips is a meaningless jumble of croaked sounds: "Mahee, yoo aw-eye?"

My mouth is so dry I can barely speak. I lick my lips, work my tongue, summoning some moisture for a second attempt as I blink, trying to wake up. Then it comes to me, what is wrong with my wife. Arms up like it's some old-fashioned stickup, fingertips nearly touching the low ceiling. Hair standing straight up from her head like a frightened cartoon character. One eye is open wide, staring at me; the other, her right, is stuck at half-mast, like I caught her in the middle of a long, lazy wink. Then there's the blo—

I turn away, wincing. My head hurts, like the mother of all hangovers, especially the right side. My right temple pulses in time with my heart, a *thud-thud-thud* over my ear. Christ, even the ear hurts. I pull a hand down—noticing now that *my* hands, too, are raised like I'm at gunpoint, the backs of my knuckles actually touching the ceiling—and explore the side of my head with tentative fingers. There's a goose egg along my temple, the hair strangely sticky and wet, and . . . and the top of my ear appears to be missing.

I look at my hand, see the fingers covered with something, the same something I saw staining Maggie's face: blood. I look back at Maggie, this time seeing the stuff I didn't want to before: her split lip and the gash along her jaw, the blood running up and across her half-open eye.

"Maggie?"

Her hair. Her arms, straight up and motionless. My own hands, both of them again, resting their knuckles against the ceiling. The pressure across my lap, a painfully tight band across my hips and testicles. The intense pressure in my head, pulsing in time with my heart.

We're strapped into our seats, hanging upside down.

Suddenly it's all there: the blizzard, the Mayday, the trees punching the Piper. The memory doesn't crash in on me like you read about in books, but is simply *there*, like it was right in front of me the whole time and I just wasn't paying attention.

I'm shocked that I could have forgotten such a thing, no matter how temporarily, but that feeling is pushed out in an instant by the thought of Maggie, hanging there with blood running across her face. Maggie, needing help.

"Maggie?" I say again, more clearly this time, fumbling at my seatbelt with numb fingers. The more I wake, the more I can feel myself, the pain of my own split lip, my hands clumsy and sausage-swollen with trapped blood from dangling inverted for so long. Jesus, how long?

"Maggie!" The shout nearly makes my head explode, a party balloon inflated to its very limit. My oafish fingers find the belt release, but the weight of my body against the buckle makes it hard to pull. I look at Maggie's eyes, one open, one squinted half-closed as if she's watching me through an oncoming migraine, and with an inarticulate sound of effort and pain, I yank the belt release with everything I've got.

A sharp, metallic pop, and the pressure across my lap is gone. I have a moment to register the strange, nearly weightless feel of falling, before the back of my head and shoulders strike the—

I wake slowly again, this time fighting it, not wanting to stir. If I thought my head hurt before, it was only because I had yet to experience my head now. It's impossible—a pain far too large to fit inside my little skull. I open my eyes but see nothing, whimpering as I push the lids back. This is a mistake. At my sound the pain spikes, sharp agony keeping me awake as my consciousness tries to creep back into the warm embrace of oblivion. It's no use, however, and I blink in surprise and frustration.

My lashes tickle, brushing against something as they flick up and down; there's something on my face. Through the pain I make out the pattern of light pressure against my skin—a familiar pattern, to be sure, but foggy as my mind is, I have to fight to place it—and then I have it.

Four fingers and a thumb. There is a hand on my face,

covering my eyes, and it isn't mine.

Pure reflex sends me scooting backward, launching myself away from this strange indignity, slapping the offending hand away.

In reality I barely manage to twitch out from under the invasive palm, my intended slap a pitiful flutter as the pain in my head makes my stomach lurch. I have a moment to make out Maggie's long hair hanging toward me—the bristle end of a blond broom, some of it stiff and dark with dried blood—and her dangling arms, one trailing hand so recently draped across my face, before I'm struggling onto my side as the vomit comes. The convulsions in my abdomen make my brain swim with agony. I lie there, huddled around my head, waiting for the world to stop hurting.

The pain doesn't stop, but dies down some. Enough to allow me to think and remember: flying over the Canadian wilderness, the storm, the crash. Then Maggie, hanging in her harness above me, bloodied and open-eyed. The more I remember, the worse I feel, though the physical pain is fading somewhat. The more the pain fades, though, the more I become aware of the cold. Cold that makes me shiver, and *that* starts to bring the hurt back. I have to do something here, no matter the agony. I really have no choice.

I open my eyes.

I'm lying on the ceiling, now the floor, I guess, facing away from Maggie, which is good, but facing the cockpit where the pilot (*Bill,* that calm part of my mind reminds me. *His name is . . . was, Bill*) hangs in his own harness. I can't see his front, and that's good too, because the back of his seat has a thick branch sprouting from its center. The tip of the branch pokes a foot beyond the chairback, jagged and white, like shattered bone, twigs, and bark stripped away on its passage through the seat . . . and Bill.

"Oh, shit."

The limb destroyed one side of the windshield when it came in to nail Bill to his seat like a spear thrown by a Titan, and that's where the cold is coming from. The glass is shattered, maybe half gone, and frigid air streams through the ragged hole. The plane coming to rest upside down probably saved me: if we'd been right-side up, the broken window would have been too high from the ground to be mostly blocked by the deep snow, and I likely would have frozen to death as I hung unconscious in my seat.

My seat . . .

I turn, stiff-limbed and wincing, to look up at my seat. The unbroken section of windshield and some of the windows along one side are above the snow, allowing me wan illumination. Hanging from the shadows between the seats, Maggie dangles. I stare, letting the tears run rather than trying to wipe them away; every movement causes my head to throb, and I can't afford the extra motion. I wonder how I'll get her down, how I'll half-stand to release her belt and cushion her as she falls, when I can barely move myself. I have no illusions about her being alive. Her eyes—one filming over, one blood-caked—still stare vacantly from a face bloated and mottled, and her hand, the palm that lay across my face, is locked in position, wrist flexed back, fingers spread and stiff and swollen.

Her blood has settled, and rigor began while I lay beneath her.

I'm not sure how long I've been lying here crying. It didn't seem long a minute ago, but now it *feels* long. *Really* long. I think my time-sense is messed up. Shock at finding Maggie? My head *does* hurt.

I investigate my head with my fingertips and find a goose egg behind one ear, and the hair is all stiff with what has to be blood. I have a sense of déjà vu, but I don't remember ever having a lump like this, even when I played football in college. And what the hell happened to my ear?

Something's wrong. Concussion? Shock? My God, I'm cold.

"I'm sorry, sweetheart," I murmur, crawling the couple of feet to where I see my coat, thrown to the floor—or, I guess, the ceiling—during the crash. "I'll get you down, I promise, but first things first."

I have to drag myself beneath the hanging seats to get to the cargo area, but that's all right; I'm not sure I could stand if I tried. When I get there, I can't tell if the difficulty in opening the Piper's door is due to the frame buckling in the crash, or because I'm just so beat up. Probably both. Eventually though, I struggle out into the snow.

Cold. The storm has passed, but the wind is still up, fierce against my exposed face and hands, and I hurry, as best I'm able, to check out the situation. I was right about standing, though: I'm only halfway to my feet before I vomit into the snow.

The plane has come to rest against a rise, along the edge of a clearing about half the size of a football field; probably what Bill was aiming for as a landing strip. The storm did its best to bury us while I was unconscious, but the same wind that's drifting snow over the plane and against the hill also scours clean the windward side; a row of windows and the door protrude from the snowbank, the one remaining wing jutting from the ground at a slight upward angle. Apart from the broken wing and shattered windscreen, the body of the plane appears intact—a miracle, considering the trail of broken trees behind it. It looks a mile long, the snow littered with pine needles and shattered limbs. Admittedly, though, I'm a city boy: anything more than a couple of blocks looks like a mile to me. I go back inside to get out of the wind.

Searching the plane is slow going, and I can see the light is changing as the sun makes its way toward the far side of the hill. Sundown is approaching, I think, and though that gives me a sense of urgency, my body doesn't seem to have any hurry left in it. Investigating the shattered windscreen, I try my best not to look at Bill, his face ribboned by flying glass. Strapped to the side of his seat, though, I make a fantastic discovery: an emergency survival kit. Matches, fire-starting plugs, a half-dozen self-lighting flares, a knife, two of those foil survival blankets, a first-aid kit, and quite a bit of other stuff. No food, though: a crumpled granola bar wrapper and several empty antacid and aspirin packets lead me to suspect Bill's been using his "emergency kit" like a medicine cabinet.

Terrific.

I look at the matches and kindling plugs, thinking of all the broken branches lying in the plane's trail, then of the rapidly fading light coming through the broken windshield. I feel the breeze coming in as well.

I can try for a fire tomorrow, I think. *When my head's maybe calmed down a bit. That's what they do in the movies, right? A signal fire? But for tonight . . . well, the plane's not heated any more, but it's insulated enough to fly at a few thousand feet, right?*

I drag myself back outside and crawl to the front of the plane, then in under the engine housing. The nose of the plane, the propeller snapped off somewhere in the crash, is held out of the snow by the cabin roof, angled slightly upward due to the way the Piper is lying. In the shallow lean-to created by airplane and hillside, I push and pack snow in front of the hole in the windshield. I'm sick again as I work, but nothing comes of it, just a dizzying bout of dry heaves; apparently, I'm empty. I cover the hole as best I can, finishing just as the sun touches the top of the hill. It's not perfect, but it's the best I can do.

Back inside the Piper I go through the luggage, just trying to see what I have, but the light is failing fast. I give up; as cold as it is, it's about to get colder. Dumping all the clothes into a pile, I tear open one of the crinkly survival blankets, as well as another find from the kit: one of those break-and-shake emergency chemical lights. In the cold, green glow of the light stick, I take off my boots, struggle out of the jeans I wore in the snow and into a dry pair, then put on every sock I can find, trying to warm my feet. I wrap myself in the blanket and snuggle into the pile of clothes like a nest. I've read somewhere that people with head trauma shouldn't go to sleep, but I've never been this tired, and sleep is coming whether I want it or not.

I look up at Maggie, still hanging from her seat. From this

angle I can't see her face, but I suddenly remember my earlier promise. I actually start to fumble with the blanket, thinking that I have to get her down from there, but I fall back, exhausted.

"I'm sorry, babe," I whisper, and I'm pretty sure I'm crying again. "I'll get you down tomorrow, I promise." Her hair is the last thing I see before my eyes close, and consciousness flees back to its hidey-hole in the black.

I wake to light from the low morning sun streaming through the windows, and my feet are numb. I peel off all those socks and see a pair of white, dead-looking things that frighten the shit out of me. I can still move them, though, and take that as a good sign, covering them with two pair of socks and wedging them back into my boots. My head feels a little better, I think, but it's all a matter of degree: I don't vomit when I move, but it still throbs like what my father would have called *a mad bastard*, and I don't feel like moving all that much. I rummage through the first-aid kit and come up with a packet of extra-strength Pain Away ("Compare to the active ingredients in Excedrin!") and bring it outside to wash them down with a mouthful of snow.

I have a few more mouthfuls of snow to quench my thirst, but I try to keep it to a minimum. I seem to recall reading somewhere that eating snow directly isn't good in emergency situations, though my head is foggy, and I can't remember why, or where I read it.

Strange, the things your mind latches onto when you think you're going to die.

It takes a while to collect enough wood to make a fire, moving carefully. Slowly. It takes even longer to build a woodpile to last me the day—the longer the fire burns, the better chance some passing search plane will spot the smoke, right? Besides, when I get a fire going, I don't want to be off gathering wood while it's burning; I'm going to sit right there and thaw my feet.

Eventually a massive woodpile sits next to the Piper. I use a pair of Maggie's shoes as shovels and clear a spot in front of the door, pushing the snow into a sort of fire-pit wall, to protect my the flames from the wind and hopefully reflect some of the heat back at me. Will snow reflect heat that way? God, I hope so. I break out the matches and one of the fire-starter plugs. The plug looks like just a stick of rough wax, but the thing lights and stays burning, and soon I have a small blaze. The twigs and branches covered with pine needles are dry from the cold winter air, and burn well once they catch, though they smoke like hell. That's good, though: I hadn't thought of it before, but the smoke might attract a passing plane. I wonder if they're out searching for us yet? I huddle closer for warmth, feeding wood to the fire—then huddle *too* close, and take a big lungful of smoke. Though the scent of burning pine reminds me of camping trips I took as a kid, and by extension hot dogs and marshmallows roasted over the flames, the smoke itself is merely choking, and I have to back off slightly, each hack and cough making my head throb as tears wash the smoke-sting from my eyes.

My tears flow in earnest later on, as I limp through the snow looking for wood again. What I'd thought of as a massive pile turned out to be only enough wood to keep a fire burning for an hour or so, just enough time to thaw my feet and get almost comfortable before realizing I was running out of fuel.

My feet had hurt as they thawed, my boots off and steaming next to the fire, my stockinged toes as close to the flames as I could stand. They'd hurt like hell, but the pain had eventually gone away—all but the underside of those big toes of mine. Peeling the socks off again, my feet had looked pink and slightly puffy, except under my toes. There I'd found a pair of fat, red blisters. I don't know if they're a sign of frostbite (isn't frostbite white, or is that just in the cartoons?) or if they're from walking in wet boots, but the effect is the same: I mutter curses at the pain of each step as I search for wood, looking for bigger, thicker, longer-lasting branches to bring back to the fire.

Those blisters are doing one good thing, I think. *At least they're distracting you from your stomach.*

My stomach. Christ, *why* did I have to think of my stomach? As if in answer, my gut rumbles, reminding me again of the bagel and coffee back in the airport. Actually—

I pull my useless cell phone from my pocket. There may be no signal out here, but the clock still works: 11:13 am. The flight left yesterday morning at 7:00 am. I try to do the math. That's *more* than twenty-four hours, right? There's twenty-four hours in a day, so I . . . I have to . . .

It's a simple calculation, one I should be able to make, and the fact that I can't figure it out, or even remember *how* to figure it out, is frightening. I start to worry if my confusion is a sign of concussion, or if there's something even worse going on in my head—and then my stomach chimes in again, like thunder rolling across the valley, reminding me just what I was doing in the first place.

I'd puked up everything I'd had inside me, but once the nausea had faded my stomach had started bitching loudly, a constant nagging, like some spoiled toddler in a department store whining for a toy, just whining and whining and . . . and when the pain from my toes isn't enough to distract me any more, here I am checking the time and trying to figure out just how long it's been since I've eaten, like knowing that will somehow cow my belly into shutting up.

I look down at the cell phone in my gloved hand, just in time to see the readout click over to 11:14. Another minute gone. Another minute since I last ate. Another sixty seconds I've spent freezing and hungry, lost somewhere in the Canadian wilderness, all because Bill the pilot said we'd be fine. Said the weather would hold off, and then had us up in the air before learning the storm had shifted, and instead of skirting it just to the east, we'd flown right into it.

I look around at the snow. The trees. The snow.

*Right into **this**,* I think, and a sudden rage takes me; rage at the hunger, and the cold, and Bill, and this fucking *phone* that won't even tell me how long this has all been going on. I cock my arm, intending to hurl it far away into the snow, where it'll never be found, so it can die all alone in the cold . . . just like me.

At the absolute last instant, I check the throw, stumbling a little as I pull the phone to my chest. It gets no signal out here. It's not a help to me in any way I can think of. The battery's even going to run out soon. But I can't get rid of it. I can't throw it away. Not while the clock works. It's my one last little reminder of my life. Of civilization. Besides, Maggie gave it to me, and I—

A thought comes through the fog that's been shrouding my head since I woke. Maggie. She's still hanging in the plane, and I promised to get her down. I *promised.*

I tuck the phone in my pocket and try, as best I'm able, to hurry in my search for wood. I have to get enough, and I have to do it quickly. I promised I'd get Maggie down.

Then, maybe, I should make some kind of signal fire . . .

I try. I try for a while, I really do. But I can't get her down.

There's not a lot of room to work in between the seats, but I wedge myself up there with her, forcing myself to try to unbuckle her seatbelt. I *have* to force myself: even though this is Maggie, I've never touched a dead person before, never mind *handled* one. Gravity tried to pull her legs toward the floor, but her shins and feet fetched up against the seatback in front of her, only allowing her knees to drop until they touched her chest; her lower half is curled into a sort of fetal position around the restraining belt. Somewhere in the middle of this knot of flesh and bone is the buckle with the belt release, but I can't get to it . . . especially since rigor has set in. I try to push her knees out of the way, but all she does is rock in the seat, inflexible as a statue.

I've seen a couple of movies where a coroner "breaks the rigor," actually snapping the tendons, but I can't do that. I barely consider it before thrusting the idea away. I can't . . . break her that way. I just can't. My headache has come back from all the activity, and the crying, and I'm so, so tired.

While I'm up there, though, I find something I missed in my search of the plane: Maggie's purse, its strap tangled on the armrest beside her. Unhooking it from its perch, I sit down right there, my ass striking the ground hard enough that the shock to my head makes me momentarily dizzy. I lean back against the bulkhead for a moment and close my eyes to let it pass.

I wake with Maggie's purse in my lap. Where the hell did *that* come from? I look up at her and she stares back with her mismatched eyes.

"Did you give me this, hon?" I say, then utter something halfway between a chuckle and a sob. That idea; it's crazy, right? Yeah, I know it is. It's almost funny. Almost.

I look down at the pocketbook. Seeing it reminds me that Maggie usually has—I rummage through the bag—there they are.

Two rolls of Certs: one peppermint, one wintergreen.

The wintergreen roll is already open, one or two missing, so I tear into that one first. I force myself to eat them one at a time, rather than just dumping the whole thing into my mouth, wrapper and all. The *his name is Bill* part of my mind points out that before yesterday I'd have been horrified at the thought of crunching through them as fast as I am; would have been slowed by the threat of a broken tooth. Nothing slows me now, though, Certs cracking loudly as I chew, tearing my way through the whole roll in less than a minute. It's been more than thirty hours since breakfast yesterday (at least, I *think* it has), and the whole time I chomp the candy I'm wishing Maggie'd had a whole oven-roasted turkey in that purse. Or maybe a ham. At least a Powerbar, for Christ's sake, but she's never carried food in her handbag, other than a little something to freshen her breath.

We were supposed to land in Saskatoon before noon yesterday, and were scheduled to go out to lunch with my mother. Why *would* we have brought food on the plane?—and then I remember that Maggie *did* bring food, one of those little bags of pretzels from the vending machines back at the airport. An hour into the flight, she'd offered to share them with me, but I'd said no thanks.

Jesus Christ, I said "No, thanks." What the hell was I thinking?

I wasn't thinking I'd ever be here, I can tell you that. I look down at the unopened peppermint Certs in my hand; while I've been daydreaming about pretzels lost, my fingers have already started picking at the edge of the wrapper, searching for that little pull-tab that opens the roll. I stop my fingers, actually have to concentrate to get them to cease, and set the roll aside. It seems a little silly, considering they're just candy, but it looks like they're going to have to last me a while. Every movie I've ever seen about people stranded in the middle of nowhere, marooned, or plane-crashed, or whatever, they always try to ration their food, no matter how meager their stores. You can't get much more meager than a single roll of Certs, but in those movies, *somebody* always makes it. *Somebody* always survives.

I want to *be* that somebody.

I set the Certs aside and tip out the contents of Maggie's purse to see if I missed anything: a wallet, keys, a cell phone (I check, but she has no signal either), a mini makeup case, a hairbrush, and a flat clamshell case I recognize as her birth control pills. I place the pills next to the unopened Certs. They must have *some* sort of nutritional value, right? When I open the makeup case, more out of curiosity that any real hope, her lipstick rolls out into my lap.

An image flashes through my head: a smiling woman with lipstick smeared across her teeth. I've seen it countless times, but never heard of it hurting anyone.

At least it's not poison.

I add it to the small pile.

Steeling myself, I creep into the cockpit, a space that's barely separated from the rest of the plane. I've been avoiding this place ever since doing what I could to stop up the hole in the windshield, because Bill is so . . . Bill is nailed to his seat by a wooden stake as thick as my calf, and his face is a ruin from flying glass, or wood splinters, or both. His eyes, though they were wide open with fear when he died, were miraculously untouched by the debris storm. Now, with his heart stopped, and gravity pulling all of his blood down into his head and hanging limbs hard enough to leave his flesh puffy and bruised, the pressure in his skull has his eyes practically squeezing from their sockets. I was creeped out by touching Maggie, but that was nothing compared to the skin-crawling that goes on while I search through Bill's jacket pockets, his bulging eyes staring, as if indignant at my actions, the countless small cuts and slashes gaping like tiny lipless mouths in the purple, swollen face hanging mere inches from my own.

I find a dollar and thirteen cents in change, a little notebook and pen, and a Big Red gum wrapper. I don't even find any keys, and I assume he left them behind in some locker at the airfield or something—especially when I notice the name patch sewn onto the breast of the jacket: Phil.

Bill, I think, *you couldn't even find your own coat, and we were expecting you to fly a plane? No wonder we crashed.*

I peruse my tiny pile of supplies: one roll of peppermint Certs, eighteen small pills in a clamshell case, and one rose-colored Maybelline lipstick. I shake my head without thinking, sending a sharp spike of pain through my temple and into my eye, my whole head throbbing in sympathy. I'm not sure when I last took any of that Pain Away, but it seems to be wearing off. I open the first-aid kit again and take four more pills, which leaves just four in the kit. I add them to the supply pile.

Suddenly exhausted, I crawl out to the fireside and throw on one of the thicker branches I found this morning. That's all I manage before I slump onto the woodpile for a rest.

It's not as if I have an axe, or hatchet, so this isn't one of those tidy woodpiles you see in images of hearth and home, all cut to length and neatly stacked. This is broken branches I found on the ground—*every* broken branch I've found on the ground—and just dragged here to the pile, an intertwined, springy mass about the size of a large couch, though shaped more like a nest. I only sit here because if I don't sit I'm going to fall, and it's a spot near the fire where I won't be in snow . . . but the shapeless springiness of it allows me to lean back, my three shirts and winter coat padding me pretty well. The fire is warm, and this is actually the most comfortable I've been since the airport yesterday. I'm exhausted. My head is throbbing. I close my eyes. Just for a minute, I tell myself.

Just for a minute.

I open my eyes to darkness.

No, that's not quite right. It's only dusk, but the difference between that and the sun-brightened snowscape I closed my eyes to is striking. Confused, I look down to the fire, wincing at my stiff neck and the *whomp* of headache the motion gives me, expecting the same blaze I'd last seen. Instead I find the thick log I threw on right before I took a seat is nearly gone, its thin, blackened remains lying in a bed of softly glowing coals.

Jesus Christ, how long have I been out?

I grab a long, thin branch from the edge of the pile under my ass and sit up, squinting at the even bigger *whomp* this causes, and start snapping it into smaller sections over my knee. It's from the end of a limb, thin, with lots of smaller branches and twigs coming out of it this way and that, and I know it'll make great kindling—which is good, because I have to stoke this fire up again. I've already used two of the six fire-starter plugs from the survival kit; keeping the fire going would be a *lot* better than having to start it again. As I lean forward, however, motion in the clearing catches my eye. I change my focus without turning my head, looking over the bed of coals rather than into it.

A wolf gazes calmly back.

I freeze, staring stupidly, feeling the cold spot in my chest where my heart has stopped. I can't remember ever seeing a real wolf, not even in the zoo. It took me a minute to spot it, its gray and white coat matching the snow well in the dusky light, but now that I've seen it I know it for exactly what it is, and even from thirty feet away it's bigger than they ever looked on television and in movies. From beneath my lowered brow the thing looks *huge*, a Shetland pony with long lean limbs and golden eyes. I've read that all animals have an instinctive fear of man, but this animal can't read, apparently: head up, ears erect, it watches me with an expression I choose to interpret as curiosity, because whatever it is, it ain't fear.

I drop my fistful of kindling onto the coals and, like the wolf itself might have done in a child's storybook, huff and puff, blowing the soft glow into a sharp red one, until the kindling flares, shooting out waves of heat and light.

The wolf watches all this without moving until I sit up from the fire, dizzy and surprisingly out of breath for such a small amount of work. When I sit up tall the wolf wheels about and trots off into the trees without a sound, a gray shadow fading into the darker shadows between the trunks. But it doesn't fade before I get a good look at it broadside: at the ribs, sharply defined in the light of the rising moon, even through the coat of fur; at the tiny waist, a thing worthy of a racing greyhound, not a beast with this one's obvious muscular bulk.

That wasn't curiosity in the thing's eyes. That great canine was looking at me with hunger—at this thought, part of my mind makes a quick count of everything left in my small supply pile: twelve Certs, eighteen of one pill, four of another, and a rose-colored lipstick—and it's not alone. As it disappears into the shadows, I make out motion here and there under the trees. I don't see another one clearly, and I have no idea how many there are, but my curious, hungry visitor brought friends. The whole pack is out there, all lean and hungry from the harsh winter.

I make the mental count again.

I wake in the plane.

I'm confused. I was out by the fire—I saw a wolf, for Christ's sake!—and now here I am, one of the dome lights, or whatever they're called in a plane, digging into my back. I open my eyes, though it barely makes a difference: it's night, and inside the Piper it's pretty damn dark. I sit up—then sag to the side as my head swims. My shoulder butts up against one of the hanging seat backs and I realize I'm in the center of the upside down cabin, below the narrow aisle between the left and right seats—lying next to Maggie, in effect, though I can't see her in the dark. The pain in my head is back, and strong, though not as strong as it's been in the past. I lie back, as gently as I'm able, and gaze through the low windows, at the moonlight on the snow: a soft glow in the night. Is my head getting better? Or am I just used to the pain?

I hear a sound, recognizing it as the thing that woke me— I'd heard it in my sleep. A wet, snuffling snort. I wonder for a moment what it might be—then remember that I'm alone here, and there shouldn't *be* a sound if I'm not making it . . . and I'm *not* making it. I roll gently onto my side, taking my weight on one elbow, turning my attention toward the sound. Toward the cockpit.

Moonlight shines faintly silver on the snow, coming in through the unbroken side of the windshield . . . and there are shadows moving. Shapes in the night, passing back and forth on the other side of the glass, like fish in a tank. I roll further, squirm a little closer, peering at the shapes outside, curious—and then my curiosity becomes fear: not all of the shapes are outside the glass. A growl, low and rumbling, burbles out of the darkened side of the cockpit, where shadows roil strangely, all movement and no detail, like shapes under a blanket.

It's pure reflex, but I'm scrabbling for some way to beat back the darkness and see what's right in front of me. The cell phone fumbles out of my pocket, the screen coming to life. The artificial illumination, so meager back in civilization as to be almost laughable, is bright enough in *this* setting to cause me to squint against the glare.

The wolf, however, does *not* squint, crouching as it is, not five feet away, half in and half out of the plane, peeking at me around Bill's seat back, its eyes golden dinner plates at this distance. Its hindquarters protrude out through the broken windshield, and I can see where the snow I'd piled there to keep out the cold wind has been cleared away. For an instant my fear is drowned out by a flood of anger: just who the hell does it think it is, coming into my plane—my *home*—uninvited like this, tracking in snow and letting in the cold?

Then I focus on the dark muzzle, at the bared teeth splitting it in a savage grin, and fear shoulders its way back to center stage. Christ, from this close those teeth look as long as my fingers, though much, *much* sharper, and . . . and as I watch, some of the darkness around those teeth drips off. It's just a single drop, but I watch it fall with amazing clarity, a droplet in high-def, tumbling through the air to strike the ceiling which is now our floor with a tiny, soundless splash. Around it I see more darkness on the floor, drips and drabs and spatters, and all but that last drop is beneath the shape of Bill, hanging in his seat.

Blood.

They're eating the pilot. They found the hole, smelled Bill through the snow or something, and dug their way in. That's what woke me: the wet sound of tearing fabric, or maybe the wetter sound of tearing flesh. Did they stop there because Bill was easy, hanging right in the entrance so they didn't *have* to come in any further? Or had they not even noticed me sleeping a half-dozen feet away, so intent had they been on this dangling buffet? And would Bill be enough to feed them all? Part of me considers all the shadows I saw through the windshield, the rest of the pack waiting its turn, and doesn't think so.

Before the thought is finished I'm struggling with the phone in my hand, rolling clumsily to my knees. From the corner of my eye I register the wolf flinching back at this sudden move. The icons on the phone's screen look tiny, and the one I'm searching for seems to hide among the rest like some insane *Where's Waldo* game. The wolf recovers, head lowering slightly, the rumble in its chest rising as it places one foot forward, the first move it's made toward me. Oh, why the *fuck* do I have so many goddamn applications on this thing? It *has* to be here, I *know* it's here—and then it is.

My thumb stabs down on the screen.

If the background glow from my screen seemed bright, the flashlight app explodes. Brilliant light, the colorless white of a lightning strike, bursts from the little machine. My eyes and head nearly rupture with pain, and I cry out, falling forward, catching myself with one stiff arm before I crash headlong. The impact with the floor ratchets the torment in my head even higher, but through teary eyes I see the wolf take a step back, then retreat another, head dropping, ears folding back sleek against the skull. Those golden orbs squint nearly shut, and the head droops lower as I kneel up tall, raising the light up by my ear to aim the blinding beam directly into the beast's eyes, like a cop making a traffic stop.

Despite the situation, I nearly giggle at the thought of a cop pulling over the Big Bad Wolf. The words run through my head, *Do you know why I stopped you?*, but what pours from my mouth are inarticulate sounds: part fear, part anger, but *loud*. Loud enough that it, combined with all the sudden movement, makes my world go swimmy. I fall forward again, still trying to catch myself one-handed so I can keep the light trained on my intruder.

The sudden light, the shout, my falling toward it—it's too much for the wolf. It backs away with a yip, just as the jolt of landing stiff-armed once again makes everything roll, like the world's lost its vertical hold. There's a flurry of movement, the flash of a bushy tail, and it's gone.

I lie on the floor, breathing hard, stomach kicking from all the fear and activity, though I don't think I'm going to actually be sick: there's nothing in there to come out anyway. I lower my forehead to the floor and close my eyes for a moment—and when I raise my head I notice my breathing is normal, my heart no longer thudding in my skull. Even my stomach seems to have settled in an instant, no longer dancing like a tap artist but offering a nice, steady, "feed me" rumble. Did I pass out? I glance around, unable to tell for sure, though I suspect that I did. How long? Are the wolves still about? My phone is in my hand, though the light is out, the screen dark: yet another indication that more time has passed than I was aware of. I touch the screen and the backlight glow fills the plane once more.

I immediately see the uncovered hole in the windshield, suddenly become aware of the cold, much more intense than when I'd woken and discovered the intruder, and know I have to do something about it. But I'm not going out into the snow, into the night, not with the pack out there, probably waiting to get back at Bill again.

Or start on me.

I crawl back and forth, towing suitcases, but they aren't enough to fill the gap. I drag myself back, trying not to look at Bill, though I'm working right in front of him. I try not to see the stumps where his left arm is missing from the elbow, his right from the shoulder, or his torn face tipped back with its mouth open wide as if he'd screamed in agony while the wolves took their treats. I simply pull myself past him to the passenger seats, jerking the cushions free.

In the event of a water landing, singsongs a flight attendant in my brain, *your seat cushion may be used as a flotation device.*

"How about keeping out the Big Bad Wolf?" I say, stretching my arm through to pull what snow I can reach back to cover the hole, then spread the cushions and cases across the gap in the glass to shore things up. "What do you think about that, Bill? Is it enough to keep out the Big Bad Wolf?" No. No way. But it's the best I can do for the moment. I slump down, my back against the cases, still trying to avoid eye contact with Bill. I want to go to my supply pile, thoughts of the hungry pack reminding me of my own shrinking, growling, howling belly, but I'm just too tir—

I open my eyes to daylight, and I'm out by the fire. This is where I fell asleep, sitting on the woodpile, and for a moment I suspect my nocturnal visitation was all a dream. Then I look through the open plane door. I can't see Bill from where I sit, but I can make out the edge of the stain on the floor, splashes of what I know to be blood, and I realize everything was real. The wolves were here, feeding, and they'll be back. They know they can get into the plane, and they know there's food in there—some of it so fresh it's still moving, albeit slowly.

I can't believe I may have survived a plane crash, and then the deadly cold of Canadian winter nights, only to wind up a walking take-out meal. That thought begets a short fit of giggles, but the laughter hurts my head so much I sober quickly. I know I have to do something to keep the wolves out, I have to, but just the thought of them feeding is enough to send me scuttle-crawling back into the plane looking for breakfast. Applying such a lofty title to my miniscule pile of supplies makes me grin—almost makes me giggle again, despite the pain—until I reach the spot where I left that tiny pile, and find it gone.

My head throbs as my gaze flicks this way and that, but I'm barely aware of it. It *can't* be gone! It was barely anything, but *anything* is better than *nothing*. Someone is repeating "No, no, no," in a rusty voice, and it's me, of *course* it's me, and I can't understand how the wolves got past me, slunk right past without my even seeing, to eat my food—and why would they do that when they had their own food hanging right there, in front of their entrance?

"Why would they do that, Bill?" I say, turning to him for a response before remembering his shredded flesh and missing limbs. "Why?" I say again, seriously wanting an answer. Bill says nothing, merely hangs there in his seat, his back to me.

Bill, it seems, is in a mood. Then, in a flash of inspiration, I turn to Maggie.

"You must know something, hon," I say. "You must." I look, just to make sure, and I was right: her eyes remain open, even the squinty one, keeping a lopsided watch. She *must* have seen what happened.

Unless it was in the night, says that fucking annoying, rational voice in my head, the one that remembers French tips and pilots' names. *In the dark, she may have seen nothing more than shadows, maybe not even that, and—*

"Oh, shut up!" My head pounds, hurting more with every movement, every shouted word, but this is *important*, damn it! I force myself calm, and scoot under the seats 'til I'm looking up at my wife, who stares on impassively.

"Sweetheart. You . . . *must* have seen *some*thing." I point to the curve in the bulkhead where I left the pile. "It was right there in front of you, and I see you watching all the time. Every time I'm in here you're looking at me. You *must* have seen something. Please, if you could just tell—"

I'm squirming in my urgency when my hand strikes something small that rolls a few inches before fetching up against the dome light housing. I grab for it blindly, then hold it up in front of my face, peering closely in the shadows beneath the hanging seats.

A small black tube, maybe the size of my thumb, white lettering along the side catching what light from the windows filters past me.

(Maybelline)

It's empty.

I look up at Maggie in shock. "You *bitch*! *You* took it? You *ate* it? But . . . but what about *me*? I *needed* that. You don't! You don't need it at all, so why would you do that? You're already dead."

I half-turn, twisting my neck savagely to look toward the cockpit, ignoring the pain in my anger.

"You're both dead. Why would you—"

I break off as something occurs to me, something so basic I'm surprised I hadn't thought of it before. I ratchet my head back and forth, trying to take them both in with the same gaze, though it's impossible from this angle.

"Oh, I *get* it. I *get* it now. You're both dead, and here I am, still moving around and breathing. And eating. I'm the odd man out, right? You two, you've been talking behind my back, haven't you? Deciding it's not right? Deciding, maybe, I *shouldn't* be alive? That it's not *fair*? Well *fuck* you! Fuck you both! You think you're going to turn on me behind my back, maybe do something about it? Fuck. You. Both."

I back toward the open door, wanting to get away from this place, not willing to be in the same room with them, but not wanting to let them out of my sight, either. Maggie watches me go, silent and impassive. I meet her gaze, my eyes flat and stinging despite the cold air; hers wonky, bloody, and expressionless.

"You know, you're my *wife*. I might have expected this kind of thing from him—he's a stranger, just the pilot, just the fucking help, after all—but from *you*? I expected better from you, Maggie. I expected better."

The back of my head strikes the top of the doorframe. It's not a hard hit, but what is now the top used to be the bottom, and there is still a small step built into the bulkhead right there. The step-edge catches me across the back of the skull, the sharp edge magnifying the impact. I stumble through the doorway, spinning away from the two of them. Rage fills me as, just for an instant, I think about the way they've teamed up against me, the way they've tricked me, even going so far as to distract me so I'd hit my head yet *again*. But I only have an instant, as the white wintery world outside goes watery, and then dim, and then black. I know that I'm falling, though I don't even have time to feel the snow's bitter-cold kiss on my face before everything slips away and is gone.

My eyelids flutter, my tickling lashes registering the snow's nearness before I see it, before I even feel it on my skin. I roll over, start to moan, then stop. My throat is too dry to make a sound—all the attempt makes is pain, and I've had enough of that to last me a lifetime, thank you very much. I scoop snow with clumsy movements, mashing it into my mouth to melt slowly on my tongue. I reach for more and see red streaks on my fingers. *Blood? Did I bite my tongue? Lose a tooth?* I wipe at my lips again, numb fingers scraping woodenly across an unfeeling face.

More red. But it's not quite right, it doesn't look like . . . I hold my fingers closer. Squint.

It's not blood red. It's rose red. A single word floats through my mind.

(Maybelline)

Horrified, I stick a finger in my mouth, scrubbing it against my teeth and gums. It comes out covered in a familiar rose red.

"Oh, God," I try to say, but the words are only a rough whisper. *I* ate the lipstick. And if I ate *that*, then I must have eaten all the rest as well. I cover my eyes with a hand, trying to recall the deed, to recover the taste, the feel, to remember *anything* about eating the last of what I laughingly referred to as *food*. There's nothing there, not even the dreamlike possibility of a memory . . . but I have no problem remembering something I wish I could forget.

My God, I was awful.

I roll onto my stomach and try to rise, but I'm too clumsy, my balance nonexistent. I crawl instead, dragging myself the short distance into the plane, thankful I hadn't gotten farther before I fell. Thankful also that the door wasn't closed behind me. Something about that bothers me, the wide open door (*Were you raised in a barn?* says a voice in my head, female and familiar, but I can't quite place it), but I don't have time to worry about it now. I can only handle one thing at a time, if that, so rather than think about it I simply close the door behind me, shutting up the nagging in my head.

"I am so sorry," I say, the words coming hard and slow through my dry and swollen throat. The other two say nothing, patient. "I was wrong. It was me. I had no right. Can you forgive me?"

Bill pointedly refuses to even turn to meet my eye. That hurts, of course it hurts, but not as much as the blank, dead stare my wife levels my way.

"Maggie, please." I pull myself closer to her, a little bit of feeling coming back to my rubbery limbs through use; pins and needles, mostly, but at least it's something. "I'm not doing so good here, you know? I know I said I'd get you down. I tried, but I can't. And about the food, I lost my head there. But I know it was me now, see?"

I rub a quick, painful finger across my teeth and gums and hold out the reddish-pink result for inspection.

"See? I know, you know"—I wave a hand behind me—"even *Bill* knows. I was way out of line before, okay? But please, *please* don't shut me out. Don't ignore me, I couldn't take that. I'll never make it on my own. Please."

Maggie's expression doesn't change a whit. It's like talking to a stone.

"What do you want? Do you want me to die? Was I right before?" I turn, throwing words at the back of Bill's head. "Is that it? Bill? Is that what you both want: for me to join you? I . . . I can do that."

Bill responds no more than Maggie, but at least I can see Maggie's face, try to gauge her reactions. I turn back her way, meeting her cold stare.

"I can do that, hon. I can *do* that. Is that what you want? Okay. Okay."

I keep saying it, like a mantra, as I pull myself over beneath the seat where I woke up the other day. Using the curve of the bulkhead and the purchase the recessed window gives me, I pull myself nearly upright.

"Okay?"

My heart is beating hard from exertion, my head pounding in time, and the plane's gone all swimmy again as I grab the nearer end of my old seat belt. I wrap it about my fist in a death grip and use it to hold myself up as I flail for the other half of the belt, dangling an arm's length away. It may be swinging, it may not; I really can't tell right now. All I know is I can't catch hold of the damn thing as it wavers, seeming to sway in the air before me. I'm still saying "Okay? Okay?" but it's less a question to Maggie and Bill than it is a tear-streaked plea to the universe to just let this happen, just let the damn belt come into my hand and let me get this done.

I want to be done.

Finally, weeping with impatience and fatigue, I lunge for the strap. My feet slip out from under me and I loose a rusty, guttural cry of frustration: if I fall I'll have to start all over again, and I just don't know if I can do it.

Twin jets of agony lance up from my knees as they impact the floor, the body-wide jolt enough to make my world go white. Unconsciousness looms large again, but I manage to fight it off, focusing on my hands, on their grips: left hand wrapped in a nylon strap, the right squeezing tight on another. Then tighter.

My lunge worked. I've got it.

Clinging to consciousness, hanging two-fisted from the seat belt, I manage to stay kneeling but upright. I struggle to my feet again, bracing my backside against the bulkhead once more. I know neither side of the belt is long enough to loop about, then tie a knot. Neither end will work alone. But together . . . together they just might get the job done.

Working swiftly, not thinking about it beyond the logistics, I snap the belt together, then grab the buckle as a whole, twist it to the correct angle, and yank it out to its greatest buckled length. Sliding my feet over the floor rather than lifting a foot and maybe losing my balance, I position myself under the seat. Holding on to the belt with my right hand, I take hold of the end sticking out of the buckle with my left: the thing flight attendants tell you to yank on to pull the belt tight across your lap.

I take a breath, and slip my head through the space between seat and belt, tucking the nylon gently beneath my chin.

"Okay," I say, a return of my mantra, as I angle my head slightly, bringing Maggie into view. She hasn't turned her head in my direction, but I can tell she's watching me from the corner of her squinty eye, and there's a grim satisfaction in her profile. With the seat backs in front of me I can't see Bill at all, but I feel his silent approval radiating from the front of the plane.

"Okay."

My right arm trembles with the strain of holding myself erect; my left simply trembles, though the fingers still wrap tightly about the pull tab of a strap. *This will do it*, I think. This will put us all on even footing, and they'll stop giving me the cold shoulder. This will stop me from feeling so alone.

And so *hungry*.

"Okay." I tilt my head forward to hold the belt beneath my chin.

Wait! shouts a voice in my head, the rational, French-tip and pilot-name voice, just as my left arm yanks the strap as hard as it can. The seat belt snaps taut beneath my Adam's apple, pinning the back of my head to the seat above. My legs give out again, and my full weight falls against the restraint across my throat.

No! comes that voice again, as limbs flail, my arms and legs no longer under my control. *You wanted them to talk to you to help you survive*, the voice says, crystal clear and as annoying as ever. *Doesn't killing yourself so they'll stop ignoring you kind of defeat the purpose?*

My lungs suddenly kick into overdrive, pulling and pulling, but it's like trying to suck a shake through a collapsed straw—all that work for no reward. My feet scrabble against the floor, but the curving shell that was once the ceiling has become a slope of ice, and they can't find any purchase.

*You're doing all this to survive! You **want** to survive!*

My throat feels like an empty beer can crushed in some dumb jock's fist, but my view of the seatback in front of me is suddenly shockingly clear, the pattern of whorls and grain in the leather coming into amazing focus, even in the dim light, the high-defest of high-def. It's the last thing I'll ever see. I don't feel Bill any more. I don't see Maggie. My uncontrolled hands strike the wall, the seat, the window, my own face.

You're the guy in the movie who rations the food. Who makes the fire.

Shiny spots. Worms of light. Worms of dark. All of them invading my high-definition view, creeping in from the sides to steal the sight from my bulging eyes. My hands striking the seat. Striking my face.

*You're the guy who wants to **live!***

Striking the seat belt release.

I crumple to the floor, great whoops of air burning in and out through my bruised throat.

You see? I told you you want to live.

Fuck you, I think back, as I huddle against the bulkhead, unable to even see Maggie's expression through the tears flooding my eyes. The sobs rip through my crushed windpipe to thrust spears up into my skull, skewering all the soft spots in my head, and though I try to crawl away—not having a destination in mind, but just needing to go somewhere—my exhausted limbs won't do more than twitch. Maybe I do want to live, but I don't know if I can take it.

I don't know if I can take it.

I'm shuffling through the snow, one hand braced against the plane for balance, the other trailing behind, dragging a long, stout branch. I stagger to a stop, confused. Wondering how I got here. I know *what* I'm doing, but not how . . . how I . . .

I know I'm trying to get Maggie and Bill—at *least* Bill—to forgive me for pulling that belt release. Bill . . . Bill's in terrible shape, stumps and stubs for arms, his face a mess—it's no wonder he's a little pissed at me for still being alive. I had the idea that if I could manage to protect Bill, if I could manage to keep those damn wolves out, then he might look kindly on me, you know? I know about that idea . . . but I don't remember actually *having* it. Just like I don't remember coming out here to work on it, though I can see from the tracks in the snow that I've already made this trip up the plane. Twice. At *least* twice. I'm going to have to search out more wood, if I ever want to start a signal fire or something.

I wonder how long I've been working out here. Then I wonder what time it is. Then I wonder what *day* it is, and how long I've been here in the clearing. Three days? Four? I glance up at the sky, looking for the sun, trying to gauge whether it's on its way up or down. Tilting my head back causes me to nearly tip over, and I lean against the plane to keep my balance. My stomach chimes in as well, rumbling painfully, curling me forward, and I spend a moment just leaning there, trying to remember what it was like when I ate those mints. Those pills. That lipstick.

The moment stretches.

My calf begins to cramp from standing there so long, leaning with most of my weight on one leg. My tongue rakes the backs of my teeth, looking for a hint of taste, even the waxy, flowery taste left behind by the lipstick, but there is nothing. Nothing but the fuzzy, rancid slime coating my teeth after . . . how long has it been since we crashed? Since we took off?

My hand slips on the plane, numbed fingertips burning as they slide across the icy metal. I catch myself through pure reflex, but the jolt to my head gives me a fresh batch of pain to worry about, the accompanying nausea sending thoughts of candy and pills skittering away. I bend cautiously, grip the limb I dropped as I stood there lost in fantasy, then trudge on, sliding myself almost bodily along the Piper's slippery hull. I have work to do.

It takes some doing, but I manage to fasten some of those branches in place like crisscrossing bars, weaving the crooks of branches together like table forks with their tines meshed. You can push and pull at those meshed tines all you want, but the only way to free up those forks is to pull the whole thing apart from the sides. With some of the branches braced inside the plane, others outside, the only way those wolves are going to get into the plane again is by pulling this lattice apart from the sides, like those table forks, and they just aren't smart enough.

I give the rough lattice a shove, then a pull, easing my weight back against my grip on the crossbars. It's in there solid. I'm pretty wedged in as well, having shoved myself under the protruding nose of the plane, right in under the upside down engine, to get to the broken windshield.

I've avoided looking in at Bill, though he hangs just feet away, even when I was working part of the lattice in under the tree limb protruding through the glass . . . and Bill. He's in rough shape, much rougher than me, and—quick motion catches my eye. I peer through the glass at Bill. Did he actually move? Maybe wanting to show his approval for what I've done, protecting the plane, protecting him? That *must* be it! I look at him, right into his shredded-meat face, looking for some sign . . . but there is nothing. He's not even looking at me, but past me, as if I'm not worth his time.

Or he's looking at something behind me.

I turn, and for an instant it appears the snow is alive, tendrils rippling toward me across the unmarked surface of the clearing: the wolves are back. Running low, legs all but hidden by the snow, they come, gray upon white, swift and silent as windblown storm clouds scudding across a steel-gray sky. They're halfway across the clearing already, and closing fast.

I'm moving before I know it, sliding out from beneath the engine and heading for the Piper's door. I have to cover a fraction of the distance they do, but I'm exhausted, and sick, and I haven't eaten in days. I know I can't walk upright, never mind run, so I don't even try. Throwing myself forward, I scramble through the snow on my hands and knees, a clumsy imitation of the wolves' fluid gait. Though my skull screams in protest, I know I can't stop, rolling under the remaining wing rather than going around.

I'm just gripping the Piper's door handle with numb, clumsy fingers when I hear the whisper of fur on snow and the light crunch of running paws behind me. I don't try to look back—I don't dare—but twist the handle for all I'm worth and yank the door hard. The pull sends me off-balance again, but I'm falling in through the opening door. I manage to shift my grip to the inner handle, thanking God it's a great big bar rather than some silly little doorknob, and let myself tumble into the plane, trying to get my legs and feet in while my body weight slams the door. From the feel of my head, landing on my back in the plane may well kill me, but at least I won't wind up—

Teeth clamp onto my boot, a muscular neck twisting, trying to rip and tear. I'm jerked to a halt, by both the boot and my grip on the door, though one of my hands slips loose, the arm flailing behind me. My scream is propelled by both pain and fear, the swollen, pulsing agony that is my head vying for dominance with the primal terror of being savaged and eaten by the monsters of the forest.

A guttural yelp echoes my own cry. I look down at my trapped foot and straight into the eyes of the wolf, its head half again as big as my own. Its own lunge through the slippery snow, combined with my own still-considerable weight, has pulled it partially into the plane, the closing door slamming into its side, pinning it in the doorway.

Rather than just letting me go, however, the beast wrinkles black lips back from white teeth that look *enormous* from this close, and bears down. I feel the bones in my foot threatening to give way and flatten like a stomped-on soda can, expensive boot or not, and I howl with pain. Toes flex, claws screeching against the metal and molded plastic of the ceiling-cum-floor, and the thing gives a heave, like the family dog playing tug-of-war with his favorite toy, but strong, so *strong*, and I'm all but yanked out of the plane like an oyster shucked from its shell.

My flailing arm comes back around, palm slapping hard against the bulkhead. My sliding foot butts up against the lip of the doorframe, the bolted-on white sign with its black lettering spelling out an upside down WATCH YOUR HEAD. My mind is strangely clear, clearer than it's felt in days, and I'm terrified but seeing everything, seeing every little thing, and I note the gap between the door and the wolf's heaving shoulder as it wrestles to pull itself free and take me with it. Planted hand and foot, a death-grip on the door handle, I yank back with all I've got, slamming the heavy metal door into the animal's side again.

Another yelp, and I gain some ground in the tug-of-war.

The thing whipsaws its head from side to side in retaliation:

a terrier shaking a rat. My whole body jerks, and I scream, feeling swollen tissue tear in my throat as my knee explodes with sick pain. The wolf is winning the tug-of-war in a series of quick yanks: my hand is sliding on the bulkhead, my good leg nearly buckling from the pain in my other knee. It's almost out now, has almost taken me with it. Shapes streak past the gap in the door: the rest of the pack milling about, waiting for this one big son of a bitch to pull me out of my shell. Once I'm out there I'll be done, torn to pieces in seconds.

Screaming again in rage and pain I use my only weapon, the door, actually pushing it open a bit in order to get a good swing. I shove that heavy piece of metal away, then pull as hard as I can, throwing my weight back with it in an all-or-nothing *yank*.

The door slams like a snapping jaw, catching the wolf's head between its swinging solidity and the edge of the frame.

The yelp this time is high and shocked, no hint of a growl left in it. The grip on my boot suddenly lets go, but my hand on the door handle keeps me upright. The wolf's jaws no longer snap, its round, golden eyes are dim, and it sags for a moment in the gap, held in place by the pressure of the door. I push and pull the door again, a quick, savage movement as fast as I can, though lacking the power of that great blow. The door smashes the wolf's head once, twice, as I struggle to get both feet under me again. The beast yips and yowls, trying to pull loose as I finally manage to get myself ready to throw my body into the blow. Claws scrabble desperately on metal and plastic as I scream one last time and push and *pull* with everything I have left.

The door swings open and closed, actually slamming this time, metal on metal, and I twist the handle to the closed position, locking the wolf and its pack out in the cold. Twisting the handle finally costs me my grip, and I tumble backward, trying not to strike my head again. I have no idea whether I do or not, there is so much pain, from so many places, and I'm just so damn *tired*.

I hear a ravening growl, then another, loud and clear, not filtered through the plane's hull or window glass. I roll to my side, toward the sound, and see those shapes through the windshield again, passing this way and that. Hear them yipping and growling there at the broken window, trying to get in the way they did before. A flanking maneuver. I hope my hastily made lattice of branches will hold. If it gives way I'm done for. We're all done for.

Keep an eye on them, Billy, I think as I roll slowly away from the windshield, unable to watch. *You keep an eye on them, while I . . .*

Rolling brings the door into view, and here, lying on the ceiling, or the floor, or whatever the hell it is now, I find a new thing in the plane. There's blood on the door, dark in the fading, dusky light, and more on that upside down sign about watching your head. The blood on the sign is shaped like a comma: thick at the top, trailing down through a short, narrowing curve, almost like an arrow. An arrow pointing to the new thing.

A wolf's foot.

It lies there below the door, severed at the wrist—do they call it a wrist, when it's a dog?—snow crystals still sticking to the gray fur between the pads at one end, white bone sticking out of the red meat at the other.

The red meat.

Keep an eye on them, Billy, I think again, though all that comes out of my mouth is a low moan. And drool. My breath practically slurps in and out, and I feel moisture on my chin as I wriggle close enough to touch the foot. The adrenaline is leaving my system, though, and I can't ignore the pain any more, and the pressure in my head is growing. Grown. Grown huge, and monstrous.

I pull the paw to me, almost cuddling it: Christ, I must look to Maggie like some overgrown toddler, snuggling his Wubbie in the cradle, but I can't help it. Just by chance, I grabbed it oriented to me, stub up, toes down. Some part of me assumed it would be stiff, and stuffed-feeling, but it's not. It's flexible, and soft, and still . . . warm.

The pressure in my head is huge and pushing, pushing me

toward the darkness. Toward rest. I know I can't fight it off: losing this battle is the cost of winning the one at the door. I look at the stump of the foot, snugged up against my chest, the warm, raw, red end almost touching my chin. It's a bit mashed, a bit messy. Not the cleanest cut. Butchery by Piper.

My head propels me brutally toward the precipice of consciousness, but my stomach fights back. It's a hard, tight ball of pain and want, so shriveled-feeling as to be unable to even growl any more. My head pushes, but my stomach rolls my tongue out and into that rough butchery just as my awareness receives that one final shove, and I savor the taste, salty and sweet and oh-so-*good*, as I finally topple into the dark.

The flare is a compromise, but I think it's a good one. I woke with the taste of salt on my tongue and dried blood on my lips. It may be mine, but it may not—I'm somewhat hazy on what happened last night once the wolf got a hold of my boot. The sun is high, the day bright, and a glance through the windows shows some of the snow is churned and red, and I have this foot . . .

Did the pack turn on one of its own? Is that why my lattice held? Did I—I hold up the foot, a lucky charm from the world's largest rabbit—do this?

No matter. Not really.

I chuckle at the thought that one of the wolves that came to make a meal of us has become, instead, a meal itself. At least I think it's a laugh. There *are* tears.

Anyway, I woke holding this stiff foot like a stuffed animal, *snuggling* with it for Christ's sake! And the blood on my lips and chin, well, it's . . . it's almost as if I was sucking on the damn thing in my sleep, like some great horrific lollipop. Thinking that should, I know, make me feel ill at the very least. Should make my stomach cramp and lurch, make my throat-flapper thing work and work as I try not to be sick. It *should*, I know.

But it doesn't. Not at all.

In fact, I was looking outside to see the state of the fire when I saw the blood in the snow. But there is no fire, and no wood—I used it all to make the lattice, I think. I consider, for the *barest* instant, going to gather more wood and start a cookfire, but the thought is pushed aside immediately, *crushed* aside, by the dreamlike memory of a taste, both salty and sweet. My mouth floods with saliva, my grip on the foot tightening of its own volition, and I think *raw? My God, not raw!*

A flare! pipes up that annoying part of my mind, though this time it's making so much sense, so much *perfect* sense. *Those flares are self-igniting, and they're right there in the kit.*

So here I sit, hands trembling so I almost drop the bright and hissing flare, though I never come close to losing my grip on that foot. Part of my mind, that goddamned annoying part that chooses when and where to speak with no input from me, points out that just a short time ago I would have found that foot disgusting. Would have refused to even touch the thing, never mind eat it.

Now, though, my mouth is already open, saliva overspilling my lips as the bright white flame of the flare blackens the fur and crisps the skin, and cooks the flesh, and my stomach rumbles. The burnt-hair stink that fills the closed air of the Piper stings my nose, and makes my eyes run with tears—but it's the best, most delicious thing I've ever smelled. I manage to wait until about half the thing is scorched before I drop the flare, nearly setting myself on fire, though I barely notice.

I start out peeling back the stiff, blackened coating of fur, but that takes too long; mere seconds later I adopt a two-handed, corn-on-the-cob style of eating. My teeth make short work of the scorched wrapper encasing the meat, and I find myself picturing well-done chicken skin, and the golden-brown skin of the Christmas goose my mother used to make. This skin is crunchier, and bitter, but the flesh beneath it is sweet and juicy. I come across bits I'd never have eaten before, the greasy fat and rubbery gristle, but they don't even give me pause; I gulp them down and keep on going.

They're part of the absolute, all-time *best* meal I've ever had. I don't stop when I run out of scorched flesh, either. I can't. I'm too busy pulling apart the bones to get to the meat in between, the paw like a great big chicken wing from Delo's back home.

I've never liked chicken wings. Way too much work for not enough reward.

A part of me warns that I should slow down, that I should be eating with more care, but I can no more slow than I could stop. Besides, it is that rational, annoying part of me, and this is an opportunity to ignore it for once, so ignore it I do—right up until the puking starts.

It comes hard and fast. I have a moment to think *no, wait,* and then it's too late. My belly, so used to being an angry, empty ball of pain that I try to ignore, shoots a sudden spike of agony through me. I curl around the hurt so hard my knees strike my face, and I barely dodge a broken nose. The meat, the meal, jets out of me as I curl, a red-pink undigested froth, black-flecked and reeking, and I'm begging my body to stop, begging my stomach not to do this. This is the only meal it—I—am ever likely to have again. This is supposed to keep us *alive,* damn it!

But it doesn't listen, doesn't stop, and the thick convulsions don't even slow until I'm empty, my idiot body pumping until the well's run dry. Once I realize it's not going to stop until everything is gone and more—my spoiled child of a stomach back to demanding food without cease—I wish for the darkness to come again, to sweep me away. I've occasionally wished for unconsciousness since my ordeal began, and usually I've gotten it, but not this time. This time I lie here, curled around that jabbing stone in my middle, and I weep. I cry with tears, then without. I wish for the pain to go away, then that I could have back that moment when I felt food in my belly—not full, never that, not even close, but something is so, *so* much better than nothing—and then I almost, *almost* wish that whatever is wrong with my head would hurry up and finish me, since *I* can't seem to get the job done.

That stops me. *That* sets me to crying anew, because I *don't* wish that. I wish, with all my heart, that this was all over, but I *don't* wish for *that*. I want to survive. I look up at Maggie, still hanging there, watching me impassively. Watching me weep.

"I'm sorry, hon. I'm trying, I really am, but I don't know what else to do. I think all the wolves have to do is be patient. All they have to do is wait, and they can have us."

I lower my voice trying not to be overheard from the front of the plane.

"It won't just be Bill next time. They'll have us all. We'll *all* be food for the wolves."

I lie there, thinking about those wolves, and the cold, and the snow, trying not to think about my hunger, for a long, long time. The flare has gone out, and night has fallen, but it feels like hours before the real darkness finally comes, and I sleep.

I am eating again. I've had dreams like this before, dreams of Christmas dinners, and pizza parlors, and childish dreams of Mother telling me to clean my plate, using the image of starving children in Africa to get me to eat every bite. This, though, this is a new one.

I'm eating the paw.

*It has to be the paw. There **is** only the paw—it's not like those pizza parlors where I can have as much as I want, whenever I want, or Mother putting a second helping in front of me when I've barely finished the first. There has only been the one, there **will** only be the one, but I'm getting a second crack at it, it seems. And it is so, so good.*

*This is an odd dream, where I am aware I'm dreaming, where I know this is my second run at this thing, and I'm determined not to make the same mistakes. I'm determined to learn. To **survive**.*

*It's hard—a constant battle—but I force myself to slow down, to take it easy. I give my stomach time—a little, anyway, as much as I can stand—to come to grips with the meat. To come to terms with it. To accept it. Mother's voice ripples through my head, piped in like the music in that pizza parlor, telling me again and again, **chew your food, don't eat like a savage, chew your food**. And I do chew, sometimes counting to thirty as I do so, sometimes losing count and starting again,* *trying to focus on the numbers rather than the meat filling my mouth, determined not to just bite and swallow, like a savage.*

And the chewing. The chewing is so good. The chewing is wonderful. The meat is juicy, and full of flavor, with none of those bits of blackened fur to bitter the feast. And the eating is easy: I started at the thick end again, where the meat is plentiful, rather than in among the smaller bones of the paw, where chicken wing effort is required. Too much work for too little reward.

I open my eyes, slowly, not wanting to interrupt the dream, wishing it could go on and on . . . and it does go on. I open my eyes to the light of day and see the meat, the good, red meat, the dream-paw become flesh, right in front of me. I am surprised—amazed, more like—but that doesn't stop me from taking another bite, from chewing slowly, carefully, definitely *not* like a savage.

I look about the plane as I chew. I've no idea what time it is, but the sun seems to be high in the sky, and bright, and warming the plane a bit as it does. I don't have a fire, but I still have some of those plugs, I think, and maybe a flare or two. My wooden lattice seems to have held, and I think I'm actually feeling better. I pause in my chewing, listening to my body work in the silence.

Gurgling, an almost happy sound, with no sign of churning in my guts. I think I really *do* feel better; even the pain in my head seems . . . lighter.

I look at the paw, seeing for the first time that it's larger than I remember, longer, more than just a paw and wrist. There's more than one meal here, if I can stop myself soon. Ration myself. Maybe far more than one.

I look at the paw, with all its chicken-wing boniness. Maybe I'll just finish that now. Slow myself down. Get all of that work out of the way. I look at the claws at the end of the paw, at their clear coat and white ends. French tips, I think those are called.

Suddenly a woman passes through my head, small and dark and smiling. She holds a paw aloft, turning it gently this way and that, showing the white-tipped claws to advantage. *You like?*

she says, and I nod, smiling a bit myself.

Strange, the things your mind latches onto when you think you're going to live.

The noise is disturbing: high and whining, growing louder by the second. I think of the wolves, think that they're back, coming to try to get into my den again, to try to take me. And my food. Again.

No.

I listen further, moving quietly from window to window, peering out into the sun-splashed clearing, looking to the tree line. Seeking out movement. It's the middle of the day, not their usual time, I think, but they must be getting desperate, those wolves.

But this is not a wolf sound.

The sound, an annoying buzz that splits the air and pains the head, is familiar. Sort of. Part of me thinks it almost recognizes the sound, and a word

(snowmobile)

floats through my head, but it's not connected to anything else in there, not anchored to food, or warmth, or wolves, so it just floats on out. The noise—loud, louder, *oh God so loud*—stops. Cuts off. Leaves silence in its wake. I hunker, not moving about the den any longer but remaining quite motionless, as still as I can. Listening.

The crunch of snow.

Again.

Footsteps? Something—or *things*—moving toward the den? From the back, where it tapers to nothing and there are no windows?

"Is this it? This *has* to be it, right?"

"Dude, do you know of any *other* small planes that went down recently?"

I hear the sounds, and they are familiar, but then so are the yips and howls of the wolf pack.

"We should call this in, right? Who do we call?"

"We're not calling anyone now. We're in the middle of nowhere. There's no coverage—unless you have one of those military sat-phones I keep seeing in the movies hidden up your ass or something."

I recognize the sounds. Words. Those are words—I used to use them myself. I haven't, though. Not for a while. Not since Maggie and Bill left. They left me some food—quite a bit, actually—but they took their words with them. I turn and look from place to place, at the food they left behind. At the meat.

Not a lot left.

But it's *mine*.

I edge toward the door. Slowly. With great stealth. Surprise is a weapon, like my stick and my knife, and I will use it as I will use them. My knee still pains me, though not nearly so much, and it shouldn't slow me when I—

"What's that? Is that a fire pit?"

"I don't—holy shit, I think you're right! Does that . . . ho-leeeeeey *shit*, does that mean . . . ?"

"It's been three weeks, man! Do you really think there could be a survivor? After this long?"

Inside the den my eyes are wide, and I tremble, almost violently, from crown to heel. There are at least two of them, maybe more, and one of their sounds has echoed in my mind, has struck off something in there and bounced about a bit. Come to rest.

Survivor.

That's me. I am. No matter what, that's what I am.

There are at least two, maybe a whole new pack, like the wolves. And, like the wolves, they want what I have. What I *need*.

They cannot have it.

I burst through the door, erupting out into the sunlight and snow, my paws filled with branch and blade, teeth bared in anger and determination to protect my den and dinner.

Determination to survive.

PLAYMATE WANTED

There was one. Walking along the highway shoulder, green pack on her back, worn boots scuffing dust as she trudged along. She was just passing a sign for a turnoff ahead, but he ignored the sign, internal pressure keeping his focus tight upon her.

I hope this isn't a false alarm, he thought. *She looks okay from a distance, but she needs to be more than just okay. Oh God, let her be more than just **okay**.*

He lowered the passenger's side window as the big caddy smoothly swung to the edge of the tarmac, and Benny leaned over a bit so that he could see the girl from a better angle. He called to her. "Excuse me?"

The girl stopped walking and bent a bit to squint through the open window.

Perfect, sighed the Need within him.

Benny gazed out at a tall girl of twenty, maybe twenty-two. Her dark hair was long, the bangs cut straight across the forehead above dark, serious eyes. Her lashes were thick, her mouth generous. Her green windbreaker and matching backpack concealed most of her upper body, but her jeans were tight, and clung to curvy hips and legs. Benny had done his reading, and knew that people with his . . . *proclivities* were said to focus on types. If he had a type, then an almost perfect example of it

257

stood before him. The final test was to hear her speak. He held his breath and watched her perfect lips part.

"Can I help you?"

Yes! Deep within his chest, in the dark place where the Need lived and grew, Benny felt a thrilling little tingle at the sound of the girl's rich voice.

Benny was well aware that she saw a pot-bellied thirty-something man wearing an unfashionable blue spring jacket. She saw thinning brown hair hanging across his forehead to fall into his bleary, bloodshot eyes. She saw teeth, discolored and crooked from a lifetime of smoking and drinking with not enough brushing and flossing.

He said "Why, yes. I believe you can!"

And he was aware she saw the gun, usually kept concealed in a gym bag on the passenger's seat, but now in plain sight in Benny's right hand. He brought it up, flat and level before her widening eyes, and shot her in the throat.

Halfway home, Benny had to pull over to shoot her again. The tranquilizer dart he'd stuck her with should have kept her down for the count, but only two hours into his return trip he thought he heard thumping coming from the trunk. He turned the radio down, then off.

Yes, there it was. Rapid thumping and muffled shouts coming from the rear of the vehicle. Benny sighed, wishing he felt safe hunting closer to home; not only was there the wear and tear on his trunk lining, but he was putting some serious miles on the caddy. He made a mental note to make an appointment for a tune-up and oil change, and checked his mirrors for traffic. Seeing none, he pulled over to the side of the two-lane highway he had been cruising along, threw the gearshift up into park, then closed his eyes and just sat for a moment. The thumping had grown faster—harder—as he'd pulled over, and the shouts had grown to a muffled howling. Now, maybe in response to the car stopping, the girl began to scream. Inside he felt light and airy, almost joyous, as the Need within him fairly danced to her song of terror. When the girl's increasing struggles actually began to rock the Cadillac, Benny sighed again and opened his door.

Holding the gun low, he walked back to the trunk and pushed the key into the lock. At the slight metallic sound, the girl inside the trunk went silent. Benny took the silence as a warning, readied himself, then turned the key. The lid exploded upward as the girl inside thrust with both feet, but Benny was prepared. He yanked his left arm out of the way of the lid and pulled the trigger.

The dart thudded into her thigh, and her eyes bulged at the sudden pain, her full lips flattening against her teeth as her mouth opened wide. Her powerful scream might actually have rocked him back a step if he hadn't already been leaning forward to slam the rebounding lid back down. Her thrashing lasted for a slow five count, then faded to stillness once more.

The tranquilizer darts he was using were supposed to take down a bear in five seconds, and keep it down for a couple of hours. A girl like this . . . hell, it had to be a bad batch. He pulled a dart from his shirt pocket and inspected it.

Looks fine to me, he thought, slipping the dart into the gun. He carefully opened the trunk and looked at the girl. The yellow fletching from his darts showed at her throat and thigh as she slept, hands cuffed behind her back.

"Beautiful," he murmured, and the word echoed in his mind, buoyed by the memory of that last scream. *What a voice!*

Benny stood, looking down at her and fighting against a sudden, dark surge. This battle for control had happened before. Often, in fact. Benny likened it to bladder control. The pressure would grow, and grow, like a filling bladder on a long road trip, but more slowly. Exquisitely slowly—sometimes taking months. But then the Need would reach the painful point where it was release or burst. Having the girl right here, right now, should be acting as a balm for his condition, allowing him to relax, but that was not the case. Like someone in search of a restroom who is told there is one nearby, only to feel a sudden increase in bladder pressure that forces them to run in the indicated direction with short awkward steps, Benny fought for control. The sudden proximity of a playmate caused the Need to flare up strong; almost too strong. His hands trembled, and he licked sandpaper lips with a tongue gone dry. He looked around at the highway, the drainage ditch and the trees.

I could do it right here. I could play right here, but I don't have my toys.

He looked at his surroundings again, almost desperately.

And it's not safe. It's just not safe. Someone might hear.

"I'm really looking forward to this," he said to the unconscious woman, in a voice choked with emotion and effort. "But better safe than sorry." He fired again and a third dart appeared, this one sprouting from her belly, before he closed the lid again. He got back behind the wheel, but left the radio turned off for the rest of the drive. He preferred to remember the screams that had so recently come from the trunk.

It was like mental music that he played again and again to soothe himself as he drove. The anticipation grew as his dark twin, the one whom no one ever saw but Benny himself, and then only in the mirror while they were playing, grinned and danced to the delightful song. The tightness across his lap was a constant reminder that his body was straining with its own eagerness of things to come.

💋

She's heavier than she looks, he thought as he carried her through the large, shadowy basement, past storage containers and old coal bins, toward the back of the house. To his playroom.

It was Benny's favorite room. Stark white walls. A metal table with restraints. A wheeled instrument tray containing his *toys.* Two portable work lights. A dual slop-sink in the corner. A top-of-the-line digital voice recorder on a shelf all its own, the long wire running up from the machine and across the ceiling to dangle the microphone, perfectly placed above the table to capture his playmates' "performances." Everything was lit up by bright fluorescent lights, like a surgical suite.

It was perfect.

He had built it himself, after inheriting the huge house from his parents. His parents had come from money, and now everything was his. His money, his house, his car, his . . . hobby. He had needed a place to bring his playmates, so he had converted one of the basement rooms into the playroom. Double-thick walls, with lots of insulation. With the door closed, no one could hear his playmates scream. And, oh, how he loved it when they screamed . . .

He placed his new playmate on the table, flopping her down and spreading her limbs out toward the corners. Easier to work that way. Her head lolled to the side, and he stroked her hair. It was so soft. Lovely.

As it had on the road, the Need pulsed in his head, driving him to move faster. He made two selections from the tray of glittering objects by his side. A thin, sharp knife and a pair of scissors. With swift, sure strokes he began to cut the clothing from her body, but, with the Need pushing him, whipping him like a jockey using the quirt in the home stretch, his pace quickly became more frantic than meticulous. He pulled at the fabric to open the cuts faster, tearing the cloth. It was a good thing he was so practiced at this; many playmates had wound up in his playroom. Each slice and snip parted fabric, not flesh. Jacket, shirt, pants and panties. In just minutes his new playmate was naked, lying on the shredded remnants of her clothing.

He caressed the bare skin of her stomach: smooth, like warm silk. He was thrilled to see she was unmarked—a blank canvas that cried out for his special creativity. His eyes went to her nipples, dark and contracted in the cool air of the cellar, and he felt himself stiffening in response. He longed to touch them, but knew he shouldn't. He shouldn't even be enjoying the feel of her belly. Not yet. She wasn't ready yet. She wasn't . . . prepared. He rolled her on her side in order to pull the last bits of clothing from beneath her—and froze.

What the hell is this?

He stared at the thin line of fine hair bisecting her back.

Starting up at the nape of her neck, where her hair left off, it followed her spine all the way down her back to end at the cleft of her backside. The stripe was about a half an inch wide, and the individual hairs were a uniform length, around an inch. It was the same color as the hair on her head, and, when he stroked his hand down it, it felt just as soft. He was reminded of a horse's mane as it ran down the horse's neck, but this was . . . different.

His pulse throbbed in his temples and groin, the Need swelling in her presence to a nearly tangible thing. He had to prepare her. Quickly. Tearing his gaze from her strange mane, Benny yanked the scraps of cloth from beneath her and lowered her onto her back again. He circled her, stopping to secure each wrist and ankle with the leather straps and cuffs bolted directly to the table.

Once she was safely spread out like a frog pinned to a dissection tray, he paused again, admiring her. Limbs long, and well toned. Torso lean, breasts not overlarge, but firm. Athletic. *Look at that muscle,* he thought. *No wonder she's heavier than she looks.* He ran his hands along her arms and legs, over her ribs, marveling at those expanses of perfect, unblemished skin. He wondered what to use first. The scalpel? The saw? The drill? He quivered at the thought of punching patterns into that perfect skin. Carving designs. There was a sound, and he glanced at the girl before realizing he'd moaned aloud. He was so hard it hurt, and hurried to finish his preparations. The dark twin was more than ready to play.

Her nails were long, and strong, but unpolished: that would never do. He filed each one, shaping them neatly, then applied some fast-drying polish—Ruby Red, his favorite. He fetched the makeup tray and moved to the head of the table. Her head was rolled to one side, a stream of sleep-spittle connecting her mouth to the metal, and he wiped her face clean with a towel. She wore no makeup, her natural beauty probably making her feel it was unnecessary, but that wouldn't do for a playmate: it wouldn't suit his twin. Benny went to work with eye shadow, eyeliner, mascara and blush, applying them with heavy, broad strokes. *Whored up*, his mother would have called it.

"Whored up," he said, holding her chin in one hand and applying lipstick with the other: more Ruby Red.

"Yes. Whored up," he murmured, only barely aware he was doing it. "Oh, God, yes."

Her eyes opened, and he snatched his hands away from her mouth, his heart skipping a beat, then recovering with a strong, fast rhythm as her eyes drooped closed again. *No wonder*, he thought, considering the three darts he had used to get her here. He hoped she would throw off the effects soon. If she didn't, he would have to inject a stimulant. He needed her awake to play. He slapped her cheek, gently.

"Wake up."

Her eyes opened. Then closed.

"Wake up!" His palm cracked against her beautiful, whored-up cheek. Her eyes snapped open, rolled once, then focused on him. He slapped her again, harder. "I said wake up, lover. It's time to play."

The girl's head lolled left and right as she took in her surroundings. The white walls, the lights, the table. When her eyes focused on the tray beside her, on the array of shiny, sharp instruments, the leather restraints snapped tight as the muscles stood out in sudden, stark relief along her long and lovely limbs.

"Over here," he said, snapping his fingers to attract her attention.

Her gaze found his again, her eyes round and rolling, and she bared her teeth at him. He was surprised at the aggressive expression on her face, in her eyes. He would have to change that. He slapped her a fourth time, then grabbed her face again, digging his fingers mercilessly into her cheeks and jaw, holding her head still so he could lean down to stare straight into her wide eyes.

"Scream for me."

Her head thrust forward in a sudden, powerful motion, catching him by surprise; only his startled recoil saved him from

injury as her white teeth snapped closed a fraction from his nose.
"Jesus!"

She was strong—very strong—and seemed to have thrown
off the effects of the tranquilizer with amazing speed, but it was
more than that: she was struggling, as they all struggled, but he
stood frozen in surprise, realizing that she was straining not to
get away from him, but to get *at* him.

He was unnerved. Wrong—this was all wrong. She was *his*
playmate. *His*. He needed to regain control of the situation. To
regain dominance. Steeling himself, he touched her, trailing his
fingertips slowly down her body, from the base of her throat,
down between her heaving breasts and over her taut, quivering
stomach. The muscles beneath her skin felt like shifting stones.

"You're a strong one," he said. "It's going to be fun to break
you. And I *will* break you. You *will* scream for me, little girl."

Her only response was a growl, a grinding rumble deep in
her chest, as she continued to strain. Beneath her growl, and
beneath his own sharp, nervous breathing, Benny swore he
heard the leather restraints creak.

He weighed the idea of giving her another dose of
tranquilizer. *I **will** break her,* he thought, *but better safe than sorry.*

"I'll be right back. Don't you go anywhere!" He forced a
laugh, striving to sound casual. He turned from her and went out
into the main basement, letting the playroom door swing shut
behind him, and started walking toward the stairs.

He wanted the dart gun.

He was at the top of the stairs, pushing the door open,
when he heard it.

A thump, down in the cellar.

He half turned, looking down the stairs. *I shouldn't hear
anything,* he thought. *I built that room to be completely soundproof.*

Leaving the door to the kitchen open, just in case, he slowly
made his way to the bottom of the stairs again. The cellar was
spooky. It consisted of three corridors, all running parallel,
separated by storage closets and old coal bins. The light switch at
the top of the stairs turned on only the lights in the main

corridor, leaving the side corridors and the spaces between the bins swathed in shadows. He looked down the central aisle toward the playroom, and saw a sliver of light along the floor.

The door was ajar.

Well, that explains it, then. He had forgotten to close the playroom door all the way, so some sound was leaking out into the real world. Simple.

It didn't feel simple.

What the hell is the matter with you? spoke a voice from somewhere behind his eyes, the voice of his dark twin—the voice of his Need. *Look at you! Frightened by a helpless playmate! You need to be a man, take control! It's **your** game! It's **our** game!*

Benny had put off his Need for quite a while before he'd gone hunting this time, and it had grown so, *so* strong. Almost without a thought, he took a deep breath and started toward the door. He tried to ignore the shadows that loomed to his left and right, in the dark spaces. He needed to shut in the sounds, and shut out the world. He needed to close that door, and fetch the dart gun. Then he could get on with his game.

Fine, said the twin behind his eyes. *Go get the gun. Bring it back; then we can play. We can play **hard**.*

As he approached, his hand outstretched to push the playroom door closed, something felt wrong.

Why can't I hear the girl?

She should have been screaming for him. Or crying. He should be hearing the sounds of her struggling, pulling futilely at her straps and sobbing. But he heard . . . nothing. Unnerved, he opened the door wide.

The cuffs were empty, the torn straps lying loose on the table. The room was silent.

The girl was gone.

"Shit!" He looked at the shadows shrouding most of the basement, wondering how long it would take him to find her down there, when he suddenly remembered that he had left the—

The kitchen door at the top of the stairs slammed shut.

"Shit!" The bitch was *getting away*! He sprinted for the

stairs. Shadows loomed on his left and right as he ran toward the exit, arms and legs pumping, mouth open and shouting in time to his slapping feet.

"No! No, no, no! No—"

He was almost to the stairs when something burst from the shadows to his right and hit him. He caught only the barest impression of motion from the corner of his eye before the impact lifted him from his feet and drove all thought and breath from him. Whatever it was hit him and didn't stop, Benny's own weight not slowing it at all. His feet never touched the ground as he was driven sideways into the door of the old coal bin, *through* the door, breaking it to splinters with his shoulder and back. Benny was carried along until he smashed into the back wall of the bin, hard enough that some of the boards broke. He slumped to the dirty cement floor, paralyzed by pain. His body struggled to draw a breath while his mind looked for something to focus on. As he sat there, he noticed he only had one loafer on, the other foot clad in just a black sock.

Hit me right out of my friggin' sh—was all he had time to think before his breath came back, rushing down into his lungs with a loud *whoop*. Then a second. And a third; inhalations so strong he rocked as he sat there. He focused on counting his breaths so he wouldn't have to look at the feet.

Right there in front of him, pale in the dim light leaking through the shattered door: bare feet and legs. Female. Shapely. He could only see them to the knees, but he refused to look up. A sound came from up there, above the legs, but he didn't want to think about it. Growling, low and guttural and growing. Beneath that sound, Benny was aware of a sound from his own throat; a high, terrified whimper, like that of a frightened dog.

Hands gripped him, shockingly strong; they squeezed his shoulders and lifted him off the ground. His back was pressed hard into the wall, his feet dangling; the one without a shoe felt cold. His eyes were closed, and he intended to keep them that way. This was playtime, and playtime was supposed to be fun. But this was not fun.

"Look at me."

He felt her breath upon his face, warm, and moist. He tried to jerk away, smashing the back of his head against the wall. He did not care. All he wanted was to get away from whatever was holding him. He twisted in her grip, trying to turn away from that mouth, so close to his face.

"Look at me!"

Flecks of spittle sprayed Benny's cheek and neck. It smelled of decay. The voice was deeper, rougher than before. Louder. More insistent.

"No . . . please, I—no . . ."

As Benny heard himself begging, part of him searched within his head, poking into the shadowed corners of his imagination for the backup he always found there; this was playtime, his dark twin's favorite time, and he would know what to do. He would know. But the vaults of his mind were empty, with no sign of his powerful twin.

He was on his own.

No . . .

He gasped as the grip shifted, and something—a thumb?—pressed against his collarbone. Hard. Harder. His gasp became a high-pitched mewling cry when, with a sickening crack, and an explosion of pain, the bone snapped.

"Look—at—me!"

The voice would not be denied, and when Benny felt a similar pressure start to build on his other clavicle he turned his face toward the voice, its breath fluttering his eyelashes.

He opened his eyes.

Her eyes glowed, red in the dim light, but it was her mouth that captivated him. It was inches away, and it was wide. Too wide. The teeth were long and white; almost luminescent in the gloom. The lips were drawn back, baring the teeth in a snarl. As he watched in horrified amazement, the mouth grew even wider, the teeth longer. Through the growl that issued from between those teeth he heard . . . cracking. Snapping. The sounds of bones shifting, moving and locking in place. The jaws opened, impossibly wide, and within that cavernous maw a tongue, long, and black in the shadows, writhed. Flicked along teeth growing longer still, thicker, stretching their sockets in the pink gums. The jaws came together, slowly, lips stretching down to cover most of the teeth, the tongue slipping out to moisten the lips. The voice came once more, but the halting, straining quality of the speech hinted at a mouth no longer suited for forming words. As that mouth spoke, straining to articulate, Benny noticed that those impossibly wide lips were stained with color.

His favorite. Ruby Red.

"*Give . . . me a . . . scream . . . lover!*"

He did.

Edith Hammond saw the girl hitchhiking on Route 1 in Ipswich, and she just had to stop. Edith was seventy-two, and people said she shouldn't drive anymore, but her eyes were still good enough to see that the poor girl was wearing cast-off clothes. Her jeans were too big, and that blue spring jacket was far too large for her. They didn't look like something a young girl would wear; not at all. She almost looked as if she were wearing her father's clothes.

"I don't usually do this, dear, but I just had to stop for you," said Edith as her Buick pulled away from the curb. "A young girl like you shouldn't be out here alone, hitchhiking! Where are you going?"

"I'm going to Spreewald, Maine, but as long as you can take me north, that's fine."

"You need to be more careful, dear! You can meet some dangerous people out here on the road, you know."

"Yes, ma'am," Valerie Redfern replied, a small smile playing across her Ruby Red lips. "I am aware."

ABOUT THE AUTHOR

ROB SMALES is the author of *Dead of Winter*, which won the Superior Achievement in Dark Fiction Award from Firbolg Publishing's Gothic Library in 2014. His short stories have been published in over two dozen anthologies and magazines. His story "Photo Finish" was nominated for a Pushcart Prize and won the Preditors & Editors' Readers' Choice Award for Best Horror Short Story of 2012. Most recently, his story "A Night at the Show" received an honorable mention on Ellen Datlow's list of the Best Horror of 2014, and was also nominated as best short story by the eFestival of Words in 2015. More about his work can be found at **RobSmales.com**, **thestoryside.com**, or on Facebook at **facebook.com/Robert.T.Smales**.